ABOUT THE TRANSLATOR

TERENCE MCENENY is from upstate New York. His MA from the
University of Nottingham examined irony in the poetry of Dryden.
From 2005 to 2014 he taught conference interpreting at the University
of Novi Sad, Serbia, before moving to Texas and becoming a staff
interpreter in the federal court. Other literary translations include
Destiny, Annotated (*Sudbina i komentari*) by Radoslav Petković
and a collection of Montenegrin short fiction.

OTHER TITLES IN
THE WORLD SERIES
SERBIAN SEASON

Filip David, *The House of Remembering and Forgetting* (translated by Christina Pribichevich Zorić)

Dana Todorović, *The Tragic Fate of Moritz Tóth* (translated by the author)

PETER OWEN WORLD SERIES

'*The world is a book, and those who do not travel read only one page,*' wrote St Augustine. Journey with us to explore outstanding contemporary literature translated into English for the first time. Read a single book in each season – which will focus on a different country or region every time – or try all three and experience the range and diversity to be found in contemporary literature from across the globe.

Read the world – three books at a time

3 works of literature in
2 seasons each year from
1 country each season

For information on forthcoming seasons go to
peterowen.com / istrosbooks.com

FEAR AND
HIS SERVANT

Mirjana Novaković

FEAR AND HIS SERVANT

Translated from the Serbian by
Terence McEneny

PETER OWEN
WORLD SERIES

WORLD SERIES SEASON 3 : SERBIA
THE WORLD SERIES IS A JOINT INITIATIVE BETWEEN
PETER OWEN PUBLISHERS AND ISTROS BOOKS

Peter Owen Publishers / Istros Books
Conway Hall, 25 Red Lion Square, London WC1R 4RL, UK

Peter Owen and Istros Books are distributed in the USA and Canada by
Independent Publishers Group/Trafalgar Square
814 North Franklin Street, Chicago, IL 60610, USA

Translated from the Serbian *Strah i njegov sluga*; first English-language edition
published by Geopoetika Publishing, Belgrade, Serbia, 2009

Paperback ISBN   978-0-7206-1977-5
Epub ISBN   978-0-7206-1978-2
Mobipocket ISBN   978-0-7206-1979-9
PDF ISBN   978-0-7206-1980-5

A catalogue record for this book is available from the British Library.

Cover design: Davor Pukljak, frontispis.hr
Typeset by Octavo Smith Publishing Services

Printed by Printfinder, Riga, Latvia

For my parents, Milica and Ljubiša

'What the novel can't stand is history.'
Ljiljana Pešikan Ljuštanović,
Professor of Serbian Folk Literature,
Novi Sad University

Part the First
BEHIND THE MASKS

ONE
In the Fog

'Master, please step out.' With these words my servant woke me from the light sleep into which I had fallen upon leaving Petrovaradin.

'One of the wheels is on its way out. We have to replace it before it breaks.'

I yawned, stretched and got down from the carriage. The six white horses stood still, while the coachman and my servant readied the new wheel. It was a cold morning. I shall never understand why I always let myself be talked into travelling at the very crack of dawn, when I hate the dawn – and whatever crack it crawls out of.

I turned around where I stood, twice, having a good look at the thick fog that was rolling in from all sides across the flat black earth. The endless plain. This land is said to be quite fertile. For wheat.

The coachman drew near enough for me to smell the previous year's inferior vintage.

'Sir,' he said, 'could you mind the team while we change the wheel?'

'All of them at once?' I asked.

'Oh no, sir, it's only the leader you have to take in hand.'

How clever of him to have realized. The night before, when I'd hired him, he'd struck me as somewhat slow. Clearly, alcohol had the opposite effect on him, sharpening his wits. He really ought to give it up.

'My dear coachman, if you only knew,' I answered. 'Holding the leader by the reins is fine, of course, but I'd much rather have them all.'

No sooner had I said these words than I heard a distant whinnying and sound of hooves that could belong only to another carriage heading in our direction. I couldn't make it out through the fog, but it was coming closer, of that I was certain.

The moments passed, and the horses grew restless. My servant drew his pistol and loaded it, although this was unnecessary. I have no enemies among the sons of men. I am beloved of all.

And as I stood there, thinking of love, out of the fog came a wide carriage of black and yellow. A six-in-hand like my own. Its driver brought the team to a halt, the door emblazoned with the imperial coat of arms swung open and out of the imperial interior leaped a young man. He was dressed quite as well as myself. Tall, with broad shoulders. He bowed and spoke in German.

'My dear sir, you seem to be having some trouble. May we be of some assistance?'

'Thank you, my fine young gentleman, but I trust my servant and coachman will manage to change the wheel and that we shall shortly be on our way again.'

'And where are you headed, if I may ask?'

'To Belgrade.'

'As are we. But please, allow me to introduce myself. I am Klaus Radetzky, physician and special investigator in the service of His Imperial Majesty Karl VI.'

'And I am Count Otto von Hausburg, a distant cousin to His Imperial Majesty. How odd that we should happen to meet like this. It was only the other day, as I was leaving Vienna, that His Imperial Majesty received me, and yet there was no mention of any special investigator.'

Radetzky squirmed. The situation was awkward for him, not because he'd been caught in a lie but because he'd been caught in the truth.

'His Imperial Majesty does not wish my – I mean, our – business to be a matter of general knowledge,' he said, stumbling over his words.

'And yet I hardly had to drag it out of you, did I?'

'I was . . . how should I . . . I cannot explain . . .' As he stammered, a way out suddenly occurred to him. 'I was struck immediately by your resemblance to His Imperial Majesty and knew right away that you must be related.'

'Indeed, I am related to His Imperial Majesty's half-brother, but it's one of those half-brothers of the illegitimate persuasion, and the connection is all on the half-brother's mother's side, so one could say that I'm not actually kin to His Imperial Majesty. Or even kith, as far as that goes. But no matter. What matters is the love and esteem in which His Imperial Majesty holds me. It was by personal service in the English colonies that I earned my title and lands and not by inheritance.'

Radetzky, having disgraced himself even further, was dumbstruck. He could only look around, hoping perhaps that something would come out of the fog to save him. There was, however, nothing to save him. How could there be? Out of the fog?

'Well now, as you've already told me so much, you might as well tell me your business in Belgrade. Always finish what you start, as they say. Stories first and foremost.'

He considered for a few moments, then bravely swallowed. It seemed such a big thing for him – to swallow, I mean.

'My lord,' he said, 'you would be sure to learn of it in Belgrade anyway. I belong to a special commission, one personally chosen and sent by His Imperial Majesty to Belgrade, so recently under Turkish dominion, in order to investigate certain occurrences there of a strange and horrifying nature. I am accompanied by two other men of science, both of the rank of Graf.'

Fortune had smiled on me at last. After the bony Hungarian girls in Pest, the clever coachman and the broken wheel, now was my chance. I had only to get close to Radetzky, gain his friendship and everything I wanted to know would be dropped right into my lap. So the news had reached the emperor after all. My journey had not been in vain.

I gave the young man a nod, and he turned and leaped into his carriage. Again the escutcheon flashed before my eyes, and then the carriage vanished into the fog.

But barely had the clip-clop of hooves and the creaking of the carriage wheels faded away when from the thick mists appeared a new figure. This one was alone and walked on his own two feet, and was therefore either a wandering beggar or a fool. Same thing, really. As he approached I was able to make out some of his features. He was exceptionally tall, had long pale hair and a beard and was dressed in rags.

He drew near, but not too near, and called out, 'Need any help?'

What a question, coming from the likes of him. The man must have a good heart, I surmised. There were any number of his ilk wandering around in the fog. I don't like them. They don't bathe as a rule, thinking that cleanliness doesn't matter. And so they stink. Other people, put off by the smell, give them a wide berth. It's easy to be good when you haven't actually got to deal with other people. However, it was not the offer of assistance that surprised me, coming as it did from a man who was attired – if you can call it that – in rags. No, what surprised me was the language in which he spoke to me. It was Russian. I answered in the same language, '*Nyet!*'

Then he cried out, 'Oh! Brother of mine!' and came running.

Ah yes, there was that smell.

'No, *not* your brother,' I said in Russian, thrusting my hands out to ward him off. The Russians love their kisses. And always in sets of three.

'But you are Russian!' he exclaimed, still giving signs of wanting to embrace me. 'I am Nikolai Leskovich Patkoff of Moscow.'

'I am Boyar Mikhail Fyodorovich Tolstoyevski,' I responded, taking special pleasure in my introduction. 'And where might you be going, Nikolai Leskovich?'

'To Belgrade,' he answered, greatly pleased for some unknown reason.

'To Belgrade? From Moscow to Belgrade? That's rather a long way.'

'Yes, my lord, the way is long. It was last summer when I started out. But the journey must be made.'

My servant informed me that the wheel had been changed and that we could continue.

'Well, Nikolai Leskovich, all the worst! Er, all the best, rather,' I said, and got into the carriage. The six-in-hand set off with a jolt, and the Russian continued to stand there. He'd make it to Belgrade in time for dinner. As long as he didn't lose his way in the fog. As for me, yes, it would be just as well to reach Belgrade before the commission did. I removed four kreutzers from my purse then put one back. I shouted to the coachman.

'Get us to Belgrade before that other carriage, and you'll have' – I slipped another kreutzer back into my purse – 'two kreutzers for your trouble.'

I heard the crack of the whip.

TWO
Still in the Fog

It had been years since my last visit to Belgrade. And I was missing it. I was curious to see what twenty years of Austrian rule had done for the place. The last time I'd seen it, it was an Oriental bazaar, the skyline bristling with countless minarets, the air filled with the stench of tallow and the wailing of muezzins. In Pest I'd heard how the city was nearly destroyed in the siege of 1717 but that the fortifications had since been tripled, making it even more impregnable than during its time under the Turks.

We made our way on to the bridge over the Sava, our vision obscured on every side. I stuck my head out as far as it would go but was unable to see the city. All was blanketed in thick fog. I could just make out, at the very top, the fortress of Kalemegdan.

We stopped while my servant spoke to the guards, and soon I heard the heavy gates creak open. The imperial and other state credentials I carried were the work of Jewish master craftsmen. I've got every conceivable pedigree – from German princedoms, Italian city states, the empires of Austria and Russia, the Kingdom of France . . . Although something tells me the French papers have nearly outlived their usefulness.

Once again I was Otto von Hausburg, Graf.

'Master,' said my servant, 'the guards say to go straight to the regent's.'

This struck me as odd, but I merely nodded, and the carriage jolted back into motion.

At long last we reached our destination, and servants dashed out to meet us and unhitch the team. A promising welcome, I thought to myself. I watched my man speaking to the servants, and the servants all shaking their heads. At once I beckoned him to me.

'What are they saying?' I asked. If you want to learn something important, always ask the little people.

'Master, they say that no one must go about once the sun goes down.'

'Ah well,' I said, playing the part, 'it's always that way in a city, isn't it? As if one would go wandering about Pest or Vienna at night! No shortage of cutpurses and brigands anywhere, is there? And here we are in the middle of an entire garrison, so one can just imagine what they get up to when they've been drinking . . .'

'No, master, they don't mean soldiers or brigands or any of the other things that strike fear into a city. Soldiers may be soldiers, but at least they're flesh and blood, and robbers are flesh and blood, too, as you yourself know, master – but the danger in the night they are speaking of is something else.'

'What?'

'They wouldn't say. They're afraid. The regent doesn't want it spoken of.'

Well, of course he doesn't, I thought. His position as regent was at stake. But keeping quiet never saved anyone – quite the contrary, you might say.

I didn't pursue the matter, not wanting my servant to grasp the real reason for my presence. I couldn't trust him. Naturally, when he'd first learned of our destination, he was beside himself. 'Why, master? Why Serbia? They're still fighting the Turks.'

'Because it is good for you to see your homeland.'

'I cannot believe you'd do such a thing to me, master.'

'Then don't believe,' I'd answered.

And yet I must bear with him, as it's so hard to find good help these days, *willing* help. I've got any number of people actually working for me, of course – practically everyone you can think of, in fact, but more in a roundabout sort of way, inconspicuously. Very few people directly on the payroll. However, my Serb was an exception in every sense.

After losing the war the Serbs beat a hasty retreat from the Turks. This particular Serb hadn't stopped for breath until he had reached Pest. Which is where I'd found him in 1706.

The first time I laid eyes on him was in a tavern called the Fat German. He was roaring drunk, but I liked him instantly. I don't know why. He had an intelligent look about him, and beautiful hands. What's the use of a clever servant with nice hands? I wondered. The second time I saw him was outside a tavern called the Second Encounter. To this day I wonder at the name. Such an odd choice for an alehouse. It was indeed our second meeting, and I took it as a sign. This time I couldn't resist. He was drunk again, and I had to crouch down to speak to him.

'Would you like to come and work for me?'

He fired his answer back like the best Austrian cannon. 'For *you?* Get thee behind me, Satan!'

'Yes, quite. Although, frankly, I don't know how you expect to get ahead in today's Europe with such an intolerant attitude.'

'No use being open-minded when I'm always drunk,' he retorted, and right away I knew I was dealing not only with a clever man but a wise one. Just the sort of servant I like. Without wasting time I got straight to the point. The meaning of life.

'I'll pay you ten forints to be my servant.'

'Seeing as you're the Devil, sir, you could be more generous.'

'Generous? Ha! And I suppose old Fishmouth is generous, is he?'

'Fishmouth, sir?'

'You know, that old Jew. The Jew with no teeth in his mouth. How much is *he* paying you?'

'Nothing yet, but he's very open-handed with his promises.'

'Have you a name to go with all those wits, my man?'

'The name's Novak. *Twelve* forints.'

'Eleven,' I countered. 'You're quite the drinker.'

'Twelve, because I do my best thinking when I'm drunk.'

Everyone's always telling me how accommodating I am and how it's one of my very best weaknesses.

I accepted, and he fired a question at me. 'But tell me, sir, what is it you do exactly? I've always wondered.'

'I deal in seven things and seven only. These seven things, in order – and the order is of the utmost importance, mind you – are as follows: pride, avarice, lust, envy, gluttony, anger and the despairing neglect of eternal salvation called sloth.'

And that was how he came to work for me.

But that was thirty long years ago.

In such a fog, everyone was sluggish and in disarray, and it was quite some time before I was able to enter the hall. At least there was no fog indoors. The walls were mostly bare, with the occasional decorative halberd in that narrow-bladed Saxon style of Johann Georg I. There were also some tufted maces lying about, and some hussar sabres, and a pickaxe, nearly a dozen daggers, five or six rapiers, a two-handed broadsword that even Hercules would find cumbersome, a pair of yataghans, three katana, a pair of Scottish flintlock pistols and one otherworldly Chinese landscape on silk.

The man who received me was a Baron Schmidlin. He was an adviser in the administration and was just over forty years old. Already bald, shortish and sporting a beer gut. He had a hearty manner that went beyond the merely polite, and it didn't take long for him to open up. As we all know, fools rush in where angels fear to tread.

'Herr Graf,' he said excitedly, 'I know that you are sent from Vienna to investigate the terrible events that torment His Majesty's subjects.'

Excellent, I thought. The man thinks I'm one of the emperor's special investigators. Why didn't he just assume I'd been sent because of the war Austria was waging to the south? Following its initial victories and the conquest of Niš, the imperial army had suffered defeat after defeat. Caribrod and Pirot had already fallen, and Niš was under siege by the Turks.

'Indeed,' I said evenly, 'I am a special imperial investigator, and I shall expect your full cooperation in bringing our investigation to a swift conclusion.'

'I'll tell you everything I know, but you must go and see it with your own eyes.'

'See what?'

'It,' he repeated, 'the thing with no name.'

'Very well,' I said, quite sure that I wouldn't. 'I shall.'

'And you are not at all afraid?'

'No,' I said resolutely, although I was afraid. Had I felt no fear I would not have come to Belgrade. 'Now tell me.'

'When the time is right,' said Schmidlin, nearly whispering. 'We expect the regent to return from the hunt at any moment. You see how thick the fog is. The hunt is sure to have been a failure, and the regent is very angry when he comes back empty-handed.'

'From what I hear, he's always very angry,' I said, making a bid for closeness with Schmidlin.

He grinned and nodded.

'That is so. And please do not forget, he does not like to be called President of the Administration, which is his real title here. Address him as Regent of Serbia.'

'I shall bear it in mind.'

'One other thing. Tonight there is a ball here at the Residenz. You will certainly attend, but I beg you not to speak to the regent of your business here. It will only provoke him.'

'But I am an imperial . . .'

'Vienna is far away, Herr Graf, and here there are terrible crimes in the dark.'

'Very well,' I said, nodding, 'but I must advise you that there is another commission on its way, one that knows nothing of me and has been sent by His Imperial Majesty to conduct an investigation alongside my own. They are not aware of me because, among other things, I must oversee them as well. The commission is led by a young doctor, Klaus Radetzky.'

'It was to be expected,' said the baron. 'For Vienna to send a doctor was only to be expected.'

He said nothing else, and I felt that he was holding something back.

As I expected, he was kind enough to escort me to the chamber that had been prepared for me. I entered the room, which was not especially luxurious, and lay on the wide bed. I was pleased with myself. I fell asleep and was only briefly awakened by the first cock-crow.

THREE
Love, the Mother of All Ills

'Love is the mother of all ills,' whispered the hostess of the ball into the ear of a fawning lady. But still the words reached me. So that was why Maria Augusta, Princess of Thurn and Taxis, was looking so pale and wan. Afflicted with the age-old woe of the idle, she had barely noticed me. Too long in the tooth for my taste anyway. True, she was barely thirty, but I do feel that's quite enough for any woman. Her rich diet had amply padded out her hips and bosom. She was stocky with dark-brown eyes and a dark-brown wig like all the members of the Thurn and Taxis clan. I shall never understand what causes entire families to go in for matching wigs.

I assume that her marriage was the result of careful planning and skilful negotiations. The wedding had not taken place until her husband's position as Regent of Serbia had been assured. Only then had she been dispatched to this side of the Danube, there to complain of love as the mother of all ills. But what could this foolish woman know of troubles and cares? Nothing. I could speak of such things for years and decades and centuries and still not be done. Yet, who would listen? There was no one I could tell.

'How can you love him?' asked the lady confidante, with what seemed to be distaste. 'He falls so short of perfection in every way.'

Maria Augusta heaved a great sigh and said, 'I did not fall in love because I was looking for boundless strength, or flawless beauty, or bottomless wisdom. On the contrary, it was when I noticed the imperfections that I began to love – the weakness running through the strength, a hint of ugliness, the foolishness of an idea or opinion . . .' She paused then continued, 'It is not possible to love someone who is too strong, too beautiful, too wise. That is the price they pay.'

'Yes, but . . .' the lady began, only to fall silent, whether because she had realized that the princess was right or because she disagreed entirely, I could not tell.

But Baron Schmidlin was talking nineteen to the dozen, as they say. Why nineteen, I've always wondered? Why not eighteen, or twenty, or even my old favourite, thirteen? At any rate, I said to myself, I ought to join his listeners. I knew it would be best to win the man over completely, and there's no better way to make people like you than by following their stories attentively. Even for someone who's been around as long as I have it's deuced odd – inexplicable, even – to see the most ordinary attention so readily taken for love.

That young doctor, Radetzky, was after the same thing apparently, as he was making a show of nodding and assiduously following as Schmidlin perpetrated his abuse of the language. There were two other gentlemen with them, dressed in the latest Viennese fashion. I concluded that Baron Schmidlin must be bending the ear of the real commission. No doubt he was taking pleasure from the false knowledge that a secret commissioner to His Imperial Majesty was also present in my own person. The time I have spent among the rabble of mankind has taught me that people love and enjoy nothing so much as their belief that a lie is in fact the truth. Our man Schmidlin was positively blooming from the dung-heap of misrepresentation I had prepared for him.

I approached, observing how Radetzky started at the sight of me. Baron Schmidlin bowed slightly and introduced me to Doctor Radetzky and the other two men of science, counts whose names I have forgotten. One's wig was blond, and the other's was red. Naturally, I was introduced as Count von Hausburg, passing through on my way to Niš.

'I've just been telling the young gentlemen from Vienna how we repaired and rebuilt the Fortress of Kalemegdan. The work was led by General Nicolas Doxat de Démoret, whom you'll meet in Niš. He was also the one who recommended following the plans of the ingenious Marshal Vauban.'

'Vauban, Sébastien Le Prestre de Vauban? Do you mean the marshal who got a whipping from our very own Prince Eugene of Savoy?' asked Radetzky.

'That's the one,' the baron agreed, adjusting his wig, which still sat crookedly. 'But, lest we forget, in his day, Marshal Vauban won every battle he fought. He was actually an engineer by training, with his specialities being the fortification of cities and siegecraft. Every city he laid siege to would fall into his hands – and, may I remind you, gentlemen, that his successes include Lille, Maastricht and Luxembourg, among others – while every city he fortified was able to fend off its enemies.'

'So, a master of both defence *and* offence,' I said, working my way into the conversation.

'Well, you must know how an attack is conducted', said Schmidlin, 'in order to prevent one. And by the same token, you must understand how defences work in order to break through them. General Doxat followed all of Marshal Vauban's basic instructions for laying out proper artillery fortifications. In our library you can consult a small tract by the marshal on sieges and defence works – if you know French, of course. It's entitled *De l'attaque et de la défense des places*. It was published this year in Paris.' He stopped for a moment then spoke again. 'Why, tomorrow we could all see the walls together.'

'You simply must take us around those fortifications,' said one of Radetzky's companions, the one in the blond wig, politely.

Schmidlin struck his forehead and declared, 'I'd almost forgotten, tomorrow night is the costume ball. It's the most important social event of the autumn, and anyone who's anyone in Serbia will be here with the regent at the Residenz, all in their masks and fancy dress.'

'Perhaps you could tell us something about why we've come?' asked the other man of science, the one in the red wig. Radetzky looked at me, then looked at Schmidlin, then at the man with the ersatz red hair, then at the man with the ersatz blond hair and then back at me. With a meaningful look the baron sought my permission, which I granted with a slight nod.

'The first complaints from the Serbs came in the autumn of '34, if memory serves, but none of us paid them any mind, thinking it was all just superstitious nonsense. More complaints and accusations followed in the spring of '35, and again we dismissed them without further enquiry. However, just before Christmas that year one of our tax-collectors disappeared, in the very same area where most of the complaints had been made. We suspected renegade peasants in the matter, those highwaymen as the Serbs call them. It made sense, as they certainly have no scruples about robbing and murdering ordinary men, so why not a tax-collector returning with laden coffers? Not only would they make a rich haul they'd increase their standing in the eyes of their countrymen by stealing back what had been taken from them – you know what the Serbs think of taxes. The unfortunate man had been travelling with an escort of five soldiers. They'd all fallen asleep without leaving a single one on guard. Drunk, as we quickly established. The next morning they woke to find the tax-collector and the money gone. Naturally, we had their effects and persons searched at once, suspecting that the soldiers had conspired to kill the tax-collector and divide the spoils. However, the search revealed nothing, not a single kreutzer. Besides, if they really had done it they'd hardly return to Belgrade; they'd have gone elsewhere to drink away their ill-gotten gains. We also observed that the soldiers were behaving strangely. They were silent, pale, unaccountably fatigued. They stopped drinking, a most serious symptom. Our suspicions soon shifted from them, and we concluded that the crime must be put down to Serbian brigands.'

'Could we speak to the soldiers?' asked Radetzky, interrupting the baron.

'Oh no, good sir. Shortly thereafter we had to let them go. They were no longer fit for military service. I believe all of them have long since departed Belgrade. But you could speak to their colonel's physician.

Although you can't, as a matter of fact. He's been sent to Niš, if I'm not mistaken. And, as you know, the situation in Niš is rather grim. We'll have to send for him. Although he won't be able to come. We can't very well leave the colonel without a doctor while he's busy defending the city from the Turks. They say they're eighty-thousand strong now, the Turks.'

'Do continue,' I said impatiently.

'Yes. So, we had the guard doubled and ordered them to remain on the alert at all times, thinking in that way to foil any attempts by the brigands. Indeed, that seemed to be the end of the attacks. And so we would have put the matter behind us, satisfied with our prevention of further evil, but for something else that happened, something most strange. On their way through the area, two of our Serbian *Oberkapitäne* happened to discover, quite by chance, in the cellar of an alehouse, the tax-collector's body. The body was . . . it was . . . The captains were there last summer . . . six months after the tax-collector's disappearance . . . The body was . . . it was . . .' Schmidlin had not ceased to fiddle with his wig, which was perched on his round head in positions of ever-increasing absurdity. 'The body was . . . it was . . .'

'Out with it, man!' I snapped. 'The body was what? This is intolerable!'

'The body was . . .' Locks of hair stuck out wildly. 'The body was . . .'

And as he spoke someone shrieked. I turned around and saw a wig. On the floor. A black wig. Looking down at it stood Maria Augusta. Without her wig. Her hair was white. Quite entirely white. And cropped short.

That woman . . . I thought. That woman is truly suffering. Why, she's scarcely thirty years old. And her hair is already white. Quite entirely white.

'What's happened?' asked Radetzky.

'I don't know,' answered one of the other two.

But how white the woman's hair was. A suffering soul.

A soul.

I could not tear myself away from the sight. A servant ran to retrieve the wig and attempted to restore it to the princess. And yet she would not take it. She only turned and rushed from the hall. Her departure was not proud but abashed, as if in flight. Only after she had left the hall was I able to turn my attention again to Schmidlin and the physicians. The baron's fingers were still at his wig. I was beginning to lose my temper.

The red-haired count and man of science wrinkled his nose and said, 'It smells in here. Of brimstone.'

Radetzky was quick to regain his composure, unlike me. 'What about the body, then?'

'The body was . . .' Schmidlin repeated, and I could see his mind was no longer on the words he was mouthing. I wanted to strike him.

'Please excuse me. There's something I must . . . do,' said the baron, and then he was gone.

I tried to remain calm. In spite of all. First, some captains had found a body. A body. So the tax-collector was dead. That made all the difference. He was dead. Second, the captains were alive. Schmidlin hadn't mentioned anything happening to the captains. Third, the princess's hair was white. This was not reassuring. This distressed me. All in all, not counting the princess, of course, I had nothing to worry about. Other than perhaps the body. What *had* the body looked like, if Schmidlin was unable to utter the right words?

'The baron is sure to return,' said Radetzky, addressing me.

'I do hope so,' I answered, as politely as I was able.

'What is your opinion?' Radetzky continued.

'In regard to what?'

'The body.'

'I've no idea,' I said.

'Nor have I, although it must have been horrible.'

'But you're a physician. What could seem horrible to you?'

'I don't know. Probably something I've never seen before.'

'You should speak to those captains,' I said, trying to be helpful.

'Most certainly,' said Radetzky, lost in thought.

They were all disappearing on me. The princess wasn't coming back, neither was Schmidlin. The prince regent hadn't yet even appeared.

It struck me that the members of the household were behaving very oddly. I tried to work my way into several conversations but was unable to find out from anyone how the princess's wig had slipped or been knocked off, or the nature of her affliction. Was it connected to her unhappiness in love? They either couldn't or wouldn't say. Although if people know something they're usually quick to volunteer information. They just can't help themselves.

The orchestra struck up a tune, and the dancing began. I couldn't see anything through the swirl of ball gowns. I took a seat and wondered whether to leave or to stay a bit longer. I was hoping to hear something important. I was hoping that Schmidlin would come back and finish his story. I was hoping the princess would return.

And return she did. She was wearing the very same wig. She was despondent, although she smiled. Between her feelings and her outward expression stretched the chasm of pain known as *noblesse oblige*. I decided to draw closer but without addressing her. Even when I know someone quite well I avoid speaking to him (or, especially, her) in times of difficulty. The princess sat and rested her chin on her hand. For some time she merely watched the lords and ladies dancing – her gaze not focused on anyone in particular, I noticed – and then she began to fan herself, as if suddenly flushed.

Her fan was Chinese, painted in bamboo ink. Along the middle ran the Great Wall, dividing it nearly in half. Orderly rice paddies could be seen in the lower half, with industrious Chinamen standing up to their knees in the water. Off to the far right, closer to the handle of the fan than to the Great Wall, a procession of officials marched on its way. Perhaps the emperor himself was among them, although I could not see. The peasants were bowing low to the ruling power as it passed. Under the last row of peasants was the finger of Maria Augusta. Below it extended her pale and delicate hand. On the other side of the wall lay the desert, its great white expanse unbroken by anything but scattered, stunted vegetation. On the left jutted rocky mountains, although on which side of the wall it was hard to tell. Directly overhead, the black sun (the image being in no other colour than black) illuminated or darkened the entire scene. Beyond the black sun and the white sky was the ball, the coloured gowns, the prim dancers and the music.

The princess snapped the fan shut, quite as suddenly as she had spread it open, and then a footman came to me and murmured, 'Your servant awaits you outside. He says it is urgent.'

I could well imagine how urgent it was. For me to lend him drinking money. I was forever lending him money. Then deducting it from his pay. Then lending him more. I was beginning to feel like a bank. And here in Belgrade there was no end of places to drink. A good two hundred, I'd heard. The best place in the city was said to be the Black Eagle. German beer, Hungarian wine, Serbian *rakija* – all straight down the gullet of drunkards galore. Why had I ever taken this man on as my servant? Couldn't ask for anyone worse. Not only did he drink, not only did he always owe me money, he also gave me no end of cheek. I remember telling him once how I'd had a laugh at old Fishmouth's expense. By Fishmouth I mean, of course, the Old Fish Himself, ΙΧΘΥΣ. That's a good one. But where was I? Oh yes, one day in Jerusalem, among the multitudes, during one of the Jewish holy days, I run into Fishmouth. He doesn't recognize me, of course, but I know him straight off. So I ask him, 'Who do you take after, Fishmouth? I've seen your mother, and she's got a fine mouth on her, so it must be your father. Ha, ha, ha.' And he says –

'Hold, master, this was not our agreement,' Novak interrupted me.

'What do you mean, not our agreement?'

'We agreed that I would serve you, not that I would listen to your stories.'

'But don't you find my stories gripping and great fun?'

'To tell you the truth, no. Besides that, I don't like it when you call Our Lord by the name of Fishmouth.'

'Lord, you say? *Lord*? *I* am your lord, and for twelve forints to boot.'

'No! You are *a* lord, but Christ is *the* Lord. You are my master, but Christ is Our Lord.'

And that's how he was always throwing me into confusion. My servant, I mean. Serbian bastard. Just see if I'd give *him* any money. Let him stay sober. Let him suffer.

And as I raged within I spotted Schmidlin. I went straight to him and dragged him off into a dark corner. I didn't want to be seen by Radetzky or those other two idiots from the commission.

'Baron,' I said, 'finish your story about the body. I must know.'

'To be clear, I did not see the body myself. At the time I was in Vienna. Yes, it was July, and work had just finished on the Fortress of Kalemegdan. The cost was enormous, you understand, and I *am* chief commissioner for financial matters.'

'So, you don't know what the body looked like?'

'I do, though. It was described to me. Only I can't be sure as I didn't see it myself. You do understand?'

'Quite, but tell me what you were told.'

However, no sooner had I said these words than my servant appeared at my side. My faithless servant.

'Master, you must come with me at once!'

'Why?'

'Because I have found what you are looking for.'

'You fool, you have no idea what I'm looking for.'

We were speaking in Serbian and Schmidlin could not understand us.

'But I do know. You're looking for vampires.'

FOUR
Unter Ratzenstadt

1

Schmidlin gave a start, as if he had understood.

'You can't seriously expect me to *meet* the vampires,' I said, my legs beginning to tremble.

'Of course not, master. I've arranged for you to speak with some men who have seen them.'

'And these people who've seen them . . . they're not vampires, are they?'

'No, master. They're just ordinary people like you and me. I mean, like me.'

'There's no danger then?'

'No, master, none at all. If we take the measures they've explained to me, there's no danger at all.'

'What sort of measures?'

'You'll see, master. Just don't get upset. You know you always smell of brimstone when you're frightened.'

'That's not true!' I protested, raising my voice.

'Let's say no more about it for now, master. They're expecting you in Unter Ratzenstadt – Lower Belgrade, as we call it in Serbian.'

I took my leave of Schmidlin, who seemed greatly relieved at not having to answer any more of my questions, and went with my servant out of the hall.

'Wrap up well, master. It's very cold out. And foggy.'

'And dark. You're the one who said that no one here goes about at night.'

'I did, but we'll have protection.'

He did seem convinced – and, besides, he was coming with me himself. Whatever happened to me would also happen to him. And he was far too fond of his own skin to risk it. I could be sure of that.

2

We stepped outside, into the night and the fog. Soon we came to the King's Gate on the Sava River, the fortified entrance into the Fortress of Kalemegdan and the way out into the town.

At times the moon would slip behind the clouds. It was only a sliver away from being full. The cobblestones were uneven, and both of us stumbled more than once. Along the narrow, winding lanes we went. I confess I would have got lost had not my servant been there to guide me. Despite his years away from Serbia and Belgrade, he made his way unerringly through the maze of streets. I was not afraid because we were still in Weissburg, the German part of the city. As Novak had explained, the vampires had yet to make an appearance on this side of Prince Eugene's line. Apparently they respected borders, unlike ordinary mortals.

But when we reached the outermost gate that separated us from Ratzenstadt, my heart sank. The soldiers let us pass at once, and then we were beyond the pale. Ahead lay only darkness. I could see nothing at all. Not the moon in the sky, not the houses on the ground.

'And now, master,' said Novak, 'for our protection . . .' And from the folds of his cloak he produced something which was at first hard to make out. But I could smell it. It was a string of garlic bulbs.

'Don't be stupid! Did you actually think that would be any use against vampires?'

'It's what saved the people we're about to meet.'

'But don't you know it's also supposed to protect people from *me*?'

'Yes, master. But just because it's not true in your case doesn't mean it's not true for vampires. Besides, it can't hurt to wear it around your neck.'

'Of course it can't hurt. It's *garlic*. This whole thing is asinine. And if that's your idea of protection, I'm not taking another step. If the best you can do is something from the spice cabinet, count me out.'

'Why won't you trust me, master? Here, I'll put one on as well. Do you really think I'd put myself in any danger? I'm sure it's all right.'

'I'm not going!'

'But there's no danger at all. We've got pistols, too.'

'I doubt you'll find pistols much help in stopping *them*. And why can't we meet these Serbs tomorrow in the daylight?'

'They're hajduks, master, wanted as bandits by the Austrians. Not only that, they're very keen to meet you.'

'You haven't gone and told them who I am, have you?'

'That I have. And why not?'

'You're mad. You're not supposed to go around announcing it. I like to remain incognito.'

'I admit it, I made a mistake. But you've got to appear now. You wouldn't want to let your devotees down. They've done so much murdering, raping, thieving and torturing – it would be a true shame for them not to meet you.'

'But are they vainglorious and proud and grasping and envious and . . .'

'Yes, yes.'

'All right then. Give me that garlic.'

'Here you are, master. One more thing, though.'

'What?'

'Something else you'll need for protection.'

'What?'

'Well, I don't quite know how to put this . . .' And without another word, he pulled it out. From under his cloak. I couldn't believe my eyes. It was a cross.

'I'll kill you for this! So help me, I will!'

'Master, remain calm. It's only a cross.'

'You want me to wear a cross? *Me*?'

'They go together. Truly, master, that's what they told me. The garlic's no good without the cross.'

'You want *me* to wear a cross? Me, its greatest foe.'

'There's no need to look at it that way, master.'

'How then?'

'Let's say that a great sinner was to wear a cross. What would you say to that?'

'I'd say that's hypocrisy.'

'There you are,' my servant said triumphantly.

'I fail to see your point.'

'Hypocrisy is a sin. Fishmouth disapproves of it. Doesn't He even say somewhere "Ye Pharisees are whitened sepulchres" or something along those lines?'

'Aha, so it's Fishmouth now, is it?'

'Therefore, I see no reason why you shouldn't do something that will offend Fishmouth.'

I had to admit it, his reasoning was quite sound. I put the blessed thing on.

3

The streets led downwards. In the dark, we headed who knows where, with no obvious rhyme nor reason. But towards a goal. It's always like that. Never an ounce of sense but with a goal. My servant led me, stopping at every corner to get his bearings, to turn around, to look up at the black sky.

Placing one foot in front of the other, step after step, down we went into the swirling mists and the pitch dark. In the utter stillness no sound could be heard but my own footsteps. Novak stepped so lightly I could not hear him at all. We did not speak. They were out there. I knew they were. The vampires. Each step might be the last. Should I duck around the next corner? Turn back? Go on? It made no difference. I adjusted my pistol.

We passed windows. Shuttered. Behind them may have been life. Uneasy sleep. But we saw nothing. Down and down we went. Nothing but my footsteps, hollow footsteps, along the empty streets. My tread. The echo. Breathing in and out. On and on. Should I have asked to turn back? But no. To go faster? But no. To stop and rest? But stopping to rest is never the answer.

'Incredible, the smell of brimstone you're giving off tonight.'

Heavy footfalls. And heart. I could smell the river. We'd gone as far down as we could. What did the city look like? Or the river? It must be black. There was no gleam of water, no moonlight. When there's nothing to shine upon it, it isn't there. It doesn't exist by itself. But I could smell its oozing mud. I heard the straining of ropes. They creaked and groaned. I heard the water lapping against the sides of boats.

A shadow. A grey shadow in the black night. Vampire!

I caught hold of Novak.

'What is it, master?'

'A vampire. In that doorway, straight ahead.' I squeezed his arm. 'A vampire, I tell you!'

'I don't see anything, master.'

'Let's get out of here!'

'But there's nothing there, master.'

The end of days. The final book.

'No, I didn't say anything, master.'

A wave splashed against an anchored boat. Again. And again. The shadow bent over the water. Listening to the irregular sounds. Suddenly it straightened up, perhaps recoiling from the spray. And then it vanished.

For a long time we followed the river. Moving more swiftly. Again and again I glanced over my shoulder.

'Your eyes were just playing tricks on you, master.'

Were we heading upriver or down? Why, since we were not in the water, it made no difference. The current meant nothing. It flowed along, carrying everything with it. But I was not in it, and it was not carrying me. And it was not in my way either. Upstream merrily, merrily; struggling downstream all the way.

You should never give in. Never go against it. You should stand outside it all.

4

The public house was named after its neighbourhood, Ekmekluk, Turkish for 'Bakers' Alley'. There was no sign, but my servant told me that everyone knew it. I could barely see the interior through the thick smoke. The tobacco from around Varaždin is highly spoken of. And here they were, happily puffing away. Rough faces sized us up. We really were rather overdressed. Also, we didn't stink. Extraordinary how one can always detect, through a veritable cloud of stench, a mere hint of eau-de-Cologne. It offends more than the slightest whiff of a bad smell amid an entire Versailles of perfumes.

'And what brings you gentlemen here among us?' asked one man, rising to his feet. He was the biggest of all.

'We're here to see Vuk and Obren,' answered my servant.

'Austrian spies,' said another, also standing up. He, too, was huge. His eyes were hidden behind bushy brows.

'Traitors to the Serbian nation,' chimed in a third. I needn't mention how large he was.

'Just like that turncoat Branković at the Battle of Kosovo,' added a fourth. A strapping great figure of a man.

'German swine,' said a fifth. Quite a small fellow, this one.

They circled around us. I felt for my gun under my cloak. I'd be able to kill one of them. Novak could take one more. The other twenty would have us. A pistol wouldn't be much help. I fingered the garlic. But these Serbs weren't vampires. The cross? Well, they were Christians after all. A cross would hardly protect me from Fishmouth's own believers.

'Would you look at the crosses on these two!'

'And the garlic!'

'It's to keep the vampires away.'

'Vampires, Austrian scum.'

'They'll be wishing it *was* vampires after they see what we've got in store for them.'

Laughter.

They were moving in on us. Taking their time, and with pleasure. I drew my gun. I'd be taking at least one of them with me.

5

When down they went the field of Kosovo,
The field of black that nae could blacker be . . .

Everyone stopped in their tracks and turned around. In a far corner, in the shadows, sat an old man. He could not have seen us. He was blind. Everyone watched him in silence. For moments on end they stood stock still. Then one of the group stirred and moved towards the old man. The rest followed. And the old man reached deep into the pocket of his rough cloak and took something out. At first I could not tell what it was.

'He's got a gusle.'

'A gusle.'

'He's a gusle-player.'

There were cries of delight. The gusle was an unprepossessing instrument, no longer than the old man's forearm. The short bow seemed lost in his big hands. He propped the gusle on his lap, tucked the scroll end under his chin, and began to rub resin along the bow while blowing on the end. Only then did I realize that the instrument had no string.

As if no one else were around, the old man moved with ease and grace. All eyes were upon him. They had forgotten all about me. The first sound filled the air, and the gusle-player began to tune his nasal voice to the non-existent string that scraped and wailed as if it were actually present, would tightly. Then he threw his head back proudly, his Adam's apple jutting from his throat.

'Sing us a song of Kosovo.'

'How we lost the kingdom.'

'How we lost our lands.'

'Innkeeper. Beer for the old man.'

'Austrian beer, old man – the best beer.'

Novak and I took the table by the door. No sense looking for trouble. We ordered a beer for good measure.

The gusle-player began with a drawn-out wail – *Aaahaaaaah* – then launched into his cryptic verse:

> A hawk took wing, the bird of feather grey,
> He left Jerusalem, the holy place,
> And carried he the little swallow bird.
> It was no hawk, the bird of feather grey,
> But Elias the sainted one was he.
> Nor carried he a little swallow bird,
> A book he from our Virgin Lady had,
> That brought he to the king in Kosovo,
> On royal knee the saint the book did set,
> And the book itself to the king began to speak . . .

The Serbs were crowding in around the player, their breathing hushed, their eyes moist. Faster now, the passion growing in his voice, the old man sang on. Or whined, depending on one's opinion of the gusle. The very fire in the hearth seemed to leap up and burn brighter.

I regarded my servant. He was straining to follow the gusle-player's every note, as though something unexpected might happen, as if one of the ten-syllable lines might suddenly turn out to have twelve, as if the pause might land on a different syllable and not just the fourth. Serbian folk music offers no such surprises – never has and never will.

Despite its predictability, however, that very song had just saved my life.

And so I watched my servant and thought about him. Why was he serving me? I am no believer in those tales of selling one's soul to the Devil. There was that Englishman who wrote about it – Marlowe, I believe. With that awful first name I'd rather not say. I mean, who sells his soul to the Devil? No one, that's who. All the men and women who serve me, every last one of them, fell into ruin long before meeting me. Besides, I'm not interested in buying. Like everyone else, I want gifts that come from the heart, the gift without a price. I've wandered this earth for such a long time, I've worn myself to the bone, but I have yet to meet a soul that will offer itself to me freely and not ask for anything in return.

'It's love you're looking for, master,' Novak said once in the middle of some story I was telling, some tale of woe.

'Don't be daft,' I answered. 'Love is easy to come by. I'm not looking for love.'

'Easy to come by, master? With so many looking high and low and so few ever finding it?'

'It's quite simple, really. If they're looking high and low, it's because they don't want to find it.'

'You just made that up.'

'So what if I have? Why shouldn't I? Where does it say that old ideas are always better than new ones? Oh, you humans! Always believing that wisdom is ancient and that the present brings nothing but dross.'

'Isn't that the way, though?'

'Of course not. Do you really think time is so mighty it can turn any ancient rubbish into today's great wisdom?'

And then – I don't know why, considering the topic at hand – he told me the story of his life and why he had left Serbia and become a drunkard. And become my servant.

As the story goes, he was the son of a rich and respected merchant. The rich and respected parts always go together. Not right away, of course. At first one is merely rich. Some time goes by, and then one is rich and respected. Unfortunately for Novak, his father was also progressive. And so the man took it upon himself to give his son an education. He found tutors, one after the other, for Greek and Latin and all the other subjects. The boy applied himself and was eager to learn – to his further detriment – and by the age of twenty was already holding forth with priests and even the bishop himself on matters philosophical. For instance, whether my fall was occasioned by envy or a lack of love, and what shall become of me at the end of the world. That's what happens to people who don't mind their own business. They end up as the hired help. His studies went well; he learned to keep the books and to handle money. But he didn't want to go into trade. What he wanted was to read – all the great tragedies, the great passions, everyone in love with someone else and any number of dead bodies piling up at the end. And so, slowly but surely, he got an idea. (He never actually told me as much, mind you; I figured it out for myself.) My man Novak got the idea that his life would be meaningless until he'd been hopelessly in love and all the rest of it, just like in stories. He had worked himself up into a proper Hamlet state of mind. However, there was no one on hand to do the father in, the mother had long since died and the only uncle available for the role had squandered all his money on drink and fawned and cringed whenever the father was around. So much for that plot. And as for an Ophelia, I need hardly mention the unsuitability of the local females. Sometime later he resolved to be Paris and even managed to find a candidate for the abduction – a cooperative young lady who had, in fact, agreed to go with him – but called the whole thing off after overhearing his chosen Helen's father exclaim, 'If only someone would take that girl off my hands, I'd give the man *five* dowries.' The siege of Troy would be conspicuously lacking in this case, he realized. Not long afterwards he convinced himself that he was another Odysseus. Lacking a Penelope, however – even though many of the Serbian girls had skilful fingers from weaving. ('Well, not *that* many,' he later admitted.) His father, saying that all his plans had gone to Hell – which I can assure you was most certainly not the case, and I should know – resolved to marry him off. He even found a bride for his son, a rich young girl from a good family. But no, the son would not agree. He would *not*. At least not until the father threatened to write him out of the will. Only then did Novak say to Hell with it all and gave in. The wedding followed, and the first night of married life. The poor girl frightened and miserable. Novak rough and furious. In fact, that's when he began to beat her. It was all her fault, he thought. And so he cursed her and beat her.

Things would have continued smoothly in this way had not Austria and the Ottoman Empire interfered in their marriage. It was 1690, a black year for the Serbs. The Turks had routed them and driven many of them as far as Belgrade in reprisal for their service under the Habsburg banner. Belgrade itself was under attack by the fiercest troops of Albanians and Tatars, and on 29 September these forces crossed the Sava and the Danube and entered Austrian territory. In the ensuing commotion, as people fled for their lives, Novak's wife was killed. That is, she drowned in the Sava. When it happened, he told me, something inside him snapped ('I could feel something inside me just give way') – and from that moment he never looked at another woman and swore off all pleasures. Except for drink. Although drinking was no pleasure, he assured me, which I found hard to believe. ('It's penance for every time I hit her. It's penance for every time I cursed her.') His father died, and rather than take over the business he drank away every last penny. And that's how I found him in Pest, at the alehouse.

'Work for the Devil? All right, I will. That's just what I want, to burn in Hell for eternity. I deserve nothing less.'

'You could burn for all eternity just as easily by committing suicide,' I answered. 'But, of course, this way you're also enjoying yourself in the meantime, thou wretched sinner. Anyway, you can't atone for one sin by committing another, if you really must know.'

But people are always doing that, making up for one sin with yet another: they ruin a woman's life, so they enlist in the army, supposedly to redeem themselves, and they end up slaughtering heaps of other people. Or they stuff their pockets with stolen goods and then gamble it all away. Or they fail at love then make up their minds never to love again.

But none of this would have happened in the first place if Novak hadn't been reading books. Before books existed, men and women didn't know anything about pure, exalted love; they believed that a great true love was one they could actually get their hands on. Only after they had started reading books did they come up with this business about love being attainable only for the most fortunate few. Mark my words. They shall burn with me, all those scribblers and their damned books, the ones to blame for people no longer loving each other, for everyone waiting to see what comes along next, for letting their eyes wander, and changing their minds, and wanting something better, wanting only the best – and all without questioning whether they themselves are worth it, or recalling the old saying 'you get what you deserve'. And the more these men and women burn, the more they'll think they deserve better. That's how I stay in business. I simply adore books, and their readers even more.

The night was wearing on, through smoke, drink and the defeat of Kosovo, and still the hajduks had not arrived. It occurred to me that they might have been frightened off. Indeed, that happens sometimes. The very worst criminals – murderers, rapists, kings and poets – simply quail at the sight of me. Men and women who never blanch at acts of evil cannot bring themselves to face Evil Itself. I've often wondered why. Of course, they're mistaken in believing me to be evil through and through, as if there were nothing else to me. They don't understand, the foolish creatures. If I were pure evil I would be God. Because God is God so that He might be nothing but good, and that is the same as being nothing but evil. God is God because God is One and nothing else. All the rest of us, from the angels to the children of men to myself are a mixture of good and evil. Now, the individual *proportions* are a different matter altogether. These men and women, the worst of humanity's worst, fear the One. Whether good or evil. They cannot stand before God, and they cannot stand before me.

Besides, they go in terror of me for another reason. And quite rightly.

They know I outdo the worst of them. And such creatures fear no one but those who are worse than themselves. The violent, the cruel, the sinful – they fear only violence, cruelty and sins greater than their own.

'Is there any point in waiting?' I asked Novak.

'You can't expect outlaws to be punctual,' he answered sagely.

'Very well,' I said. 'We'll stay for one more beer.'

We ordered the beer, and as Novak was listening to the gusle-player with such rapt attention I made no attempt at conversation. Instead, I cast my eye around the room, thinking perhaps to find an interesting soul.

Which I did not.

I'd had quite enough by then and told Novak it was time to leave, that it was pointless to continue waiting. Novak got to his feet reluctantly, no doubt displeased at being deprived of the gusle-playing. We headed for the door, and I said, 'That instrument we've been listening to, I simply must have some set up in Hell. That way, if we get someone who happens to enjoy a roaring fire, we can always use the gusle on them instead.' Novak only narrowed his eyes but said nothing. To my surprise.

But at the door, as if from nowhere, two little men appeared: one was bandy-legged and had a very large moustache; the other had a very large moustache and was bald.

'Arr you the Devil?' asked the bald one, addressing me. He rolled his Rs.

'I am he,' I answered. And then, just to make a point about the Rs, I added, 'That's rright.'

'Then it's us you want to see,' said the bandy-legged one. I didn't know what his Rs sounded like, as he hadn't used any yet.

'*These* are your hajduks?' I said to Novak. He frowned and motioned towards the table. We all sat down.

This is my number. Or so they say.

So here we sit, the four of us. I'm the first to speak. 'Out with your story, then.'

'Money firrst, up frront!'

'The money!'

How odd, as if they thought they were saying two different things. I set the purse on the table.

'And now for the story,' I said.

'Well, since you arr wanting to hearr it . . . It happened like this . . .'

We all drew closer to the table and leaned towards the story-teller.

'The Austrrians sent a tax-collectorr down this way, and two soldierrs with him.'

'I was told there were four,' I interjected.

'Two, five, makes no differrence. We knew that he liked a drrink, and the soldierrs liked a drrink, and so we lay in wait one earrly morrning, down the rroad. They'd always come that same way, the tax-collectorrs would.'

'Because it's the *only* way,' said the other hajduk. Again, I couldn't tell anything about his Rs.

'We knew they'd be hungoverr. And it was foggy out, like today . . . So they'd harrdly be cutting acrross the fields . . . The morrning goes by and us still waiting. The afternoon goes by and not a sign. We head forr the inn. Then we see, not a horrse in sight. So they'd gone by in the morrning afterr all.'

'We hadn't expected that,' said the other. Still no Rs.

'I'm not interested in what you were or weren't expecting. It doesn't matter,' I said, trying to speed the story along.

'Rright. So I say to him, I say, they've gone off, the drrunkards, and got lost in the fog. Shall we go afterr them?'

'Let's go after them.' Aha, an R at last.

'And so we head off along the rroad, like, looking rright and left. Going on and on. And afterr a while the fog clearrs out. And the sun's beating down . . .' From Schmidlin's account I couldn't recall what time of year it was when the tax-collector disappeared. '. . . and us all thirrsty. And I say, shall we go back to the inn?'

'Let's go back to the inn.'

'So we have a drrink, and we settle the bill like decent folk, and off we go, back down the rroad. They could have turrned back, couldn't they? What with being drrunk and taking the wrrong way, they'd turrn arround and come back. So we head back. It's a hot day, and us rriding along. Rriding, rriding along, and noonday in summerr. I say, shall we go back to the inn?'

'Let's go back to the inn.'

'So we each have two drrinks morr. Maybe by now they've found the rright way. Out on the high rroad. And so we look again, left and rright. And no sign of them, like the earrth has swallowed them up.'

'So you thought you'd go back to the inn,' I offered helpfully.

'Just what I said myself. I say, shall we go back to the inn?'

'Let's go back to the inn.'

'So we each have anotherr two drrinks.'

'Two.'

'And I say, shall we go back again, the same way? They've given us the slip, they have, if they set off this morrning. So there we arr again, looking left and rright. Nothing, no sign of them. Shall we go back to the inn?'

'Let's go back to the inn.'

'So back we go. And the innkeeper says, "You've drunk me dry, you have." Not us, I say, not with the wee bit we've been sipping. "You and that other lot downstairs," he says. What other lot would that be then? "Why, those Austrians." Downstairs? In the cellarr? And what about the horrses? Where's the horrses, then? "They had me set them loose in the meadow to graze." So, the cellarr. Down to the cellarr we go. The soldiers, dead drunk. The tax-collectorr still with his eyes open. We slit his throat. We take the money. We leave the soldiers where they arr, nothing we can do to them in that state.'

'We can't do it if they haven't got their eyes open.'

'You can't slit someone's throat unless its owner is looking at you?' I asked, not quite clear on this point.

'We cannot. We did trry waking them up. But they werre dead drunk.'

'Just like the dead.'

'We take the tax-collectorr and burry the body so no one can find it.'

'Where do the vampires come in?' I ask.

'Ah, that comes later, Devil, sirr.'

'Go on.'

'A year later, a man goes and dies. And we put him in the same cellarr. The Austrrians . . .'

'Our own lads, those über-captains . . .'

'That's rright, our überr-captains go and find him. We tip them off, don't you know?'

'No, I don't know.'

'Because this parrticularr man . . .' he said, chortling through his Rs, and breaking into guffaws.

'What's so funny?' I said then looked at Novak. But he was also at a loss and merely shrugged. The man with the rolling Rs was now rolling around with them on the filthy floor. The other man had greater composure and was merely shaking with laughter where he sat. Then the laughter was picked up by the neighbouring table. And the next. And in less time than it would take for me to remember my last ten good deeds, the entire alehouse had erupted into Serbian laughter.

'The man, Devil sir, the man was . . .' But unable to finish his sentence, he, too, fell to the floor.

I had it! The man had resembled the tax-collector. And they set him up, the man who had just died, to make it look as though he *was* the tax-collector. After a year or half a year he would have seemed quite fresh. That's what Schmidlin had been trying to say. The corpse had seemed extraordinarily well-preserved.

I struck the table with my hand. So, that was the story of the vampires – that they were nothing but a story. Just like that, they had vanished.

As had my purse. And the hajduks.

7

At least I can stop worrying. Although they certainly cleaned me out. But then, everything has a price. Whether you're finding out that something exists or finding out that it doesn't. So, there are no vampires. The whole fuss was caused by two little men who couldn't get their tongues around the letter R. And the matter had gone as far as the emperor in Vienna. To say nothing of myself.

If that's how things stand I can return to Vienna and from there to Paris. Lots of work waiting for me in Paris. This business with the Serbs was nothing but a temporary diversion and setback. My only regret is not being able to spend more time with that wonderful soul, Maria Augusta of Thurn and Taxis. But now that I think of it, why not? Matters in France will be none the worse for my spending another month or so in Belgrade and collecting that prematurely aged soul. Why not indeed?

I told Novak we could go.

We stepped out into the fog, which had lifted a little even though it was not yet dawn. Back we went along what I assume were the same streets, but uphill. Novak was moving quickly and did not speak. I didn't know whether he was disappointed that there were no vampires or had simply failed to understand what was happening. Perhaps he was still under the spell of the gusle-player's song. I myself am interested in folk traditions. I've heard all the Serbian stories about St Sava and me and about me and my apprentice. Too bad for storytellers who have no love for me in their hearts – it's only in stories that you'll find me playing the fool. I've never even met their St Sava, never hired an apprentice. All I've ever had is servants, as I do now. A servant not an apprentice. Because an apprentice wants to learn, to take over the shop some day, while a servant wants only to serve out his time and not be bothered.

'*Haaalt!*' came the ear-splitting command. Startled, I looked around me yet saw nothing but the fog.

'Master, it's the guard at the gate.'

I answered in German, saying who I was and asking to be let back into Weissburg.

The voice asked for the password.

'What do you mean, password?'

'Off with you then.'

I looked at Novak. He looked at me.

'Now we can't get back into the German part of town. We don't know the password. You didn't tell me there was a password. It is your duty as a servant to keep track of such things.'

'Don't get upset, master. Let's wait a bit. Someone from the German side who knows us may come out and be able to vouch for us.'

'Someone who knows us, you idiot? There's no one but Schmidlin and Radetzky, and they're not coming out. Or rather, Radetzky might, but not until the commission does.'

'There, see?'

'No, I do *not* see. What are we supposed to do until then? Assuming they ever do come out. I don't like it, I don't like being on the wrong side of Prince Eugene's line.'

8

In helpless fury I stood cursing my servant. The fool!

It was still foggy and dark, and I could see no further than a few feet in front of me. How humiliating to sit waiting at the gate. For any waiting is always a humiliation, no matter what you're waiting for. I had to go somewhere, but where? And so I craned my neck and looked around me, not wanting to say another word to Novak.

But Novak spoke first. 'Someone's coming, master.' I couldn't hear anything and merely waved his words away. But again he said, 'Believe me, master. Someone is coming this way.' Again I pricked up my ears, but still I heard nothing. I gave him a scornful look, but he said for the third time, quite in the spirit of the Serbian songs we'd been listening to, 'Master, I'm sure there's someone coming.'

And then from out of the fog came a pair of oxen. Behind them was a cart, and in it sat a peasant holding a switch. The cart drew closer and closer, and still there was no sound. From time to time the peasant would flick at the oxen, but no swish or crack could be heard.

'Shall we go with him?' asked Novak.

'Go where?'

'What do you mean? Surely you just heard him ask if we're going to Dedejsko Selo.'

'No, I didn't hear that.' I thought I must be going mad. 'Well then, why not?'

The peasant halted the cart, and Novak and I climbed up.

I sat beside the driver, while Novak sat behind us facing the other way. No one spoke a word, at least not that I could hear. An unpleasant feeling took hold of me. Whenever I feel uneasy I pay attention to the little things around me. This occupies first my attention and then my thoughts, and in a little while I stop feeling anything at all. Now, the little thing I had spied right away was the sack the peasant was holding on his lap: it was of leather, but old and worn. There was something inside it, something I couldn't make out.

For a long time we rode along, and the only sounds were Novak and myself as we shifted in our seats. The fog lay thick and heavy.

If I were anyone else I would have assumed that the utter stillness was the work of the powers of darkness. As it was, I could only suspect the other side – so to speak.

I cleared my throat, just to have something to listen to. The fog seemed to be getting thicker and thicker, and the peasant seemed to be driving by memory alone, or else the oxen themselves were following a path they knew by heart, as the way could not be seen. At one point the fog began to shine. The sun must have been struggling to rise in the east, its rays illuminating the mists. Shortly thereafter the sun must have gone back down. And still I could hear no sound.

Our path was suddenly blocked by a small fortified gate. On either side stretched low defensive walls made of wooden palings, scarcely higher than a short man.

'This is what they call the field line,' said Novak. 'It protects the Serbian town, the one outside Prince Eugene's line.'

For no reason I could see or hear, the doors swung open. We passed through the gate. The fog was starting to fill with light again.

Just on the other side of the gate our way was blocked by a stream. The peasant urged the oxen forward, but they baulked at first. No sooner had the cart entered the water than we sank into the mud. And there we sat, not moving. The peasant shifted in his seat, not wanting to lash the oxen and not wanting to get down and lead them across. At last he made up his mind to step down. It was the moment I had been waiting for. As soon as he had his hands full with the oxen I grabbed the sack he had been holding. Quickly I undid the string and opened it.

Inside there was a cone of sugar.

I couldn't resist, and I nibbled a bit off the top. The sugar was sweet, of course. No surprise there. I quickly tied it up again in the bag and put it back.

The peasant was still dealing with the oxen. Novak joined him, and by working together they were able to get the oxen moving and free the cart from the muck. When we reached the other bank the peasant and Novak climbed back into the cart.

We had not gone much further when Novak announced importantly, 'We're here.'

We jumped down from the cart, and the peasant vanished into the fog and the night.

'A good man, that peasant,' Novak said.

'You know I loathe good people.'

'But you'll ride with them.'

'I certainly will. I've got a sweet tooth for taking advantage of good people. This whole thing has left a most delightful taste in my mouth, in every sense of the word.'

9

I was exhausted, and I sat down on a good-sized rock beside the road. The rough surface was uncomfortable, but it was still better than squatting in the dust like a beggar. I've always thought you can tell the masters from the servants first and foremost by where they sit: the masters will always be sitting *on* something, no matter how uncomfortable, while the servants will always be sitting *in* something. Novak confirmed the rule once again, of course, and I looked down at him and asked, 'Where are we now?'

'Why, in Dedejsko Selo.'

'Ah, yes. And how far from Kalemegdan?'

'I couldn't say for sure, master, but I reckon we're an hour's stiff walk from the gate we came out of.'

Too far then, I said to myself. We shouldn't have come so far out of our way. I decided that the best thing was to have a rest, perhaps a bit of sleep, tired as I was, and then to make our way back to the Fortress of Kalemegdan. There had been no point in riding this far. The fog was slowly lifting. The moon's false sheen was giving way to true and burning light. I don't care for mornings, and I knew this one would be no exception. As I sat there thinking, I heard the sound of horses and loud voices.

'Someone coming, master.'

'I'm well aware of that.' My keen sense of hearing had returned.

I looked around but could see nowhere to hide. By the frightened expression on my servant's face, I could tell that he was faring no better. I drew my gun and said calmly, 'If they're bandits, we fight. If they're gentlemen, I shall introduce myself.'

'As the Devil or as Otto von Hausburg?' my servant asked.

'Don't be stupid! Even if I did introduce myself as the Devil, who would believe me? They'd think I was out of my mind. It's happened before, as you know perfectly well. I can't stand it when you play the fool.'

The riders were nearly upon us, and it was clear that these were no hajduks. They wore armour and wigs, leaving no doubt that they were, in fact, Austrians, and noble ones at that. I slipped my gun back under my cloak.

The middle horseman, unlike his companions, had no wig. He wore his hair very short, his head nearly shaved. He had the neck of a bull and hands so massive he could easily have felled a horse with them. From his appearance, he had clearly dressed in haste or without care. He was well fattened, but muscular. Only when he had reached us did I notice the scar that stretched from his left ear to the top of his head. He was not particularly young – perhaps fifty years old.

On his left rode an old man. Neither the blackness of his wig nor the straightness of his posture could conceal his age. Everything he wore was spotless and shining, and a mantle of noble crimson hung over the back of his horse, brushing the ground.

The third horseman, on the right of the man with the scar, was young, barely twenty years old. He had a great black moustachio and I knew at once that he was a Serb. He wore the uniform of an *Oberkapitän*.

These three were followed by some ten others, all well-armed, while bringing up the rear were horse-drawn covered wagons.

The riders halted at a signal from the middle horseman. He looked at me for some time then said, 'You are the Devil himself.'

You said it, I thought. But aloud I said, 'The Devil indeed. I am Otto von Hausburg.'

'You can't fool *me*. And you seem to be in a tight spot. Hardly to be expected of the Devil. But then, you're no stranger to me.'

'I am to be addressed as *Count*.'

He laughed heartily then called out, 'A horse for the Devil!'

'And his servant,' I added.

'The Devil and his apprentice. Horses, and make it quick!'

He did not introduce himself. None of them introduced themselves. Such behaviour is the mark of either the extremely self-confident or the extremely insecure. The latter are ashamed of their own names – that is, they consider themselves unworthy of having a name at all – while the former simply assume that everyone already knows who they are.

I was given a mare to ride and managed with some difficulty. Apparently the horse was unaccustomed to being ridden, and made this point rather clear. We all set off – me struggling to keep the mare in line, the others without any trouble.

As we rode towards Belgrade and left Dedejsko Selo behind, I wondered about the identity of this man and his curious retinue. He must be a nobleman of some sort, as was the man in crimson. It occurred to me that the best way to find out was to drop Baron Schmidlin's name then see how the conversation developed. I spoke up. 'Yesterday, when I was speaking with Baron Schmidlin . . .'

'Oh, talking to Schmidlin, were you?' interrupted the man with the scar. 'He must have told you never, ever to refer to me as head of the administration, but as Regent of Serbia.'

So, this was Alexander of Württemberg, Regent of Serbia, great commander under Prince Eugene of Savoy and husband to that wonderful woman, that long-suffering soul.

'Schmidlin's an ass,' I said with pleasure.

'Yes,' laughed Württemberg, 'but don't even think of mentioning the word administration in my title.'

I said nothing. But how very galling it could be, the behaviour I had to put up with sometimes. And from human beings. Do people not read books, the New Testament? Does it not say quite clearly that I am Prince of this World? Doesn't that come straight from the Old Fishmouth Himself, that vile Jew, and from that other vile Jew, Paul? People don't believe the words of their own faith. Here was this petty bureaucrat instructing me – me, mind you, ruler of this world and all it holds – on the finer points of addressing him. On one side, the lord of all the world; on the other, a head of administration.

'Your Highness, Lord Regent of Serbia, was the hunt a success?' I asked just to pass the time.

'I'm not satisfied.' Then he began to speak, at great length, about the trifling events of his hunts as if they were veritable battles, with the fate of kingdoms hanging in the balance. Many kings and princes have I known, many high rulers, in many lands and many times, and

I find them to have one thing in common: they all consider their personal matters and amusements to be the most important things in the world; they all imagine their hobbies, their hunts, their amorous escapades and dances to be ever so important, to be taken ever so seriously. At the same time, they show considerably less effort and concern when it comes to ruling their lands and people.

He went on talking, but I wasn't listening. And, as I had nothing better to keep my mind occupied, I naturally began to follow the conversation between the Serb horseman and one of the other soldiers. They were speaking of the victory at Belgrade in 1716. The Serb with the moustache was explaining.

'The fortress had to be taken before Turkish reinforcements could get there. As quick as we could, we set up a pontoon bridge across the Danube, and do you know who the first man across was? Our glorious prince, Regent of Serbia, Alexander of Württemberg. Then we headed towards Vračar and laid out the first line of attack. Blast after blast, we kept up a barrage from every cannon we had, and once we even managed to hit a powder magazine in the lower town. Our engineers had planned out the assault on the walls. When you take a city the battle almost always goes the same way: you keep firing the cannon until you breach the walls. Meanwhile, the infantry is filling in the defensive ditches with earth, loose stone – anything they can shovel up.'

'But isn't the point,' I said, 'to get through the gates?'

'Not very often, not very often at all. It's best to keep the gates as they are, best to take them intact. Normally the gatehouse will have its own detachment. And an army can get into a city just as well through any old hole in the wall,' he responded.

'But even when you blast an opening in the wall, doesn't the defender simply double his forces on the spot?'

'Sir, you are apparently not familiar with siegecraft. The prevailing custom, you see, is to offer the city a chance to surrender, once its walls have been breached. If they accept, the city is not sacked, and the defenders even have the right to leave the city under armed guard.'

'And you offered such terms to the Turks?'

'No, our artillery never made a scratch in the walls.'

'Then how did you take Belgrade?'

'The reinforcements sent by Halil Pasha had reached Belgrade, but they were unable to enter the city because Mustapha Pasha Čelić, commander of the Fortress of Kalemegdan, had ordered all the bridges destroyed to prevent his own army from fleeing. Halil Pasha dug in at Ekmekluk. We locked forces on the field at Mali Mokri Lug, 16 August, just after midnight.'

'Mali Mokri Lug?'

'Yes, that's the name of the village. We broke through their ranks with our first charge, at least our right flank did. Then the Turkish cavalry seemed to rise from the dead, and they nearly turned the battle around. At that moment a thick fog fell all around us, making it impossible to see. We stood there, waiting, as did the Turks. Our generals all wanted to wait out the fog until morning then strike at first light, but Prince Eugene of Savoy ordered us to attack immediately. In the fog our flanks got separated. The Turks quickly realized what was happening, but then Prince Eugene himself and his second line charged into battle and fought all the way through to the second Turkish line. The only thing that saved us was his incredible courage. If only you could have seen the man, charging through the darkness and fog against the Turks. The same Eugene of Savoy who was turned down by Louis XIV of France as being too short for military service. There never was a man to match Prince Eugene! Our very own regent fought in the same battle. In Vienna the wagging tongues say he is under Prince Eugene's special protection, but in that battle he received the wound you see on his head at the hands of a janissary. If that's what you can expect from special protection, you can keep it. Evil tongues have done more damage to our regent than enemy hands and sabres. We killed fifteen thousand Turkish soldiers, took their entire camp, and Halil Pasha retreated and didn't stop running until Niš. Mustapha Pasha Čelić was still refusing to surrender the city, and we beat him again. Two days later the commander of the Fortress of Kalemegdan signed the surrender of the city. That's why the fortress itself was never taken. We beat the Turks *outside* the fortress. Under the terms of surrender the city's garrison and any surviving Turks were allowed to leave for Ottoman lands with their women and children and whatever bags and weapons they could carry on their shoulders and tie around their waists. They went to Niš.'

'I see,' I said.

'And now we've built an even stronger fortress, one that no one will ever be able to conquer,' he concluded through his moustache.

Someone began reciting in Classical Greek: '*Sing, O muse, of Achilles and his wrath, son to Peleus / Whose fury on Achaean heads a thousand woes did wreak . . .*' The same voice continued, 'Is there any city that has ever withstood a siege?'

I turned around, but the only figure directly behind me was the man with the crimson cloak, and the set of his lips implied that he had not spoken at all. He didn't seem like the type with nothing to say, however. Indeed, he looked like someone who has quite a lot to say but who is keeping his mouth shut in order to seem serious and grand. People often imagine that silence is a sign of weighty decision-making or profound meditation on the meaning of life. Which it is.

'Are you happy now that you've freed your land from the Turks?' I asked the moustachioed Serb in his own language. He was obviously surprised that I could speak Serbian. His eyes widened. To avoid answering right away he took out a bag of tobacco and began to stuff his pipe, a Turkish chibouk. His horse was well-trained, and the Serb didn't spill much tobacco. He was a dab hand at it.

'What's it like in Hell?' came the question from the regent instead of an answer from the Serb.

I replied. 'In Hell it is cold, and the sun warms it not. Further north than north itself lies Hell. And everlasting night is there, a starless, moonless night . . .'

'Unholy sir, I'm a mercenary. As far as I'm concerned, the best side is the one that's paying the most,' said the man with the moustache.

'. . . a mantling blackness wraps around it,' I continued, 'and never any light, no, never a gladdening ray shall fall on those who dwell there.'

'Dark,' the regent concluded.

'Right, can't see a thing,' I retorted.

'Not much of a punishment then if there's nothing to see,' Württemberg said wisely.

'Your Highness, King of Serbia, just knowing is more than enough; one needn't actually *see* it.'

'But most people are bloody fools and only know what they see,' continued the indomitable administrator.

'We don't get that sort in Hell.'

'Ah,' Württemberg said, then fell silent.

Here was my chance to continue the conversation with the moustachio. 'What's your name then, young hero?'

'Vuk Isakovič, unholy sir.'

As the words left his mouth, the man in the crimson cloak frowned at him, almost angrily, as if the young man had revealed a secret meant to be guarded from strange ears. Isakovič flinched and sped his horse forward; he dropped back again, but so that the man in crimson was now between us. It was obvious that Isakovič was no longer allowed to speak to me. I wondered what sort of power the other man must command if Vuk Isakovič feared him more than me.

We reached the little river and the gate in the low wooden walls. We were about to enter the Serbian town. One of the soldiers called out, the door swung open and we forded the stream and galloped through the gateway.

Novak rode alongside to speak to me.

'Why are you talking to that captain? He's getting fat on the blood of his own people. He steals from the Serbs and gives to the Austrians, and all the while he's lining his own pockets. And why ask him if he's glad the land is free from the Turks?' Novak seemed to think that Isakovič had hesitated to answer for some other reason, and not just because of the man in crimson.

'Well, why not?' I said, playing innocent.

'Of course he's glad, now he can get back to thieving. Under the Turks he wouldn't have been able to.'

'And what about you? Are you happy that Serbia has been liberated from the Turks?'

'That's a hard question to answer.'

'Oh? How so?'

'Because it all depends on what you're expecting.'

'Expecting? Serbia's been under Austrian rule for a good twenty years now, and it was under the Turks for quite a bit longer,' I said.

'That's not what I meant. It's like this: if you're expecting the worst, or something only a bit better than the worst, you'll be happy with whatever actually comes along. But if you were hoping for the best, anything that falls even a bit short will seem terrible.'

'Will it?'

'And once the Turks were gone the Serbs were expecting the very best.'

'And had their hopes dashed.'

'Yes, but that's not all, meaning the worst is yet to come . . .' Again and again he paused.

'I'm listening.'

'The Austrians won't be staying much longer in Serbia. Everyone knows the Turks will be back, and everyone's expecting the worst.'

'And?'

'What's it like in Hell?' asked the regent, as if he had forgotten our conversation of only moments earlier.

I was caught off guard, but maintained my composure and replied, 'In Hell it is hot. Further south than south itself. The sun never sets. Everything is lit up, and anything that can burn, burns. The sky is yellow, and there is no shade, no shadows. The sheer light, which never goes out and never diminishes, makes it impossible to see.'

'What kind of punishment is that if you can't see anything?' he asked, as if he had never asked before.

'There is no need to see it. Just knowing is enough,' I answered, playing along.

'But there are any number of fools who only know what they see.' I couldn't believe my own ears.

'True, Your Highness, and those fools are all in Hell.'

'The Turks won't make the same mistake they made fifty years ago,' my servant cut in, 'when they took revenge on the Serbs for what happened with Austria. And this time things won't be anywhere near the worst. Do you understand?'

'Not exactly.'

'Expectations are too high. To the Serbs, the Austrians seemed like ferocious beasts. The Turks will seem like gentle lambs. That's life for you: you expect the best of good people and are always disappointed; you expect the worst of bad people and always end up pleasantly surprised. It's no wonder we're always in such bad company. Goodness is hard to bear. It's never quite good enough.'

'Are you insinuating something, you impertinent menial?'

'I don't understand,' put in Württemberg. 'How it can be cold and the sun never shines and also hot and the sun never stops shining. And how can there be no fools in Hell and Hell be full of fools? Which is the truth?'

'Both,' I answered.

Before us rose the gate that guarded the way into the German part of the city. Just as we were about to cross Prince Eugene's line, I noticed that the man in crimson was gone.

FIVE
The Fortress of
Kalemegdan

1

I am Maria Augusta, Princess of Thurn and Taxis, wife to Prince Alexander of Württemberg, the former Regent of Serbia. I have three sons, all named Eugene after my husband's protector, Prince Eugene of Savoy, and one daughter, Katarina. I came to Serbia, to Belgrade, in 1730, and I left at the beginning of 1737. All the children were born after my departure from Belgrade.

The man you ask about was introduced to me in Belgrade in the autumn of 1736. He was said to have appeared a day earlier, but I saw him for the first time when Baron Schmidlin was taking him around the Kalemegdan Fortress in Belgrade.

What did he look like? Ordinary, quite ordinary. Medium height, brown hair and eyes with no distinguishing features. No, he didn't limp. He spoke flawless German, although one sensed it was not his native language, and Serbian and Hungarian besides, as I was told. I know he was reading some books in French and English. No, it didn't strike me as suspicious – in fact, I thought at the time that it was a rare opportunity to meet an exceptionally well-educated man.

You want me to tell you everything just as it happened? I am sorry, my hearing is not good.

Not to leave out a single unimportant detail?

You'll decide what's important and what isn't?

It was exceptionally sunny and warm for the lateness of the season, a real Indian summer. I had gone for a walk by myself. I was fond of walking alone around Kalemegdan. I passed through the King's Gate and climbed to the promontory, to the left of the cistern, and stood looking out over the Sava and the Danube where they meet and at the land on the far side of the rivers. At the time I did not realize, although I know now, that this very spot offers the first and best view of Europe. Shall I explain? I say the first view because it's where Europe begins, and the best view because you can only appreciate the meaning of Europe, its true vulnerability and its true might, by standing outside it, sometimes regretting that you cannot enter and sometimes glad you're not inside it. You don't follow my meaning? No matter.

As I say, I stood there looking out over the Sava and the Danube. The rivers were different. The Sava was brown, and the Danube had more of a bluish colour. And I wondered whether the colour of rivers depended on their length, whether the water could only be purified by flowing long enough. Or does the clarity depend on the lands through which the river flows, the rocks and soil, and the people who enter its waters? Is purity the result of a long struggle, carving out a channel to flow in, twisting and turning all the while, or does it just come drifting along on the current, carefree and easy? Or does a river remain the same from its source all the way to the end, and nothing along the way can alter it?

Unimportant details? Well, you're the one who asked for the whole story.

As I stood there thinking I was interrupted by Baron Schmidlin, who approached me with four other gentlemen. Three of them were members of the special vampire commission and the fourth was von Hausburg.

Soon after the first three left with Schmidlin. But von Hausburg, or whatever his name is, stayed behind. He offered to accompany me on a stroll around Kalemegdan, and I agreed. We walked in the sunshine and made small talk. No, we didn't discuss God. Although . . . I do remember something von Hausburg said later, on another occasion.

He said, 'There's nothing to be said about God. He's already said it all himself.'

Is that important? Shall I continue?

I asked him what he meant by that, and he answered, 'He spoke the world into existence. Let there be light, let there be this, let there be that. He didn't do anything else, just spoke. Doesn't the world he's made tell you quite enough about him and the language he speaks?'

But that came later. That first time, on our walk around Kalemegdan, we didn't talk about God.

He was most courteous, more than was called for. Yes, it did occur to me that his intentions towards me . . . that his show of goodwill went further than it should have. At one moment he abruptly bowed and seized my hand. And smelled it. I didn't pull my hand back because I didn't think he would do any harm. I wasn't frightened, merely surprised. I was about to ask him the meaning of his gesture, but he told me first.

'There is no odour of brimstone about you.'

I was at quite a loss, and he took advantage of the moment to bow once again, say goodbye and hurry off. That was the first time I thought the man's mind might be disturbed.

I bent down to pick up my fan, which I had dropped in surprise. Fortunately, it wasn't soiled. It was my favourite fan. Chinese. All across one side of it was painted the Great Wall. The artist had rendered it as massive, mighty, impregnable. Near the handle were muddy fields of rice, with peasants wading through the water and bowing before a motley procession. On the other side of the wall was a wonderful landscape of the most beautiful trees, flowers, birds and a crystal-clear river full of fish, flowing swiftly past evergreen forests and snow-capped mountains dotted with monasteries. The people were reading scrolls or conversing . . .

What's that you say?

I'm not sticking to the point?

Was I surprised at von Hausburg's behaviour?

No, I wasn't surprised. Nothing surprises me any more. I grew up and ceased to be surprised. Growing up means understanding that things are not the way we were taught, that things are quite often just the opposite, that people go on living and bearing things that are considered unbearable, and God only knows the consequences. Why are we brought up that way? So that we'll be better people, striving to achieve the unachievable? Or will we become even worse one day, when we realize that we shall never attain the ideal, and we start hating those who taught us otherwise and those who still stand by their claims?

But I must ask, dear cousin, why all these questions? And after so many years?

2

I never had any interest in the Fortress of Kalemegdan. And why should I? I was tired of sleepless nights, of the regent and his never-ending questions. The man in crimson was a worry. At least I'd laid the vampire business to rest. I wanted to get some sleep.

The instant I'd dozed off Schmidlin woke me up and dragged me off on his tour. He talked and talked and never stopped talking. First the history of the fortress: the Roman legion of Flavius IV, driven out by the Huns, followed by the Byzantines, who were driven out by the Magyars, then the Serbs, who were driven out by the Turks. And what about us? Who was going to drive us out? I asked Schmidlin. He didn't answer that one but rattled right along.

'Did you know that Belgrade was a dowry? The Serbs didn't conquer Belgrade, they received it as the dowry of the Hungarian princess who was given in marriage to King Dragutin.'

Sometimes it pays to get married. That's the only point in its favour.

As for the two types of fortress that exist, and the fact that Belgrade used to belong to the first type, I confess my ignorance. According to Schmidlin, fortified cities (meaning all of them, so I'll just say 'cities') can be divided into the categories of Christian and Crusader. How so? Christian cities have few protective walls and are surrounded by shallow defensive ditches, their bastions are unstrategically placed and their cannon are only good for short-range engagement, but their defenders are numerous, courageous and unbeatable. On the other hand, we have the Crusader type . . . And this is merely a way of referring to them, the baron warned, and should not be construed as denying the status of Christian to the Crusaders let alone implying that the Crusades themselves were not a Christian undertaking. To continue, the Crusader type of city was surrounded by the strongest, highest, thickest walls with the deepest moats and ditches and the most far-reaching artillery, all of which required great numbers of defenders – numbers that were simply not to be found in the Holy Land, which is why you could hear a pin drop in the streets. Well, Schmidlin didn't put it quite that way, but the point was that Acre, Jaffa, Ascalon, Safed, Samaria and even Jerusalem itself had no one to defend them and that their very builders had relied more on stone and mortar than on the people within. And such mighty fortresses attracted the very worst mercenaries and cowards, men who trusted in architecture not in themselves. And, least of all, in the good God above (as he put it).

In the time of Jan Hunyadi, Belgrade was as Christian as Christian can be, the baron informed us, while now – by God (as he said) – it was both Christian and Crusader.

Then he stuck out his chest as far as his stomach would allow and said, 'You must see the cistern. It's a masterpiece of modern architecture. It took us twelve years to build. We completed it five years ago.'

We passed through the King's Gate and immediately to the right was the entrance to the cistern. Although the day was sunny and warm, the air inside was damp and stale. We walked down a wide tunnel that had water dripping from the ceiling. In the left-hand wall three semi-circular niches held burning torches. Only steps from the entrance, on the right, there was a small chamber. I looked inside. There were three fountains. I continued down the tunnel and came to a great chamber with a high domed ceiling. Every surface was wet. A dozen torches provided illumination. In the centre was an enormous hole, surrounded by a barrier. A short flight of steps led to a raised walkway that ran around the hole. The three men from the commission were already staring down into the great hole, and Schmidlin was telling them about the dimensions of the cistern. At the bottom of the hole would be water, I presumed, and I declined to climb up and look down.

'If Belgrade should ever find itself under siege, this cistern will do away with any worries about water,' Schmidlin said. Suddenly there was a strong gust of wind. Out went all the torches. We stood in utter darkness. I thought I would scream.

Schmidlin spoke. 'I'll be right back.'

He must have felt his way out through the dark. I heard some rustling. I was alone with the three fools. Fortunately I couldn't see their wigs. But I still somehow felt it would be nice to hear their voices. And so I struck up a conversation.

'Have you learned anything more about those captains?'

'Oh, not a thing,' said a voice I recognized as Radetzky's. 'But Baron Schmidlin has arranged for us to spend tomorrow night in Dedinaberg. But you must know this already.'

Of course I didn't know. And I didn't care either. The vampires were nothing but a hoax perpetrated by two hajduks. But I had to stay in character, and so I said, 'Yes, I know the place.'

'You've already been to the watermill?' As always, Radetzky was ready to spill the beans.

'Of course.'

'Did you see them?'

'No.' I didn't want to stretch the lie that far. But then I had a wonderful idea. I felt like having a bit of fun with the Austrians. 'Although some Serbs I spoke to last night did tell me that a vampire has been seen at the mill.'

'I know. Baron Schmidlin has even told me his name,' said Radetzky's voice.

'Whose name?' I asked.

'The vampire's,' said Radetzky in hushed awe.

'And what *is* the vampire's name?'

3

'Sava Savanović,' came the answer, as if a great secret were being revealed. 'Do you wish to accompany me to the mill?' Radetzky added.

'No,' I hastened to answer. 'I'm supposed to be keeping an eye on things. You understand.'

Light shone out. It was Schmidlin with a torch. 'I beg your pardon, gentlemen, for the inconvenience. Please, follow me and we shall soon be out.'

We stepped outside and the first thing I saw was *her*. The princess, bathed in the late-summer light. In Serbian they call it St Michael's summer – a name I can't stand, of course. Nor can I fathom that phrase, 'bathed in light'. Next thing you know, they'll have everyone 'soaped up in sunshine' or some such nonsense. But she looked even more sublime, even more *soulful* than on the previous evening when I had seen her by candlelight. Instantly I remembered the gruesome scar her husband sported on his face. No wonder her heart belonged to another. Which was bad news for me. I would have two rivals to contend with: one with a wedding ring and another without.

'Aren't you going to introduce us to the regent's wife?' I asked Schmidlin.

'Oh . . . of course, Herr Graf.'

Schmidlin brought us to Maria Augusta. She was facing the rivers and was looking out over the place where they met, or at the land on the other side.

'Your . . . Your Highness,' said Schmidlin awkwardly. When she turned around he was completely at a loss. 'Allow me to introduce you . . . these gentlemen, the commissioners – I mean the count, the doctor – or rather, not the commission – do forgive me. These gentlemen arrived yesterday. I – they are . . . Count Radetzky of Vienna and Count von Hausburg and counts, erm, of science, whose names at the moment escape me . . .'

Maria Augusta smiled pleasantly and said, in the world's softest voice, 'Baron, I beg you, no apologies. It is best to allow the gentlemen to introduce themselves.'

'I am Klaus Radetzky, physician in the service of His Majesty Karl VI. And now you will excuse me. Matters of state await me.'

It was quite rude of him. Not allowing his two associates to introduce themselves, Radetzky strode away, beckoning them to follow, and leaving me behind with Schmidlin and Maria Augusta. I was surprised. What could be the meaning of such disrespect towards the regent's wife?

As soon as they were gone, a servant appeared and spoke to Schmidlin, who made his clumsy apologies and left. At last I was alone with Maria Augusta. The perfect opportunity to win her for myself. Or to throw her into confusion. Which amounts to the same thing.

'Would you like me to keep you company on your stroll?' I asked her.

'Certainly, Herr Graf.'

4

However, the princess was not in a talkative mood. She walked alongside me, deep in her own thoughts, stooping a bit and seeming tired. I know that one of the best ways to get close to a woman is to come right out and ask her what's wrong. None of them can resist a shoulder to cry on. And once they've had a good cry, they feel a bond with the shoulder's owner. Besides, women like a bit of verbal derring-do. I think they even prefer big talk to big muscles. It stands to reason. Plunging headlong into the fray with a battle cry is the unmistakable mark of a fool, while a direct question always leaves room for doubt in the listener's mind: is the man asking the question simple-minded, honourable, sincere, curious, cunning or simply lacking in good manners? And women adore a secret.

'I can't help noticing that you are in low spirits today. And such a mood cannot show even the most beautiful woman to advantage.'

She glanced at me then continued to look down at the path we were following, not saying a word.

'Yesterday, at the ball, I couldn't help overhearing something you said to the lady beside you.'

'Oh?'

'You said that love is the mother of all ills.'

'I did,' she answered, with a smile that seemed to pain her. I must say, I hadn't expected her to give in so readily without putting up any fight.

'Then the cause of your indisposition this day is . . . love?' I paused just long enough for my apology to seem genuine. 'I have overstepped the bounds. I beg you to forgive me.'

'But I was mistaken, you know. Love is not the mother of all ills. In fact, of all the things in this world, love is the only one that does no harm.'

'I should not be so sure of that, Your Highness.'

'Oh, yes indeed. We only think we suffer because of love. But in truth we suffer because love is not strong enough to overcome the evils that afflict us.'

'How nicely put.'

'No flattery . . .' When she said this I knew that my tactics had worked. She wanted to open up to me, and I was drawing closer.

'If I may ask, what are these evils that afflict you that love is powerless to defeat?'

'Do you imagine, Herr Graf, that I'll tell you everything, simply because you've shown that you can come straight to the point?'

I was silent. All in all, my first encounter with the princess was going well, as we made our way towards a small outbuilding. I hadn't even noticed it at first, with its unprepossessing air, its look of abandonment. However, the closer we came to it the more her pace quickened. I suddenly realized that my presence was unwelcome and for this very reason I would not take my leave. When we had reached the shack Maria Augusta stood between me and the door, turned to me and asked, 'Do you like doves?'

'I don't know,' I lied. I hate them, and not just because they're scrawled all over churches as a representation of the Holy Spirit. I hate them because, like all birds, they can fly.

'I love them dearly.'

From the shack came the sounds of fluttering wings and cooing birds. The princess clearly did not want me to step inside.

'Would you be so kind as to wait here?' she asked. 'But of course, Your Highness.'

She went inside, and I stood and thought. What could she be doing in the dovecote that she didn't want me to see? She'd hardly choose such a place for a rendezvous with a lover. And she certainly wasn't raiding the coop for raw birds. Whatever the reason, she quickly returned with a dove in her hands. The dove had a slightly upturned beak, no doubt a defect of birth. The princess took a few steps towards the fortress walls, paying no attention to me at all, and then flung the bird high into the air. The bird took flight, at first in tight circles, spiralling higher and higher, then swooping in ever-widening arcs, until at last, just before it was lost to sight, it flew off to the south. The princess stood and watched, and only when the bird had vanished over the horizon did she turn back to me, smiling broadly and as though she had done nothing out of the ordinary.

'Did you know that tonight is the costume ball?' she asked.

I had forgotten, because I don't care for such things. Winning a soul at a costume ball is most difficult.

'Think what sort of costume and mask you'd like then send your man to Count Schmettau. He's in charge of the ball. Don't worry, there's still time for you to have something done up. Our tailors are quick-fingered, and the other guests will all have their costumes by now, so this afternoon won't be too busy.'

'Have no fear, Your Highness, I shall be disguised in such a way that everyone will recognize me.'

Maria Augusta laughed, and I wanted to seize the opportunity, for if you can make someone laugh, that soul is yours for the moment.

I asked, 'And how will you be disguised?'

She didn't answer. We took leave of each other, and I hurried off to my chambers to rest before the costume ball.

When I awoke some hours later and looked out of the window I saw that dark clouds were gathering and a stiff wind was blowing. A storm was brewing. I called for Novak and briefly explained the plan.

'Tomorrow Radetzky will be spending the night at the watermill in Dedinaberg where vampires have been sighted. This time they really will appear, you understand? I want Radetzky scared into believing they do exist. One of them, preferably the most frightening one, must introduce himself as Sava Savanović.'

'Sava Savanović?'

'You've heard of him?'

'Yes, he's a real vampire.'

'What's the point of saying that now? Haven't those two thieves already explained that there are no vampires?'

'Master, they only said that vampires were not involved in one particular case, which doesn't mean that vampires aren't real.'

'You reek of drink, and you're babbling.'

'Your biggest problem, master, is that you only believe what suits you. And I don't understand why you're so interested in the vampires. You're obviously afraid of them, but here you've come all this way to Serbia on account of them.'

'I'm not afraid of vampires, and I haven't come to Serbia because of them, and they don't exist.'

'As you wish, master.'

'I wish you to go and pay some wild-looking Serbs' – as if there were any tame-looking ones – 'to introduce themselves to Radetzky. And I'm not giving you any money for it either because of your insolence, so you'll just have to take it out of your own wages. Less money on *rakija*, more on your duties.'

And off the lout went to the Serbian part of town while I made ready to pay a visit to Count Schmettau.

I was shown into his workroom. He was sitting at the desk and drawing something with the help of a rule. Papers were falling from the piles on the desk. The man barely raised his head to squint at me. He was clearly short-sighted. He was young, no older than thirty, and he wore a grey wig. The young always want to seem older, the older want to seem younger, and no one considers himself to be just the right age. There comes a certain point in life when everything is reversed, as in a looking-glass; then people begin to complain of the thing they once pined for and long for the thing they once grumbled at. For instance, first men run after women and then suddenly swear off them, or they complain of other people's love of money and then become avaricious themselves. Only a few cross this line in their twenties and are still going strong in their thirties, while fools experience the change in their old age. Hypocrites call such a change maturity, as do I. Schmettau had spent his life until his twenties despising everything and would now spend the rest of his days longing for it all back again. I knew something that Schmettau didn't: that every moral virtue, no matter how short-lived, leaves an indelible mark on the mind and soul.

To top it off, Schmettau was the very model of a German count. Clever, young and ambitious. His interests coincided with those of the state, his stately bearing revealed his interests and all of it could be summed up in one word: authority. I could read him like a book.

'The princess has sent me to see you about a costume for the costume ball.'

He jumped up abruptly, as if I had slapped him. Then he took his seat again and resumed drawing as calmly as if he had never left the chair.

So, he was mad, and I had utterly misread him. I repeated myself, knowing that the custom of the place was to say the same thing several times. 'The princess has sent me to see you about a costume for the costume ball.'

He looked up from his drawings slowly, investing each movement with significance. This might work on Hungarian princesses but not on me.

'What can I do for you?' he asked, and I knew that not only did he not want to do anything for me, but that he would have gladly blotted out every trace of me. But then, no one can destroy the Devil.

'I want a mask and a costume for the ball,' I said.

'Almost everything has been taken,' Schmettau answered, considering this pronouncement reason enough to return to his plans.

'You don't say,' I said sardonically.

'I do say,' he responded equally sardonically.

'Perhaps I'm looking for something you haven't yet given out.'

'Perhaps,' he answered rudely, not lifting his head at all.

'Perhaps I'd like to attend the ball as Fishmouth.'

'I do not know who Fishmouth is,' he answered coldly.

'Christ. Perhaps I'm looking for a dirty old robe and a crown of thorns.'

'Already taken.'

'Perhaps I'm looking for the suit of armour worn by Joan of Arc.'

'Taken.'

'Perhaps I'm looking for . . .' (inspiration was failing me) '. . . the vestments of a saint who never ate meat or lay with woman.'

'Taken.'

'Or maybe I'd like the tunic of a Greek philosopher.'

'Taken, several of them.'

'The garb of a poet with a crown of laurels?'

'So many requests that we had to order laurels from Vienna.'

'Serbian hajduk?'

'Taken.'

Now that I had found out what sort of grotesqueries would be on hand at the ball, I could at last reveal my true wishes.

6

'The Devil?'

'We've got one.'

'I'll take it.'

Schmettau got up grudgingly and went into the adjoining room. I stole a look at the plans he had been working on. As far as I could tell they were fortress ground-plans: ramparts, bastions, curtain walls and whatnot – nothing I cared about. There was also a book, the one by Marshal Vauban on defending and attacking fortified places. This was the book recommended by the bumbling Schmidlin and was clearly something of a must-read in Belgrade. I opened it to the first page and ran my eye down the first few sentences. I must admit that it began interestingly enough:

> The art of fortification was devised so that the rights of man might be safeguarded. Community could exist only in human innocence. Once the heart was consumed by vice, divisions necessarily arose. Conflicting interests set men apart: the strong aspired to greater things while the weak withdrew. From such origins have sprung cities and the fortifications of which we shall treat.

I found the marshal much to my liking, for, if I understood him correctly, the weak and wicked made their homes in cities behind defensive walls while the strong and wicked dwelt outside the walls and spent their days plotting to break through them.

And all of them, all of them wicked.

No sooner had I slipped the book into the secret pocket of my cloak than Schmettau returned carrying a neatly folded costume with a mask on top. The costume was, of course, red. I spotted a pointy tail. The mask was also red, with a pair of stubby horns and some ghastly teeth. And really, I do cut such a handsome figure. But that's the lying Christian creed for you.

I returned to my room and flipped through Vauban's little book. I didn't care for its style. In addition to its practical bits and useful theories, it also offered a sideline in philosophy. As if it weren't enough to just build a bastion without ascribing some higher meaning to the whole thing. Obviously, bastions get built for one reason: to defend against attacks.

But, thanks to me, this sort of writing is on its way out, and writers are quickly learning to stick to the point. I look forward to the day when all writing gets straight to the matter at hand and never veers off at a tangent. As specialized as can be, the more precise the better, and no philosophical distractions. There's nothing worse than trying to make things meaningful.

Vauban didn't stick to his own topic. He went out of his way to be a know-it-all and had at least two explanations for everything. Everything had its 'higher' cause; everything led to 'greater' consequences.

The only part I liked were those opening sentences, the bit about everyone being wicked, with the weak putting up walls for protection and the strong breaking through them. It followed, therefore, that the weak had set about founding cities that the strong would promptly invade, and that this state of affairs had spawned all the ramparts and other feats of engineering associated with fortifications.

Some thoughts are quick and some are slow, and time passes at the speed of thinking. I must have been thinking swiftly because the hours of daylight were already coming to an end when my servant knocked at the door.

7

'It is time for the ball,' he announced in formal tones. Then, seeing the devil costume and mask, he rolled his eyes. But, wisely, he refrained from commenting.

'Hold your tongue,' I said, and he obeyed. He helped me on with the costume. Unfortunately, the eye-holes in the mask were set too close together, making it hard to see out. And as it was already quite dark, both from the lateness of the hour and the dark clouds overhead, I could hardly see at all.

It was starting to rain. Drops were coming in through the open window, lightning flickered in the corner of my eye, but none of it could stop me from being my usual self, shining with the brightness of the morning star.

'Have you hired those Serbs as I told you?'

'Nothing to it, master. I had my pick of any number of them. Everyone wanted the work.'

'Well? Who's the choice?'

A clap of thunder shook the room.

'A handy lad from Požarevac. He seemed to be the most capable and trustworthy. Just back from Kosovo. Glorious Kosovo.'

'Speaking of Kosovo, I've always wondered, what *is* it you Serbs are always celebrating? It was your great defeat after all.'

'Defeat at Kosovo was our reward. If we'd won, who knows what evil would have befallen us.'

'Hm, I really couldn't say, but precious in the sight of Fishmouth is the defeat of the great . . . What's the lad's name then?'

'Don't know. Didn't ask.'

'That will be all. You're not needed until morning.' Novak hurried off, glad to have the night ahead of him for drinking, and I put the finishing touches to my costume. I was ready. I turned to look in the mirror and found myself face to face with the Devil. There was a flash of lightning. I bowed and said, 'Please, allow me to introduce myself . . .'

I grinned with satisfaction, but the face of the Devil in the mirror hidden behind its black-painted mask showed no change. I spun around and heard the answering swish of the red robe. Again there was a crash of thunder overhead.

I stepped out into the hallway. It lay in gloom with only a few torches for illumination set some twenty paces apart in their holders. With unsteady steps I made my way to the stairs, now slippery with the rain that was blowing in at the open windows.

Lovely weather for a costume ball, I thought, peering out happily at the night and rain.

Just then I thought I saw someone. Without knowing why, wanting to get a better look, I stuck my head out through the window. Outside, in front of one of the buildings, stood some figures. I wondered who they were and why they were exposing themselves to the storm. What weal or woe did drive them thither?

In my mind's eye I saw a storm of years long past. Lashing rain; a dark night. A man on the back of a donkey riding towards the city. He was soaked to the skin, and his shoulders were stooped. I was standing under an olive tree and was only slightly less wet than he. I knew he would be coming, and I was waiting for him. I watched two caravans enter the city and one come out. At times the shouts of the cattle drivers would reach my ears, and that was the only sound to pierce the rain.

There he came on the back of an ass. The rain stopped, but the true storm was about to begin. I noticed that his mount was treading palm fronds under its hooves. They must have fallen from one of the carts and scattered across the road.

The moon had come out from behind the clouds, and that was why I noticed the branches.

At the gates of Jerusalem.

A flash of lightning lit up the courtyard.

There were three figures in the rain. Two of them had enormous moustaches. Of these two, one was bandy-legged, the other bald. No doubt about it, it was the highwaymen, Vuk and Obren. The third man had his back to me, but I could clearly see his Austrian officer's uniform. An instant later everything had gone black again, and through the dark and the rain I could no longer be sure that the figures were even there. Then the thunder burst in my ears, and I involuntarily stepped back into the hallway.

What on earth could two hajduks, men with an Austrian price on their heads, be talking about with an Austrian officer in the middle of the Fortress of Kalemegdan? I knew that they were up to no good, for good deeds do not seek the cover of storm and dark of night. The only question was, who could they be plotting against – Fishmouth or me?

SIX
The Costume Ball

1

At the door stood a footman, waiting to usher me into the carriage that would convey me in comfort to the residence of Princess Maria Augusta. The party was being held in the grand building she had received as a wedding present from the regent upon her arrival in Serbia. The residence stood outside the fortress walls, a short ride away through the town gate, and we soon arrived at the extravagantly illuminated building.

I hurried through an anteroom and from there into a great hall. I heard a servant announce me at the entrance, clearly and unmistakably: *the Devil*. And, once again, clearly and unmistakably, as on so many previous occasions, I found myself among the very first at the party. Anyone with an iota of self-regard takes care to arrive fashionably late. Who else would have rushed to be there ahead of the rest? No one but me, that's who – always getting it wrong, no better than the biggest clod of an officer, no better than the most dim-witted lady-in-waiting.

The hall held a small scattering of seated people, most of them puffing away on Turkish pipes: a pair of poets, or perhaps Apollos, it wasn't clear which, a madman dressed as a gamecock, and one woman dressed as Madame de Pompadour. In the centre of the hall stood our proud host, the regent – wearing no mask. He spotted me and beckoned me to him.

'Wise choice of costume you've got there,' he said.

'And how do you know who I am?' I asked, altering my voice.

'Only the Devil would disguise himself as himself and still not find anyone to believe it.'

'Precisely for that reason, Your Highness, precisely. Everyone thinks there must be something quite different behind the mask. And as for those who don't think at all, they're just happy to see me looking as the priests describe me.'

'Clever. As you can see, I, too, am in disguise.'

'Indeed? How so?'

'My face and the figure I cut are my own best disguise. I need no other.'

'How nice for you, Your Highness. And now if you will excuse me, I have a soulmate to find.' Under my breath I added, *Meaning, your wife.*

In the meantime, other guests had been arriving. There still weren't many, perhaps twenty or so. But which one was Maria Augusta?

Madame de Pompadour?

Joan of Arc?

Or could she be disguised as a man?

My precious, suffering soul. I made my way among the costumed partygoers, trying to listen in on the conversations. It wasn't easy, partly because I rather stood out in my Devil suit and partly because the thunder was still booming. The orchestra struck up the music, minuets and rondeaus and all those other dances I don't know the steps to. How I hate all the things I don't know!

The dancers paired up, bowed to one another and began to grate on my nerves. From beginning to end, their dancing was a ridiculous imitation of human relationships: first seduction, then love, then betrayal and abandonment, all ending in pretend harmony. Weren't they dancing this particular number all the time in their day-to-day lives, and did they really need to perform it now to music? Since nearly everyone had joined the dance very few guests remained for me to engage in conversation or on whom I could eavesdrop.

Just as I was sidling up to Joan of Arc a revolting snout thrust itself into my face. The mask was so repulsive that I wanted to tear it away and prove to myself that the face underneath was just as awful. Jug ears jutted out from the sides of the mask, the right ear more prominently than the left, and from the mouth grinned teeth that only a rabbit could be proud of. The two upper incisors protruded, while the remaining teeth were rotten.

'Sir,' it said to me, 'a word in your ear?' It spoke English with the accent of the colonies.

'No,' I said curtly.

'I think you'd better hear me out,' it continued with a threat in its voice that was underscored by a flash of lightning as it said *hear me out*. 'You're making a big mistake if you think this is about vampires. It's not. It's not even about Wittgenau ...'

'Who on earth is Wittgenau?' I said. There was roll of thunder.

'It doesn't even matter, since this isn't about him,' it answered.

The logic was quite sound, but I still wasn't satisfied. That's why I'm the Devil.

'It's about the doves.'

'The *doves*?'

The figure looked around to make sure there was no one near by. It noticed at the same time as I did that the regent was approaching. Lightning flashed through the south windows.

'I have to go.'

'Wait,' I almost shouted after the retreating figure. 'Who are you?'

Through the rolling thunder I could just make out the answer. Something like 'Tristero'.

The regent was already standing before me. The man just wouldn't let me be. I almost thought he might suspect me of having designs on his wife. But then, I was quite sure he was not interested in his own wife. In the wives of others, maybe ...

'If I may ask, where will you go next?' he asked, and on his breath I detected the strong smell of Tokay wine.

Now, a drunken man will tell you the truth. But that's not all. You can also tell *him* the truth, right to his face. The alcohol washes away his memory to make room for more emotion.

'I'm off to France, Your Highness, to Paris.'

'Is that so? What takes you there, if it's not a secret?'

'No secret,' I said, although in truth it was. I told him that deliberately, because otherwise he'd try to remember. This way it would go in one ear and out the other. 'I'm going to see what the Third Estate want. I hear they've been protesting against the rights of the nobility, even against the king and the Church. There's been talk that the burghers, the ones with the money and red blood, have grown so powerful that they're demanding a republic.'

'Ha. Not counting on the Third Estate to get rid of the nobility, are you?'

'Not only am I counting on it, I'm going there to lend them a hand,' I answered rudely.

'So that's it then.' He was silent for a moment, and then he marshalled his best German artillery and opened fire. 'You are gravely mistaken if you think that some Third Estate can do away with the nobility. Not that blue blood won't disappear, mind you. Not because of these upstart nobodies but for another reason entirely. Because of gunpowder. We nobles are accustomed to armour, but armour cannot stand up to muskets, pistols and cannon. Armour was protection from the arrows, spears, halberds and maces of the sixteenth century, but defending yourself from these new weapons takes more than wearing something on your own body. The nobility have trouble understanding this because a nobleman is the unity of body, mind, weapon and armour, of attack and defence. And today's armies are made up of *Minds that fight not / Bodies with weapons*. Defensive operations are now beyond the reach of any one man. And as for the Third Estate, that bunch of *nouveaux riches* . . .'

'But surely one of your own distant ancestors must have been just such a *nouveau riche*?' I said, egging him on.

'Nonsense. We have true blue blood, and we're all descended from the ancient Roman aristocracy, which was founded by the heroes of

Troy, who were the offspring of the gods. But, to continue, the Third Estate knows how to do one thing, to make money, meaning they know how to steal. The whole lot of them, robbers and cutpurses, opening banks in the cities and charging interest like the Jews. But they still don't know how to spend it. I know they do spend it, but on what, I ask you?' Before I could get a word in edgeways, the regent continued with his broadside, 'They spend it on gambling and whores. And the nobility do not spend money on gambling and whores. We spend it on first editions of Shakespeare, Old Masters and other such gimmicks.'

'Gimmicks?'

'What do you think art is, if not the biggest gimmick ever invented? Calculated to deceive, and not just once but every time, and not just some people but every last one.'

'Hm, indeed. I've always thought that one can fool all people some of the time, and some people all of the time – but as you say, art fools all of the people all of the time.'

'And whose idea was it anyway, this art? As the Devil, you must know.'

'Of course I know. And I shall tell you right now.'

SEVEN
The Secret Chapter

I don't understand. Why should I suddenly leave off telling you about von Hausburg? To talk about Count Wittgenau?

I barely remember him. He was only briefly in Belgrade. Ten days or so. I think he arrived at Christmastime. No one knew the real reason for his visit. I've heard several accounts, and I doubt any of them are correct.

But I am quite sure that General Doxat was not to blame.

You're not interested in what happened back in '35? I can't hear you. You want to hear about the costume ball?

I don't remember what I was wearing. Well, it was a long time ago. How should I remember all the masks I've worn in my lifetime? There have been many fancy-dress parties and many things to change into and out of. Now I'm old and I don't remember, especially now that I know that all of those parties never did me a bit of good.

Why do it then, you ask? That *is* what you're asking?

It happens all the time. Someone invites you, or you invite someone, to a costume ball. That's how one lives, you know.

Wittgenau.

So, someone must have been having a little joke, or sending a warning, or making an accusation – I never knew which – and arrived wearing a mask that looked just like the face of Count Wittgenau. No, I never did find out who it was. I know who it wasn't. My husband, because he was the only one to spend the entire time without a mask. At first I was frightened, for the mask seemed alive. I mean that it didn't seem like a mask. I could have sworn that the wig really was Wittgenau's. The hair was grey with bluish strands.

Yes, the custom was to change one's wig for a costume ball. I mean, we'd have recognized one another with our own wigs on. Naturally, the quickest and easiest way to identify anyone was by utterly artificial things such as wigs.

That night, yes, it's coming back to me now, there was a terrible storm. Thunder and lightning, just like summertime. But it was only an Indian summer. I arrived late. I know it's hardly the done thing for the hostess to be late, but something had happened, I no longer remember what. One of my maids was giving birth, perhaps. Something like that. And right away I noticed the trickster in the Wittgenau mask. He was speaking to the Devil, or, rather, someone dressed as the Devil. I don't know what they were talking about. I was far away, the music was still playing, and the air was filled with thunder. I don't think they were together long.

No, as I've already told you, I don't recall what I was wearing that night. I don't recall. Perhaps someone else remembers.

Something else has just occurred to me. Something I was thinking about during the party. It was often on my mind in Belgrade. A fairy-tale, a tale my grandmother used to tell me when I was very small, back in Regensburg. I no longer remember what the story is about, and even then in Serbia I don't think I knew. No, I'm sure I didn't. Probably something along the lines of all fairy-tales, a prince must defeat a monster to win a princess. But there was something special about it, something quite different from all the others. A tiny detail. Really, just the tiniest detail, but enough to make its whole meaning clear. My grandmother would tell it to me before bed. Yes, that's right. Somewhere in the middle of the story the young men are put to the test to see which one is truly a prince. All they had to do was pass through some sort of forest and reach the castle. It was an ordinary forest, no trees that could talk or do anything worse. Just an ordinary forest in the country, not particularly dark or deep, certainly not filled with yew trees. They may have been oak trees. And there was a road that led through the forest. A road paved with gold and studded with jewels. And just as there always are, there were three young men, and their task was to take the road through the forest and reach the castle on the other side. The first young man set off on horseback, but when he saw the gold he kept to the side so as not to ride over the precious metal and stones. As soon as he arrived they chopped off his head. The second young man, not knowing what had happened to the first, also rode his horse alongside the road. And he also lost his head. The third young man did not even stop to think, but galloped straight down the middle of the road, his horse's hooves striking up golden sparks all the way and crushing the priceless jewels into powder. That was the true prince, for only a true prince, said grandmother, takes the middle way along the road of gold.

That's what I was thinking about at the costume ball. What?

That night nothing else happened in connection with the false Wittgenau. How do I know he was not the real one? Because by then Wittgenau had been dead for a year. Besides that, you know more about Wittgenau than I. You know everything there is to know about Wittgenau and about who killed him. And why are you asking me all of these questions when I'm only a woman, one who knows nothing about heroic deeds and has nothing to do with politics.

Now, I've told you, Wittgenau arrived in Belgrade sometime around Christmas in 1735 and promptly disappeared. Just like that. Disappeared. All I can tell you is what I heard from the usual hopefuls at court and the servants.

Not from lovers. I didn't have lovers.

I had heard that Wittgenau was a member of the secret imperial commission which had come to look into the construction of the Fortress of Kalemegdan. And the cistern. The emphasis was always on the cistern. From what I'd heard the investigation did not concern the money that had been spent. No one ever told me what Wittgenau was actually looking for. What else is there to investigate when building is involved, if not corruption?

Yes, the principal charges were against Doxat. At least that's what people were saying. He hadn't yet been made a general; he was still just a colonel in charge of building the fortress. Yes, he was Swiss and a Protestant. But the two of them never met, you know, Doxat and Wittgenau. Doxat wasn't in Belgrade when Wittgenau arrived. By the time Doxat returned, Wittgenau had already vanished.

Who? Why do you want me to talk about my family now? You know all that. Very well.

My family hold the postal monopoly within the Habsburg Empire, Hungary, Slavonia, all the German *Grafschaften,* the Czech lands, Poland, the Low Countries, parts of France and northern Italy. My paternal uncle is Postmaster General to the Holy Roman Empire. This position has been passed down in my family since 1490. We have more than twenty thousand couriers who can deliver a letter from Paris to Buda in seven days. Or from Vienna to Istanbul in four days.

Sorry? Why would we deliver a letter from Vienna to Istanbul? I was only giving an example. That's all. Naturally our letter-carriers have passed through many lands, enemy lands among them. But we haven't carried letters for the Turks. At least not that I know of.

Who is it you are interested in, actually? Wittgenau? Or von Hausburg? Or Doxat?

You're interested in *me?*

SIX
The Costume Ball
(continued)

2

The regent was all ears. His eyes were watering, either from squinting short-sightedly or from drunkenness, and he was clutching a glass of wine in his left hand.

'You may not believe me, Your Highness, but art was invented by none other than myself.'

'I do believe you. Art is the work of the Devil.' Lightning flashed.

'It was in the very beginning, when mankind had been driven out of Paradise and first knew suffering. In no time at all people became wicked and were mine. For me, this was no fun at all. What I like is for a person to choose between good and evil, leaning first to one side, then the other, until finally coming to me. But since their lives were so full of ugliness from the very start, people were simply turning bad without stopping to think about it and never even believing in the existence of good.'

Thunder rolled.

'And then I gave them art. After that I also gave them letters, so they could write things down to have for ever. I gave them the one perfect thing that exists in this world: a complete and utter lie. Quite the paradox, eh?'

'Hm, yes. But did your adversary really sit by and do nothing?'

'He never knew what to make of art. It's not evil *per se*, you see, but it is falsehood. Not only that, but it was I who had invented it, and he never forgot it. Not long afterwards he struck back – with history. Yet another story but one that pretends to be true. That's when all the books appeared, such as the Bible. My adversary couldn't help but be on the side of truth – but as a man who knows his warcraft you can tell me yourself. What drives people to evil? History, which is true, or art, which is false?

'Power and riches.' Having said this, he abruptly turned his back on me and went off to the nearest table for more wine. I still had a few more things to tell him but decided to catch him later. I set out to find Maria Augusta. I wanted to find out which of the figures in disguise was the princess. There were quite a few women – some of them were no doubt actually men, but I hardly thought the princess would dress as a man. She had no reason to. I quickly ruled out two witches, one maiden in Serbian folk costume, three Aphrodites – two with an apple and one without, this last one surely pre-dating the bribing of Paris. I also discarded Ophelia, Lear's three daughters, Clytemnestra, Antigone and, after wavering a bit, Lady Macbeth. The court at Belgrade certainly went in for the theatre in a big way. After eliminating some others for being the wrong size, I set my sights on Joan of Arc and Madame de Pompadour.

I was just making my way towards Madame when I happened to find myself in front of a mirror. I stopped to have a look, as much as the badly placed eyeholes would allow. I bowed slightly. The figure in the mirror did the same. I stuck my thumbs in my ears, spread my palms and wiggled my fingers. The figure in the mirror did the same. I placed my right thumb on the tip of my nose, touched my left thumb to the little finger of my right hand, and wiggled my fingers again. The figure in the mirror did the same. I found myself so delightfully entertaining that I removed my mask to have a better look. The figure in the mirror remained behind its mask. Warily I stretched out my hands to touch the mirror and felt my fingers brush up against the Devil. I jumped back.

He said, 'Pleased to meet you. Did you guess my name . . . ?' And, with a burst of satanic laughter, he vanished into the crowd.

3

I was trembling. I don't know why, but I suddenly remembered my reasons for coming to Belgrade. A shiver went up my spine. I wanted to call for Novak, but I knew he was nowhere to be found. There were just too many places to drink in Belgrade.

My life truly was in danger, that much was clear again, and the hajduks and the tale they'd spun had been nothing but a trick to lull me into a false sense of security. How careless I had been!

My enemies were disguised even as my own self.

But I wasn't about to let panic get the better of me. First, to find Schmidlin and ask him whether he knew the hajduks were working for the Austrians. He might not know about it himself, but at least he'd be able to guess who had hired them. Second, ask Maria Augusta about the doves and Tristero (if that was the name). Third, ask the regent about the man in crimson. Fourth, and most importantly, ask Schmettau who else had hired a Devil costume. Back to zero, find them all among the masks, except for the regent who was standing out in the open.

I set my sights on Madame de Pompadour, and in a few steps found myself at her side. All I had to do was get her to say something; the voice of Maria Augusta would be easy to recognize.

'Beastly weather, isn't it?'

'M-hm,' she answered. I could clearly see – or rather, hear – that she was trying to avoid any answer that could be pinned down. I asked her another question.

'Could you introduce me to Count Wittgenau?'

Madame de Pompadour froze. Then with her folded fan she pointed to a group of half a dozen figures in the shadows. I started towards them, and when I looked back at Madame she was no longer there. I decided to deal with Wittgenau later. Tristero himself had said that Wittgenau wasn't important.

Next in line for inspection was Joan of Arc. It didn't take long to find her, standing and gazing out of the south windows. As her back was turned, I was able to approach from behind without being noticed.

'Are you the one I seek?'

She wheeled around as if I'd struck her. 'That depends', she whispered, 'what you're looking for.'

It was an old trick. A whisper will never give away your identity. You can't even tell whether the whisperer is a man or a woman, let alone recognize someone in particular. There was a lot of whispering at costume balls. Her whisper could only mean one thing: she thought we knew each other. Furthermore, she knew who I was, or at least thought she did. Or perhaps she thought I was the other one; perhaps she'd got us mixed up, and I could ask the right questions to find out.

'I'm looking for a woman.'

'There are many women here.'

'I seek a soul that suffers and loves.'

'Why?'

'I'm a man of wealth, a man of taste. I've got almost everything and know almost everyone. But what good does it do me without a soulmate who knows how to suffer and to love?'

'That's not much of a proposal.'

'The truth always sounds ordinary and down to earth.'

'It's more likely that you just lack the spirit for it.'

'You're right, when I'm in love. When I love, it's as if I lose the gift of speech, for true love speaks haltingly while base motives sing.'

'How nicely put. Your motives for talking to me must be rather base after all to bring on such a torrent of words.'

'Right you are.' She had managed to annoy me with her incessant whispering. If she *was* Maria Augusta there could be no hope for our union, and the woman wasn't the one for me. I can't bear petty souls. I like my souls with breadth and badness.

I offered a few unpleasantries and took my leave of the whispering wench. The way the conversation was going, I'd hardly learn anything valuable.

I poured myself a glass of Tokay and looked out of the south windows. The thunder and lightning had been raging all this time as if it were really summer, not just St Martin's. The rain fell without stopping, and the air in the hall was damp and stuffy. I had never seen a storm last so long. Again I scouted the room, hoping to set eyes on Madame de Pompadour. Anyone who runs away from you is sure to be useful. I wasn't long in finding her. She was speaking to the regent. I tried to draw near without being noticed but still couldn't get close enough to hear their voices. I watched Madame de Pompadour gently take the regent's hand and was close enough to see her make what seemed to be a slight curtsy. I saw her carefully lay her other hand on the back of his. I saw her caress the back of his hand and watched him pull away. I drew closer to them. They spoke only briefly. I heard everything. Then he left. She called out after him and buried her mask in her hands.

4

Someone must have opened the windows or doors because the wind suddenly began to rush through the hall. Wigs were flying. Madame de Pompadour gave no ground, her wig firmly in place, in courtly French style. That wig was not about to be blown away. But the music stopped, and the dancers were obliged to follow suit.

I assumed that Madame de Pompadour was one of the regent's lovers. She was certainly dressed the part, *maîtresse* to Louis XV. The regent had many lovers. It was no longer even gossiped about in Vienna. Not having mistresses – now *that* would have set tongues wagging. I've done a good job of changing people's habits over the years.

The doors or windows were still open, and the wind was blowing harder and harder. All at once it became very cold, as though a whirlwind were blasting through the court. I thought I'd better hold on to one of the columns. My hands were like ice. I shut my eyes.

I opened them again when the wind stopped, some moments later. That's when I saw him. He was standing in the centre of the hall, surrounded by lords and ladies in their masks. He wore no mask, and his white shirt was crusted with blood. His hair was slicked back, his face pale, terrible to behold in the light of the few candles that had somehow not been snuffed out. One of his riding-boots was missing its sole, his breeches torn.

His voice rang out. 'My Lord Regent!'

And the regent appeared before him.

'Lieutenant Mackensen reporting,' he gasped. 'Niš has fallen!'

Württemberg said nothing. The others began to murmur. 'Niš has fallen. General Doxat came to terms with the Turks. To surrender the city if they let the people and the army withdraw. They're on the move now. Ten thousand Serbs and some Jews with the army. They're coming north. They'll be in Belgrade in seven days' time – if the Turks keep their word and don't attack.'

'Niš has fallen,' the regent repeated, as if to himself.

Several people escorted Mackensen outside. The doors were shut now, although the wind had stopped.

The music began to play. The masked guests began to dance and the swirling skirts blocked my view of the regent.

Someone beside me spoke in Serbian. 'What happened?'

Another voice answered, 'Nothing.'

I looked out of the window. There was no more lightning, no more thunder. As if the skies had cleared. The rest of the candles were relit, and everything was brighter than before the bad news.

I poured myself more wine and looked across the table to see Joan of Arc. I called out to her, 'Shouldn't you be in Niš?'

She walked all the way around the table just so she could whisper her answer. 'It's the English I can't stand.'

I poured some wine into her half-empty glass. She was stubborn, and I liked that. Her free hand reached out to stop me from serving more wine. Such a feminine gesture.

I enquired, 'Madame de Pompadour?'

'If Joan of Arc had been a man no one would remember her,' she whispered. 'No one here is in disguise. People have no idea how to disguise themselves. Whatever they put on, they change into themselves. Our entire civilization depends on successful fakery.'

'How so?'

'Because it is easier to bear your own self if you can pass it off as unreal. Truth is indecent and not, as you said, ordinary. Truth is unbearable. I find my own self indecent and unbearable and think the same of all others.'

What torment this soul was suffering! I had not erred in my first assessment. How I adore such tortured souls, simply adore them, as well as those that have never known a moment's pain. But then, the ones that have never suffered are always perfectly happy and therefore perfectly dull.

'What then do you believe in?' I asked her.

'In the city,' she whispered, draining her glass.

'The city?'

'Yes, the city, as in Belgrade.'

The lovelorn princess had gone out of her mind, that was the only reasonable explanation. The sudden change was surely the result of madness. The princess filled her glass with more wine. She drank it down then poured again. I felt rather *de trop*. And suddenly weary.

'Please excuse me, I find I am tired from all that has happened today.'

She nodded.

I didn't even attempt to say goodbye to the regent, so badly did I want to sleep. That was a good sign. A sign that the tension was letting up. I stepped outside and jumped into the first carriage. In no time we had rattled our way back to Kalemegdan.

We passed through the King's Gate and entered the fortress. As it was nearly daybreak I could see out of the carriage window. There was the building that held the cistern and two guards standing out front. They had not been there the day before, as far as I could recall.

I doffed my mask and costume and lay down to sleep, but as unluck would have it, sleep did not come until late in the morning. I heard Novak staggering back at about nine o'clock, and only then did I fall asleep. The blasted cock crows woke me more than once, but I refused to admit defeat.

Part the Second
BEHIND THE MASK

ONE
Second Exodus

1

The story begins, I think, the day after the costume ball. I was late in rising, well past midday, I'm sure. Now that I think about it, I wonder why my husband ever invited me to accompany the vampire commission to Dedinaberg. At the time I didn't give it much thought, and an excursion outside the city walls seemed a pleasant diversion, even exciting.

I'd never been outside the city before, not in Serbia.

I insisted on riding. I didn't want to go by carriage. Before, I'd always been driven about in a six-in-hand. Alexander had them saddle up his favourite mare . . .

What's that you ask?

Who went along?

From the fortress, there was Baron Schmidlin and Count Schmettau. Of course, first and foremost were the three members of the commission: Klaus Radetzky and the two other men of science whose names I've forgotten, one with a blond wig and the other with a red one. Our group also included Otto von Hausburg, the one you're so keen to know about, and his servant. Why do I mention his servant? Because of all the servants he was the only one to ride with us; our own servants, two or three of my maids and some others, followed behind. Later, after we'd crossed the field line outside the city, we were joined by another Serb. I believe he was an *Oberkapitän* – I've always been hopeless with ranks.

Yes, there were eight of us counting the Serb.

Vuk Isakovič.

The leader of the party was Baron Schmidlin. Our destination was the watermill at Dedinaberg. The Serbs had complained of vampires appearing there. Anyone who spent the night in the place would be dead by dawn and whatnot. Radetzky thought it would be a simple matter to show the Serbian peasants that vampires didn't exist if he were to spend the night and come out alive. While he was at the mill the rest of us would lodge at a nearby house. The house belonged to the richest peasant in Dedinaberg, and, although it was hardly up to the standards at court, it could offer a hearty meal and a good night's sleep.

At the gate leading out of the fortress my horse shied and would go no further. I had to spend quite some time stroking her and calming her down before she would reluctantly continue. That's when I saw the poor little girl. She was begging at the gate, in rags, barefoot, sad and alone. God had taken away both her reason and the power of speech, and I felt a boundless desire to help her. It's a terrible thing to witness human suffering. I have also suffered – on silk pillows, but it's suffering just the same – and if only someone had looked kindly on me I'd have been so grateful. The poor child had no one and was probably afraid of people. There's no worse punishment than to live in fear of others. She had no one and nothing to call her own. I got down from my horse and took her in my arms: let her see that not everyone is a brute who passes by with a cold heart, a sharp tongue or ready fists. I knew that the five kreutzers I was giving her was next to nothing, that it would buy her no more than a few meals, but it tugged at my heartstrings to hold her and kiss her. And I began to weep. I was longing for the love of one man, and here this child was longing for the love of anyone at all. I felt how warm, how gentle she was, and – knowing that I had at least shown her my own gentleness and love – I was happy to have been able to help the poor child even that much. What a joy it is to give to others!

We had to keep going, and I left her, promising myself that I would bring her into the palace when I returned.

What?

Very well, then, back to the story.

At the time, I hadn't given the vampires a moment's thought. I believed them to be a superstition for the ignorant. The conversation I heard between Count von Hausburg and his servant Novak only confirmed my belief that the Serbs were superstitious and that there was no such thing as vampires.

The servant was telling him what the Serbs were saying, how the Archangel Michael had come to Belgrade. When he heard this von Hausburg nearly fell out of the saddle. He turned pale and began to ask questions: when did he arrive, where did he arrive, what did they say was his reason for coming, what did *he* say was his reason for coming and so on. It occurred to me that the count was not in his right mind because he clearly believed the story of the archangel's appearance. His servant began to laugh, and I felt uncomfortable at witnessing such unseemly behaviour.

When his laughter had died down he said, 'It's not the real archangel. Remember that Russian we met on the way to Belgrade, the tall fair-haired one. From the description, I'd say it's him. The peasants are saying that the archangel speaks heavenly Serbian, that he's tall and fair and all in rags, because that's what angels always do: they pretend to be poor because the human soul shows through in the way we treat the poor and the simple and the sick.'

When his servant had finished speaking, von Hausburg also began to laugh, but with a great guffaw, in a way that struck me as rather forced. He added, 'And here I thought the human soul could best be seen in its dealings with the powerful and the more intelligent and the rich and the happy. For even the worst of men can summon up a little compassion, but even the best find it hard to resist envy, hypocrisy and cowardice. I don't understand why angels and saints don't come dressed as kings and counts or poets decked with laurels.'

'Because those are *your* favourite roles. You want to see the worst in people, and angels and saints want to see the best.'

'Hence their ignorance of the world.'

The conversation did not surprise me. If you only knew all the things I've heard you wouldn't ask that. Besides, what did I know? I was still young, and a princess at that. And what can one possibly learn or understand in trappings of silk and velvet? It was only when I began to suffer that I began to think, first about myself, and then about others. What good have they ever done me, those easy days of peace and happiness? But that's why the times of suffering mean so much to me, the arduous, sleepless nights, the tears, the pain and fear, the sorrow and hopelessness. For those months, those years, built up the best in me, while the carefree days were nothing but ruin. There's no deep wisdom in what I'm saying. Every hero in every fairy-tale my grandmother ever told me, unlike the false heroes, always takes the dark and difficult and thorny path to vanquish the dragon at the end. The ones who take the broad, smooth road never get anywhere.

Yes, all right, back to the story.

We had not yet crossed the city's defensive line, meaning that we were still in the part called Unter Ratzenstadt, when Count Schmettau approached me.

No, of course he wasn't my lover. I've already told you that I didn't have lovers. With Count Schmettau I had never exchanged more than a handful of pleasantries. And I was surprised at his forward behaviour.

Count Schmettau was . . . he was responsible for the fortress. He was an architect or something along those lines. I know he was always at his drawings. I think his plan for Kalemegdan was the first to be accepted by the administration. Later it turned out that something wasn't right, I don't know what, and his plans were rejected in favour of Doxat's. That's how Doxat became chief engineer. And the fortress was built under Doxat's personal supervision, right up until we declared war on the Turks for the second time. Then Doxat was sent to lead the second regiment. He was a very able man. He took Niš in a matter of months after the fighting had started. That's why he was promoted to general.

So, Count Schmettau rode up alongside me and said, 'Do you know who's coming to replace your husband?'

Such effrontery caught me quite off guard.

'Why should the regent be replaced at all?'

'Because of the defeat. Because of the loss of Niš and the south of Serbia.'

'I take it you know who is to be regent?'

'Let's see . . .' he said slowly, staring me right in the eye, and then he spat out, 'Count Wittgenau!' before bursting into mad laughter.

'I fail to see the humour in that.'

'Oh?'

We rode along in silence for some time.

'Your impudence can only mean that someone is coming to replace my husband, someone who will protect you. There can be no other explanation for your behaviour.'

'That's right. And now at last your husband and his band of toadies will answer for all their crimes. He struck fear into the heart of Serbia, surrounded by his miserable servants. In one week he will be servant to his own fear. And I'll tell you which investigation is to come first: the murder of Count Wittgenau.'

'Is that a threat?'

'Yes. For the new judge and master will be Count Marulli.'

2

As for me, what am I to do? And who will stand with me? The Devil's strength is in his own hands, as they say. I have a servant who is a cross to bear but who also comes in quite handy. If there are questions I am prevented from asking by my breeding and position, I send Novak, for low origins entitle one to behave in the worst possible manner. How else would one family ever rise to replace another? The first thing

I told him to ask about was Tristero. Next, Wittgenstein. Third, who was wearing what at the costume ball.

He was able to discover nothing. Granted, he hadn't much time. He woke me at noon, for we had to prepare for the journey out of Belgrade to the watermill. We were to set off at the first hour after midday, and Novak had to pack my things. I left the room to have a walk around the fortress and a look at the two rivers. I was agitated, as if I were about to embark on a long, important voyage. I smoked some tobacco, hoping to be calmed by the slow, deep breaths. But I was not.

I walked to one of the bastions on the southwest side of the fortress. Below me was the Lower Town. The army was drilling formations. Men ran to and fro, the *Oberkapitäne* sat and smoked. Beyond them flowed the murky Sava, the blue Danube. Rivers are like people. Too many obstacles, too many painful twists and turns, and they become bad. But I simply haven't the time to make everyone's life bitter myself, so I've had to come up with certain schemes for getting the job done.

Novak came to find me, and we went to meet the others at the designated place. In front of the cistern. Already waiting there were Princess Maria Augusta of Thurn and Taxis, Count Schmettau, Baron Schmeddlesome, and the three members of the vampire commission. Counting myself and Novak, there were eight of us.

Schmidlin called out to the guards, and the great doors of the King's Gate swung wide open.

3

No, I didn't know General Marulli then, nor did I ever meet him. Do you think we should have met?

That's not what I think. I think it was for the best, the way things actually were. Even in the idle hours when my mind wanders through the past and all that happened, among the friends and faces I knew long ago, I realize I made no mistake, considering what I knew at the time. By the time I found out, it was already too late. That's the nature of knowledge – it always comes too late. If we knew beforehand it would have to come from another mind, either God's or the Devil's, it doesn't matter which.

Why do I say in the idle hours, you ask?

Because all the thinking and all the knowledge in this world comes from having too much time and being bored. That's why the poor are simple fools and the nobility are high-minded and progressive.

What happened next?

It's not far from the fortress to Dedinaberg. I exchanged a few words with everyone in turn, but mostly with von Hausburg. My conversation with Count Schmettau ended the moment we left Unter Ratzenstadt.

I no longer remember how the talk turned to the deadly sins, although it struck me at the time that they were one of von Hausburg's favourite topics.

4
Von Hausburg on the Sin of Pride

'In my dealings with people I encourage and support egotism and vanity. And pride – whether overweening or under. I fill their sails. They take to it quickly, like mariners with a fresh wind at their backs. Full sail ahead they make their self-satisfied way over the open seas, knot by knot. What a delight! Months away from any safe harbour, the stars changing places overhead and the great waves cavorting and gambolling like a court jester before a king. The straining white canvas carries them ever closer to the line where the waters meet the heavens. Have you ever been out on the water in a little boat?

'And then, when their souls are swirling like the whirlpool, when the anchor has not tasted brine for many a day, when dry land has been lost to sight and they begin to fancy themselves their own captains and masters, no longer creatures who walk the ground but beings that float, that fly along under the heavy sails, that's when I tell them. It was I who set you here. It was I who poured out the great oceans beneath you, and filled the sails, and cast you off.'

'But when they run into a storm, don't the same full sails that were carrying them along now drag them down, straight to the bottom of the wide open sea?' I asked him.

'He wouldn't have it any other way. He won't let them drop their sails. He won't. It's not me. I'm not the one who speeds them on their way and calls up the winds. For at his word the winds leap up and grow strong. He abhors the sails, straining at their crosspieces. No one drops sails in time. He won't allow it. He delights to see ship and sailor sink beneath the waves.'

5

At the time I did not understand that the 'he' von Hausburg spoke of was, in fact, the Devil.

No, I didn't mean that von Hausburg was the Devil. I meant that the Devil is the one who won't allow the sailors to drop sails when a storm comes along.

Why do I think that? Because only a devil will not forgive. If any of them was a devil, I'd say it was Count Schmettau.

6

We rode along for some time, and then we halted at the top of a hill. It all looked the same to me, fields and woods, with a stream here and there. It was a lovely day, surprisingly peaceful and clear after the storm of the night before. There was a slight new chill in the air.

We drew up, and Baron Schmidlin immediately came to help me down. I asked whether we were stopping to rest, adding that there was no need as far as I was concerned and that we could simply keep going. Schmidlin looked at me oddly and said that we had arrived.

'Arrived where?'

'In Dedinaberg.'

'I don't see any houses.'

'Your Highness, there are no houses here in the way we understand the word. The Serbs make their homes in huts and pits. For Your Highness we have chosen the best . . . the best *place* to spend the night.'

I looked around and saw a wretched little hovel that I would have ridden right by without noticing, just like most of the things in life we fail to notice until someone points them out to us. And somehow it always turns out that they didn't matter anyway. All by ourselves we notice what really matters to us.

A peasant appeared out of nowhere. He was very old and weathered, dirty and in tatters. He bowed low to the ground and began to speak to Baron Schmidlin. Or, rather, it seemed that Baron Schmidlin was asking questions, and the peasant was answering. The peasant kept his eyes on the ground and wrung his hands as he spoke in the way of all base and servile people. I was suddenly overcome with disgust as I watched them and wanted to take a walk among the trees. At least there was no dishonour in nature. I even thought it might be better to sleep under the trees than in such vile company, among those wicked peasants and devilish counts.

Why didn't I?

Because it was too cold.

Dangerous?

At the time I saw no danger. By the time I realized, it was just as dangerous outside as within.

But Count Schmettau invited me to go inside, and as I didn't want to behave like a spoiled and capricious princess, I stepped into the hut.

It was warm inside. There was a fire going. A dirty old woman was cooking something that gave off a bad smell. In the room were three other women, two men and three children. There was no furniture, except for a three-legged stool. Dirty rags were heaped in the corners, and the only weak illumination came from the cooking fire. There were no windows.

But the room was much bigger than I would have expected from the outside. I was still hoping that there was a better place for us to spend the night. I couldn't believe that my husband would allow me to sleep in such a hovel.

Very soon, however, I understood that he wanted to show me . . . that he wanted to show me that my wishes came of sinful pride and vanity. I wanted to be loved and was dissatisfied with my lot, while these people, these peasants, had barely a place to live, let alone any hope of being loved.

Yes, it seems there is one lesson I have never learned, and that I shall never make a good Christian, for I still believe quite firmly that poverty cannot abide love. The only thing poverty can stand is more suffering.

'Not to worry, it's only for the night, and we shall take our meal in the open air. Everything is nearly ready,' said Baron Schmidlin, and I ran outside in relief. Sure enough, in a little clearing some ten steps away, the servants were setting up the tables. On another occasion I might have been surprised at eating outside, especially at that time of year, but at the moment I was just grateful for the idea.

'The meal is not quite ready. Might I suggest a short stroll?' said the count whose name I've forgotten. It was one of the two men who had come with the doctor, Count Radetzky. The one with the red wig. I took his suggestion, as I had nothing else to do. He offered his arm. We went into the forest. He didn't speak. I appreciated his silence. I assumed he was thinking about something, and I didn't want to interrupt him. I had my own thoughts to occupy me. Thoughts about love. About how close I was to the ideal love, how I still believed in such a love, unlike most women of a certain age, and how I knew the man of my life, and how that man was actually mine, and how it was all still in vain. Better not to have known all this. Better to have been empty-headed and content to dine on rich foods, to wear the finest dresses and costly pearls. Better to have been satisfied with the occasional touching, sentimental novel like the ones delivered by the Thurn and Taxis couriers. Better to . . .

'Did you know Count Wittgenau?' the count asked me suddenly after we had gone quite some distance into the forest.

'No. I saw him only a few times before his disappearance.'

'And have you seen him since he appeared again?'

'Appeared? Has Count Wittgenau really appeared since . . . since his death?'

'Yes,' he said coldly. 'Count Wittgenau has appeared since his death.'

'Where?'

'Here.'

'And where has he gone now?'

'Nowhere. He was dead. You know nothing about it?'

'No,' I said.

He turned abruptly, and we headed back. I didn't know what to ask him, and he said nothing else. And so without speaking we made our way back to that hovel.

The first thing I saw was von Hausburg. He was sitting on the ground with his servant standing over him. It seemed that von Hausburg had been taken quite poorly. He was holding his head in his hands. He might have been crying.

I passed by him, wanting to go all the way around the hut and have a look at the exterior. I walked along one side: mud and wattle, a wooden beam or two. And just as I was coming to the corner I heard Schmidlin's voice. He was speaking Serbian with a man I didn't know and kept repeating the one word I was able to understand.

The word was *diskrecija*, discretion.

In fact, both of them were saying the word over and over. They were raising their voices. The Serb had an odd way of pronouncing it, actually, more like *diskrrecija*.

As for Schmidlin's being able to speak Serbian, that came as a surprise to me.

I wasn't able to figure out what called for so much discretion. I really couldn't speak Serbian at all. Perhaps our visit to the village. Perhaps the investigation at the mill. Perhaps the vampires. Or something, perhaps, that I knew nothing about. When that possibility occurred to me I began to worry. With all that had been happening, the only thing I could be sure of was the existence of another stream of events, flowing under our feet, one I could not follow because I had not known it was underneath us.

Yes, just what I said. Underneath us.

TWO

1

I had no appetite, I remember perfectly well. And Schmettau had brought along his Chinese cook again. A year earlier, when the Chinaman was preparing his first meal for the court, I had tried to persuade my husband to dine with the rest of us, even if it meant going a day without wild game. He'd made a cutting reply:

'Like Chinese food, do you? Had it as a child in Regensburg, no doubt. Speciality of Bavarian cooks, was it?'

'Would you have me spend my whole life eating only the same things I had as a child?'

'Now do you see why I hate you? You're a dangerous woman. Always changing.'

Sorry?

You didn't know that my husband hated me? Well, really, it was common knowledge in Vienna. Yes, he hated me.

He hated me. He'd go for days without speaking to me. I was alone. Alone in rooms of Baroque looking-glasses and servants. I used to race furiously up and down the hallways in my younger days, but gradually in my solitude I grew slower and calmer. Months went by. I'd stop and look wherever it seemed reasonable. Afterwards I would sit on the garden swings. That's when the first officer came to call. He was pleasant and spoke to me. I soon realized that he'd been sent to seduce me and become my lover. After his failure came others. Most of them Serbs, probably to add to my humiliation. Who?

Who indeed. Why should I have been any different from the other ladies at court? They were all deceiving their husbands. Have you any idea how dangerous it can be not to succumb to sin in a place where everyone else is quite given over to it? The scorn hung over me, even when everyone at court was fast asleep.

Those unfortunate women, the ones they used to pillory for having children out of wedlock – even they could not have felt more singled out than I. They at least knew the truth about the mob, that the hypocrites throwing stones and rotten fruit were just as sinful as themselves. And there's nothing wrong in knowing that. I was not only held up to ridicule but I knew I was better than the rest of them, and this knowledge would lead me down to Hell much faster than their petty intrigues and adulteries ever would.

Is not pride the greatest of sins? People repent of gluttony and avarice, they repent of wrath and adultery and despair, but they rarely repent of their pride. And if they do repent of pride it's not because of Our Lord's commandments but because of whatever their pride happens to cost them.

Yes, officers were sent to call on me. And everyone knew, and everyone found it most amusing. They'd lay wagers on the Serb who would win me over. Many thalers were lost on Vuk Isakovič, who had boasted that I would be unable to resist him. He was also said to resemble my husband, for reasons I have never understood.

He was vile. Not so much because of his appearance, although he was dirty like all the Serbs, but because he would cringe like a slave before Alexander and his whims, even as he was lording it over his own people like the most terrible master, tormenting and plundering them.

In the eyes of the Serbs, who is to blame for all that happened? Isakovič and the other *Oberkapitäne*, not us. We came to them as enemies from the very beginning, not to free them from the Turks but to take Serbia from them.

But still, the Serbs were better off with us than with the Serbs themselves. Several months after the events I've been describing I asked Patriarch Vicente Jovanović to exercise the Church's influence with Serbian women to put a stop to the practice of giving birth in the bushes, hidden away from prying eyes, as if childbearing were something shameful. Children were dying, and women were dying.

After I'd sent the letter and word got out the *Oberkapitäne* were angry, for why should some Austrian princess care how peasant women went about having their children? It was a Serbian custom, and there was no reason to change it. Once they started to give birth indoors it would be only a matter of time before they'd want to stop working while they were with child, or they'd be asking for pretty dresses or some such. Their lot was to suffer. As long as they were suffering they wouldn't get it into their heads to ask for things. They'd do as they were told.

But where was I?

2

No sooner had the gates swung open than I wanted to turn back. Inside the fortress was my cosy room, the sheets still warm on the bed; peace and quiet. Later there would be goulash of venison, thick Hungarian wine and a barmaid. Everything simple, easy and lovely. Easy things are lovely.

And when the doors were opened and we were put out in the city everything seemed so harsh and difficult. Whenever I passed through that gate I never knew whether I was coming in or going out. *Out*, of course, from the fortress, but also *in*. Into the city, obviously, but where else? All the fun had suddenly drained out of everything, the made-up vampires, the mill, even the princess. But I couldn't turn back; something was driving me onwards, some power that takes people by the hand and leads them to ruin. Other people think that power is me.

And as we left the fortress further and further behind the knot of anxiety grew ever tighter in my stomach. Even Novak kept turning in his saddle, as if making sure that no one was following us, or trying to remember every inch of Kalemegdan, the King's Gate, the south-east bastion with its curtain wall and great ramparts.

We hadn't ridden far when we began to climb along a steep cobbled way that was bristling with beggars, all of them afflicted in mind or body. It hardly seemed the place for begging. Who would stop to let them have a cent while struggling towards the top? Only later did I understand: what's uphill for some is downhill for others, and the real business probably came from those who were making their quick and easy descent. From experience I know that no one shares like those who are on the way down. And not just their money but their feelings, too.

Why I noticed one beggar-girl out of the whole lot, I couldn't say. She was dirty and in rags, barefoot, a girl who would never grow up no matter how long she lived. For good old Fishmouth takes away some people's reason even before they learn to speak and to believe in him. She was standing there, her hands stretched out towards us. The dim-witted eyes were already regarding us with gratitude. Perhaps gratitude was the only thing that soul could express. As if being deprived of reason were not enough, the girl was also mute, as evidenced by the tossing of her head and the gaping O of her mouth.

'Am I the one to blame for this?' I asked Novak, who maintained a prudent silence.

And then the princess did something that made me very happy. She indulged the most un-Christian of her traits. She stopped her horse, got down clumsily, went to the girl and began to caress her and kiss her forehead. She pressed a few coins into her hand. I couldn't see how much it was, although I wanted to. She embraced and kissed her again, although I didn't see her wipe her mouth afterwards. Then she clumsily climbed back into the saddle and spurred her horse on.

What a wonderful feeling! I was delighted to share it with the princess. Such a lofty, mighty feeling! From her place on high she had looked upon the suffering of the body, the even greater torment of the spirit and got rid of some pocket change she wouldn't need anyway. Now she felt so light, so noble, even a bit self-sacrificing – considering the bother she'd had dismounting and hoisting herself back into the saddle. Refreshed in spirit, she could ride right back into her high station among the blue-bloods where she belonged, something she'd never lost sight of even for a moment.

And this kind of charity is still called a Christian virtue? A charity that comes from the Holy Trinity: power, pleasure and pride. Oh, the world is mine, verily it is mine!

We hadn't gone much further when Novak turned his horse around and galloped back. I looked over my shoulder to see him with the beggar girl. I couldn't see what he was doing, but he rejoined us quickly. It didn't take him long to catch up.

He beckoned me to one side, and we rode along at a discreet distance from the others so we could speak privately.

'Here's three kreutzers,' he said, holding out the shiny coins.

I took them and asked, 'What's this then?'

'Took 'em from the beggar girl. It's what the princess gave her.'

'Oh, good and faithful servant, I had no idea you were so good. You've made me very happy.'

'I am good, no matter how much you twist things and call what's good both evil and good, and what's evil both evil and good to boot. And I didn't take the money to give it to you but to save the little beggar girl. Everyone saw her getting the money. She's just a poor little mite, and they'd take it from her and hurt her while they are at it, maybe even kill her. Now she's safe. She's got nothing.'

'So why not take the money for yourself? Aha, I know why. If you take it, it's a sin, plain old thieving. Now it's a good deed, but the money's still ended up in the hands of the Devil. You might have taken those three kreutzers, you know, and bought her something to eat right away, and some plain shoes that no one would think to steal.'

'I hadn't thought of that.'

Count Schmettau in the meantime had somehow ridden up alongside me. No doubt he had noticed how often I was looking back, and so he launched into the how's and why's of rampart-building.

'Did you know, before cannon were perfected, that the best and most important defence for any city was a high wall. And, as the invaders would have no way to topple the wall and could only hope to climb over it, its height was crucial. The greater and more important the city, the higher the walls. Then the art of mining was invented. Walls that were high and therefore thin (for no city is *that* rich), could be brought down easily. Oh, did you know that Belgrade was the first city to be mined? Imagine, the very first mines exploded right here, under those very walls. And, best of all, the defenders mined the Turkish trenches that were coming dangerously close to the fortress. That was in 1439, the work of Vran, who had learned his trade in Italy. In those days everyone looked to the Italians when it came to the art of war. Things certainly have changed, haven't they? Wars are fought with cannonfire now, and walls are thick and squat because no one scales them any more – they simply blast their way through them. We Germans are the leaders today.'

'Really? And here I thought it was Marshal Vauban who was the expert on attacking and defending cities.'

Schmettau's face flushed. 'Someone has stolen my copy of Vauban,' he muttered. 'What sort of person would steal a book?'

'Writers,' I suggested.

He said nothing more, but spurred his horse on.

I did the same to catch up with him.

'I beg your pardon, Herr Graf, for being so direct, but what disguise were you wearing last night?'

Schmettau reacted with a start, almost flinching. He pulled on the reins and stopped. I stopped my horse beside him.

'I wasn't dressed as Ludwig, if that's what you mean. Ludwig was my only friend, and it made me sick to see that outrageous get-up last night. I'll find the man who did it, and a good sight quicker than he thinks, too. I only had one Devil costume, the one I let you have.'

I wasn't sure what Schmettau was talking about. But he'd reminded me of a very simple fact that I'd foolishly overlooked: Schmettau knew who had been wearing what, as he had been in charge of handing out all the costumes and probably taking them back. I suddenly realized how important Schmettau was to me. This enthusiast of fortifications was the only man who knew all the disguises worn in Belgrade. True, he had no idea who could have dressed up as his one and only friend. Odd how the most wide-ranging knowledge is often useless in matters closest to the heart.

'Were there any costumes left over?' I asked. It was the most pointed question I could think of.

'Of course. There were lots of things that no one wanted but only one Devil.'

'Yet there were two at the ball!' At last I realized that Schmettau was talking about the nastiest thing to have happened to me yet in Belgrade. 'And the other devil?' I ventured. 'The other devil was Ludwig?'

'No! Ludwig Wittgenau was the finest man alive. That revolting story our enemies cooked up was just idiotic enough for everyone to believe. Especially after . . .'

'Especially after?' I echoed encouragingly.

'After his death, when Ludwig . . . You understand? People said the forces of darkness were at work. They said that Ludwig was the Devil himself, that it was the beginning of the Last Judgement.'

'The Last Judgement.'

Suddenly he turned in the saddle and fixed a sharp eye upon me.

'You've spent too much time disguised as the Devil not to know what the Last Judgement is.'

'I don't understand.'

'Oh, you understand much more than you let on.' Then he spurred his horse forward.

3

Schmettau was getting away, and I wasn't even trying to stop him. As it always does, the mention of the Last Judgement had knocked the wind out of me. Up came Novak.

'I've been thinking, master. I was thinking about it earlier, too, but I didn't tell you.'

Was it not prophesied that in the last days the best will lack all conviction while the worst will be full of passionate intensity? Had those days arrived? Of course not, I told myself consolingly; that's the way things have always been.

'Well done. No need to share your thoughts in future either.'

He disregarded this entirely.

'I've been thinking about why you'd come to Belgrade. When you didn't want to tell me the reason, I knew right away it must be something very important. And for you, as far as I can tell, the most important thing is fear. It's your prime mover and therefore your greatest effect.'

'You don't say.'

'Right. And that ironic tone of yours is also fear and nothing but. The only difference is, when you're not so afraid it comes out as irony. When you're more afraid, it comes out as wickedness. When you're not so afraid, you do your evil with twisted words. When you're full of fear, you do it with deeds.'

'A wise man have I for a servant, indeed.'

'If you had a wise man for your servant, you'd be God. All you've got is a man who lives alone with all his hopes dashed and his wits still about him.'

'What would God need with a servant?'

'So then, I figured you'd come to see about the vampires. But I still couldn't see why it had to be vampires. Then last night, over beer at the inn, I figured that part out, too.'

'Once again the spirits have wrought their blessed work upon you, eh?'

'You can use Heaven's words for your own devices, and it won't put me off one bit. I know you're here on account of the Last Judgement.'

Twice in such a short time, the two most awful words in the world. It was more than I could bear.

'You halfwit lackey! What do *you* know about the Last Judgement?'

'I know that the dead are rising, and the Apostle John in his Revelation tells us this will be one of the signs of the Second Coming and the Last Judgement. That's what got you all worried and brought you here to check whether the dead were truly coming back and turning into vampires. And you know that when Our Lord comes again, He shall judge us for all our sins. You first.'

'For all our sins! There, you see! For our *sins* not for our good deeds.'

'For he shall judge the world in righteousness and minister true judgement unto the people,' he recited, nodding.

'Are you expecting some sort of trial, something in accordance with law? Like in England, where the judges enter the courtroom and take a solemn oath on a great big book? And bang their gavels? With a defender on the left, and a prosecutor on the right? No! That's not what happens. There'll be no one there but Fishmouth. Breaking open the seals like his angels. The seals of judgements passed long ages ago. The ink of them almost gone, blotted out in tears of pain and suffering. But what does he care? Every word, every move, the least little act – he'll read them all out. And he won't ask you why you did it, or whether it was hard, or whether you could have done differently. He won't let a single thing slip, that one. Don't you believe it. There won't be any courtroom, or anyone to defend you, or any acquittals either. For he's made the whole world his courtroom, and no one to speak up for anyone else. He himself shall be accuser and judge. There will be no law and no justice.'

'But the law is the Devil's, and justice is God's. That's how it should be, by justice and not by law.'

'The law is mine indeed, and you may say that justice is his. Only, tell me, where are his judgements from one day to the next, when people need them, and where is this justice of his here on earth? Where is he to be found when men sit in judgement over others? Where is his saving help?'

'The law is here in this world, and justice will come in the next.'

'And I say unto you, when justice cometh, all shall be judged and found wanting.' Having said this I fell silent. How could my servant, the awful man, not see that the Last Judgement meant the end of the world as we know it, and that I was bound to take the whole thing rather badly. I wanted to regain my composure. And I had nothing else to say about the matter.

Fishmouth. Fishmouth. Yes, how long ago it all was.

It was evening, not quite as hot as it can be in Jerusalem. I'd made my way up some narrow paths to the top of the Mount of Olives, knowing I'd find him there. Although I felt it was already too late, not just that night but too late for all nights.

'Have you come here to forgive? Have you come to raise the dead? To heal the sick? To play at being Saviour? Who asked you, you toothless wretch? Who asked you, and who needs you?'

'Sit,' he said through his few remaining teeth. 'Sit down, and we'll have some wine.'

And I sat on a stone for pressing olives. Where he got the wine from I don't know or can't remember. But it was sweet, like all Samarian wines.

'Love is the temple I have come to build.'

'Aha, that means, "I shall build it in a day." Fools fall in love in one day . . . Why, you're nothing but a seducer, no better than the ones who ruin decent women, making promises and then not keeping them.'

'Drink your wine and be quiet,' he said.

It did occur to me that he might be trying to get me drunk. I thought I saw someone moving about in the olive grove below.

Fishmouth looked into his cup and spoke. 'I have come for those who will drink from the cup they are given. For those who would not have that cup pass from them, even though they might.'

'Don't talk nonsense. On your feet and come with me, head high, and deny your father.' I grasped his hand. It was cold, lifeless.

Again I saw something flitting among the olive trees below.

'If we leave now, everything will go on for ever. There won't be any end of the world, or any Last Judgement, or any Hell . . .'

'But there will be death,' he said, turning a stern eye upon me.

I had a lump in my throat. I drained my cup of wine. None of his ridiculous disciples were around. On my way up I had passed Peter where he lay snoring. It might have been John eavesdropping; that was his style.

'I've got a short sword under my cloak. They'll be here soon. We can still get away.'

He looked at me for some time without speaking.

Down among the trees something moved again. It had to be John.

I never promised anything out of the ordinary. Those are the kind of promises one makes to simpletons and the mad. All I offered was to save his life, there on the Mount of Olives. All I wanted was to persuade him to flee the millstone. I never promised loaves of bread for stones, or flights through the air, or power and might. Never. They made all that up afterwards to make me seem greater and more terrifying. I had to be made into something unspeakably dangerous so he could be unspeakably good.

He didn't move from the millstone.

'I can't go on like this,' I nearly cried. 'I can't be afraid any more. I can't think about Hell any more. Just call it all off now, and there won't be any Hell. Let people do their living and dying. What more do they need?'

'Hell is there where thou art, and where thou art there, too, is Hell. I cannot help you. I have come to vanquish death, and by death alone can I conquer. By my own death.'

He fell silent. For a long time he sat on that stone and did not speak.

4

'Do you know when I'll come back? I want you to know this. I'll come back when men and women no longer spare a thought for Hell and when they're sure at last I'm dead, that they've killed me. Yes, they'll even proclaim it from the rooftops. I shall come when they have forgotten me.'

Just then came the soldiers of the Roman legion of Jerusalem, a centurion at their head.

'I am Otto Maximus,' said the fair-haired centurion. 'I have orders from the Procurator of Judaea, Pontius Pilate, to arrest Jesus of Nazareth.'

Fishmouth approached the centurion and stretched out his hands. How the years have flown by since then. So swiftly. And I wager that in all that time, no one has thought more about Hell than I.

That's right. Hell. Much later I heard what that Englishman said – the one who ended up on the wrong end of a knife in a pub over some lad. It was something similar to what Fishmouth said about me and Hell. I even heard one or two bits of our conversation being echoed here and there in other places. You'd think an entire crowd of people had been hiding nearby and listening that night.

But my servant truly was wise. He knew which way the wind was blowing. I'd brought him along because I'm no fool myself. Even the best-laid plans, the highest plans that Fishmouth and his father and the other one could come up with, still had to be carried out through ordinary mortals and their simple, predictable deeds.

'What about Wittgenstein? Why is he important? Find out.'

'Wittgenstein?'

'Yes, Ludwig Wittgenstein was the only friend of Count Schmettau. Then something nasty happened to him, apparently twice. Talk to Schmettau's servants.'

'Now?'

'Right now.'

He obeyed at once and fell back among the servants.

THREE
An Account of the Events, Containing Objections Against the Narrator (Silence Is Not Golden)

1

Then we passed through another gate and came out of the town into Unter Ratzenstadt. Novak was still chatting up the other servants, and no one was bothering me. I looked over Schmeddlesome's bald head at the Sava. It was murky from the previous night's storm. With every passing day the river had a different aspect. Didn't that Greek, the one they call 'the Obscure', say you can't step twice into the same river? There you have it, the *ultima Thule* of human knowledge. And the real point is that the same man cannot step twice into the same river or any other river for that matter. People are just as changeable as rivers.

Suddenly, between me and Schmidlin there appeared a figure on horseback. Dressed *alla Turca*. What was a Turk doing in Belgrade? I wondered. At first I couldn't see his face. It was hidden by a great red turban. His caftan was of the finest velvet, embroidered all in pearls and mother-of-pearl, draping over most of the horse's hindquarters. His stocking was as blue as turquoise, and his slipper curled out to a black pearl at the tip. Then he turned to face me, and I recognized him at once. It was the Grand Vizier Yusuf Ibrahim. A massive ornament of mother-of-pearl adorned his turban with a blinding gleam, although there was no sun to reflect from it.

I remembered the vizier's seal. It was divided in two: the first section was larger and inscribed with the words *Yusuf Ibrahim, Faithful Servant of God*. In the smaller section were the words *In Silence Is Safety*. What a cunning snare I once laid for this worthy Bosnian who'd made such a name for himself in Istanbul!

With silken words I had praised him to the sultan's agents, and the words smoothly twisted themselves into a cord around the vizier's neck. But then I was called away on other business, from the Levant to the Orient, and I set sail from the Golden Horn and left the matter behind. Later I heard that he had managed to escape the snare, and in gratitude to Allah (as if I were شيطان, or *Shaitan*) he had a bridge built over the River Žepa in his home country. Well, I could hardly let such a thing go unpunished. I sat down and penned him a letter, imitating the handwriting of one of his fellow-countrymen. In the letter I recommended an inscription to be carved into the bridge:

> When Good Rule and Noble Skill
> Did clasp hands together,
> There rose this magnificent bridge,
> Gladness of men's hearts and good deed of Yusuf
> In this world and the world to come.

Sometime later I was passing by the town of Žepa and stopped to rest on the stone railing of the bridge. The evening around me was cold, but the bridge was warm, still holding the heat of the sun within. But nowhere on the bridge was there any inscription. Again I said to myself that such a thing must not go unpunished . . .

But what could this Bosnian want from me now? Revenge? And what on earth was a grand vizier doing riding along with the Austrians? It suddenly occurred to me that he might be a phantom. Like one of the phantoms I had already encountered in Unter Ratzenstadt. He must not be visible to the others.

And as I puzzled this over, he laughed out loud and said, 'Laer si meht fo eno ylno dna eerht neve ebyam ecno ta secalp owt ni era uoy won.' His face began to change. The long thin beard vanished, the eyes grew larger, the turban lengthened into a curly wig – and the green caftan became . . .

A cloak of royal crimson!

It was the count I had seen when returning to Belgrade. The slippers with the black pearls at the tip remained and did not change into riding-boots. But this was no comfort to me at all. In fact, it merely threw me into even greater confusion.

As the man in crimson was clearly an Austrian, it meant he would be travelling with us and not disappearing in the time-honoured tradition of genies released from the bottle.

And why had he spoken to me in that manner? Either he had not wanted me to understand or else he knew who I was and meant to let me know what he was about without anyone else's understanding. Whichever the case, it wasn't good. For if he spoke so I would not understand he was mad, and the mad are to be feared even more than the wicked; and if he knew who I was, then he could be my greatest foe. The Regent of Serbia had also recognized me immediately, but the Regent of Serbia had no power to transform himself into a grand vizier. And if this was indeed my greatest foe it could mean only one thing: the end of the world was truly upon us.

'What's wrong, master? You've got the smell of brimstone about you again,' said Novak.

'Be quiet!'

'I don't see anything . . .'

'Be quiet!'

'But I don't understand.'

'*Will* you be quiet!'

And in the end, merely by being so annoying, he managed to calm me down. I slowed my horse until I was lagging further behind the man in crimson. Novak wisely followed suit. When we were far enough away, I asked Novak, 'Do you see that man in the crimson cloak?'

'I don't see anybody in a crimson cloak.'

'How many of us are there?'

'Eight, counting the two of us. What kind of question is that?'

'It doesn't matter. Have you asked about Wittgenstein?'

'The name is Wittgenau.'

Who can keep all those surnames straight? I could barely keep track of all the families of Europe and their ties. Marrying away, right, left and centre. All of them with their double-barrelled surnames and everyone related to everyone else. How I look forward to the end of this aristocratic muddle, the marriages and family names and all the other contrivances of inequality. I note that the English colonies in America have made great strides in that direction. There one finds no counts, barons, princesses or other ranks of birth; what counts is one's ability. I'm becoming quite partial towards the lads across the pond.

'Well, let's hear it.'

'He was born in Germany to a good Catholic family, but he's said to have Jewish blood. Later he went to England. From there he came to Belgrade.'

The fool.

'Supposedly he said, *The world is all that is the case*,' Novak continued.

'I don't understand.'

'No one does, but that's why they thought so highly of him.'

'I understand.'

'Anyhow, Wittgenau was particularly interested in the two cisterns that Doxat had ordered to be built over three years: the one in Belgrade and the other in Petrovaradin. Everyone was sure he'd come on some sort of inspection to see whether there'd been anything crooked about it and to make sure the work at Kalemegdan was on the level. But Schmettau's man tells me, just between ourselves, that Wittgenau wasn't sent by anyone, and certainly not by the emperor in Vienna, and that he came on his own, wanting to go down into the cistern.'

'Why? Aren't people allowed into the cistern?'

'He hardly had time to. Not long after he arrived the poor man went missing.'

'Perhaps he went down into the cistern after all? Heh, heh, heh. Only he couldn't get back out. There's the secret of the cistern for you. Once you get to the bottom you find what you were looking for, but there's no way out.'

'From what I hear, there are two spiral staircases leading to the water level. One set of stairs for going down, and the other for coming back up.'

2

You say my story is inconsistent, that I've been saying things that contradict one another? You say it's clear I must be lying?

If I *were* lying, everything I say would be perfectly consistent and all the pieces would fit together. That's because, if I were lying, I'd have thought it all through in advance, and I'd tell you a story that made perfect sense. If I were lying, I'd be sure to observe Aristotle's rules of logic. As it stands, since I'm telling the truth, I *haven't* thought it through, and so mistakes are bound to creep in. Every perfect story is a lie. Truth is full of twists and turns and doesn't stick to a plan. When we tell the truth we don't look to the logic of the thing, for truth stands on its own, not because of Aristotle. Only a lie lives by the rules of reasoning.

I beg your pardon, I cannot hear you.

What happened next?

We continued to sit at the table they had laid for us. The seven of us. Vuk Isakovič was not with us. Now that I think of it, I didn't see him at all until the following morning. And he'd been assigned as our guard.

I put on my favourite cloak, a crimson-purple sort of thing, for it had grown chilly for sitting out of doors. First we were served some jasmine tea. In those days I used to take my tea with quite a lot of sugar. But no sooner had I reached for a spoonful than Schmettau, who was sitting beside me, jarred my hand, causing me to spill the sugar on the table. He did say he was sorry, but I knew at once he had done it on purpose. This became even clearer when I tried to take some more sugar. Schmettau jostled me, again I spilled the sugar, and once more he apologized. My third attempt at sweetening my tea was also thwarted by Schmettau, and then I had to ask him for an explanation.

'One does not take sugar with jasmine tea,' he replied.

'Could you not have simply said so?'

'Had I told you, you might have listened, but also quickly forgotten. Now you are sure to remember that I was most appallingly rude and also that one does not take sugar with jasmine tea.'

'Suppose, however, that now, just because of your bad manners, I shall always do the opposite of your unspoken admonition?'

'You are clever enough for a woman not to spite your face by cutting off your own nose.'

'To what do I owe this change in your attentions? Only a short while ago you were very nearly accusing me of having murdered your friend Count Wittgenau.'

'*Was* I? I was merely speaking heart-to-heart. Who else is there to talk to? Cast your eye, won't you, over the select company of idiots that surrounds us. A count from Vienna whom no one has ever seen before, who allegedly earned his title in the overseas colonies, as if there were anything *there* that needed doing. And who, by the way, also nicked my copy of Marshal Vauban.'

'I was under the impression you'd given up reading.'

'How did you know that?'

'Word travels fast, you know, especially when it's something bad.' I smiled ever so pleasantly.

The soup course was served.

'This is a Chinese noodle soup,' said Schmettau. Silently we had our soup. I don't know why everyone had stopped talking.

Next came the spicy mung beans but still no talking.

Only when the main course was brought did Schmettau speak up.

'This is five-spice duck with moo shu pancakes. It is made by adding the duck meat to a chicken broth, bringing it to the boil and then adding soya sauce, sugar, salt, ginger and star anise. Reduce the heat, cover and allow to simmer for as long as *Much Ado About Nothing* takes to perform in the better sort of theatre.'

'But if you've given up reading, what does it matter whether von Hausburg has stolen your book?'

'I've stopped reading prose and poetry but continue to buy and study specialist literature. Remove the duck from the heat, drain, then rub the meat both inside and out with the five-spice mix, salted black beans and wine. Bread the duck with a mixture of corn and wheat flour. Allow to stand for the length of one act of a serious drama, under no circumstances substituting a comedy. Fry the duck in hot oil until it turns golden brown and then drain well. Take the moo shu pancakes, also known as Mandarin pancakes, wrap them in a damp cloth and steam them for the length of Hamlet's monologue in Act Two. To finish –'

'Why have you given up prose and poetry?'

'To finish, carve the duck in thin slices. Now, how to serve. Because I've looked, my dear princess. I seek but never find. Not one book has ever been good enough for me. They start out the way they should. They tickle my fancy, I get swept up, carried away – but in the end it's never worth it, it's always a disappointment, a big nothing. At first I thought some authors must not know what they're doing, that they could think their way *into* a plot but not *out*. But as time went by it turned out that none of them could ever pull it off the way I like. Now, Chinese cuisine attaches considerable importance to the art of serving. Sprinkle the pancakes with hoisin sauce, add several pieces of duck, top with spring onions, roll up and eat. And then I understood what was wrong. I had been expecting books, those little books, to end with an explanation of life itself and its meaning. And that's not what they were doing. They'd merely see the protagonists safely married off, or killed off, or crowned, or back at home after their long journeys. What was the point of that? I've forgotten, Princess, I am sorry, the proportions of the ingredients, *so* sorry, but we shall ask the cook if you care to know.'

'Dear Count, would you ever have your portrait done in sand?'

'Certainly not,' he exclaimed.

'Well then, would the dear Lord ever choose something as threadbare as language to explain the essence of the world?'

'I couldn't agree more, Princess – Madam Regent,' von Hausburg put in. 'Just think about language and what happens to it in the ears, let alone on the tongue. It was only the other day, you might say, that people were calling it *the changing of the guard*; now they're calling it *guard-changing operations*. Before you know it they'll be calling it *modifications to be implemented in guard-duty-provider positions*. Once they start, the Devil himself couldn't come up with more sheer nonsense. Isn't that a sure sign of linguistic impoverishment and decline? How is your man upstairs supposed to use that sort of language to express his greatest secrets, eh? How?'

'Count von Hausburg, do not forget that the Lord spoke the world into existence. By his word was the world made, and the word is greater than the world, and by the word can the world be understood, but that writers fail and know not how,' Schmettau said.

'Oh, they know it all right. They know it only too well. If he did speak the world into existence, and if the word really was in the beginning, then what does that make mispronunciations, and metaphors, and switching one thing for another, and alterations, and figures of speech? The destruction of the world, that's what. Let alone irony! The deadliest weapon of all. Imagine he'd said "Let there be light" in an ironic tone of voice and ended up creating darkness. Twist the language, and you change the shape of the world. That's the Devil's work, believe you me,' said von Hausburg all in one breath.

'But what about books with wise and beautiful sentences and a certain way of putting things, the ones that make you sit up straight, or move about in your chair, or even get to your feet because you simply must stop reading? You stretch and go for a walk. You think. The most pleasurable book to read is the one that makes you put it down and stand up for a moment. In a way, reading is like the passions of the flesh, which are just as much movements as interruptions. Interruptions when you know what just took place and look forward to what's coming next. When that happens, do you really need to have the world explained to you? Novels and poems aren't meant to explain the world or to twist it all out of shape. We're meant to journey into them, to stay for a while, bathing in an airy stream of words, verses, chapters,' I said.

We all sat quietly, and then von Hausburg spoke. 'And how do you distinguish the rules of this life from the rules of literature?'

3

Let me stop and catch my breath. I've been talking all this time. It's not easy remembering everything the way it was said and the looks and gestures that went with it. Well now.

It's been many years since then, and so much has changed. For instance, that revolution in France. Who could have seen that coming? And here you are, asking about things that happened long ago and therefore don't matter, about a country that's already been given back to the Turks . . .

What? You say there's been a book about it? What sort of book? Yes, I do understand I'm not the one asking the questions here. I do. But a book? Someone's written a book about all the things I've been telling you? Hm.

Now I see why you're questioning me. It doesn't matter what really happened, all that matters is what the book says. It's the book that's upset you, not the events themselves.

And I know just who might have written that book. I do indeed.

I know all sorts of things now. Why, I even know the proportions of the ingredients for the five-spice duck with pancakes:

four cups broth
two and a half teaspoons dark soya sauce
half a cup salt
two spoonfuls star anise
two spoonfuls ginger
one and a half spoonfuls brown sugar
one and a half spoonfuls five-spice mixture

one and a half spoonfuls black beans
two spoonfuls wine
one spoonful cornmeal
one and a half spoonfuls wheat flour
six cups oil
sixteen to eighteen Mandarin pancakes
hoisin sauce
spring onions

This is for half a duck or one whole chicken, if you'd rather not have duck meat. I believe the proportions were doubled for our meal.

I don't know what's in the five-spice mixture, as they call it, and I'm afraid I can't tell you where to find the hoisin. I get mine from China, don't you know, when our couriers travel to Tiananmen and back. My family and the Qing dynasty are on good terms.

You never really know everything that goes into a particular dish. There's always a dash of something secret. Just so you understand, the smaller and more insignificant that mystery ingredient is, the more delicious your dinner.

What was my answer to von Hausburg? I'll tell you in a bit. No need to go in strict order, is there? Besides, you already know what happened. And how. And in what order. Not only that, something important was just about to take place. Something more important to the story than my answer to von Hausburg.

One of the servants was careless with the Chinese soup and spilled some on Baron Schmidlin. He had to excuse himself from the table to change. You don't see why this should matter? During the meal, neither did I. It was only later that I understood, and then very much so. As I say, Baron Schmidlin stepped into the hut to change his clothes. But changing seemed to take him a very long time – all throughout lunch, in fact. I must confess we had quite forgotten about him.

We finished the duck off quickly, or rather the pancakes with bits of duck in them, and in my distracted state I didn't even notice when the three men from the commission began their discussion, whispering and explaining something very important to one another. I saw von Hausburg straining to listen as they whispered, but I don't think he was able to hear. I, however, have unusually keen hearing. Or, rather, I *did* have at the time. And so I was able to hear and understand some of what they were saying.

The one doing most of the talking, or whispering, was the commissioner with the red wig, while the other two listened and occasionally nodded. In fact, the whole time they behaved as though the one in red were in charge and not that doctor, as they'd given us to understand.

4

Yes, what I learned from the three men's conversation is what actually happened later. They agreed that Klaus Radetzky would be the one to sleep at the mill. It wasn't clear to me at first why the three of them didn't just spend the night there together. Later Count Schmettau explained it. The Serbs would not stop believing in the vampires if all three men stayed at the mill. Vampires were believed to strike, for the most part, when no one else was around, so nothing would be proved if all three men stayed the night.

In the meantime, Baron Schmidlin had returned, just in time to break open his Chinese fortune cookies. The fortunes are written on slips of paper and then baked into sweet biscuits. There's usually a line from Confucius or Lao-tzu, someone like that. Supposedly, it's not by chance that one gets a certain message. It's destiny, fate, speaking through the layers of sweetness.

Mine said: *Joy is along the way not at the end of the road.*

China?

Yes, the fortunes were in Chinese. Count Schmettau translated them for us. For all of us, of course. None of us knew Chinese. Although . . .

Although I do remember, as if it were yesterday, seeing Count von

Hausburg give a start when he unrolled his fortune. It occurred to me at the time that he could read what was written there, and that the words had shaken him. But still he handed his paper to Schmettau to be translated. And Count Schmettau's translation was: *Your world is the totality of facts not of things.* Von Hausburg looked at him in surprise, as if Schmettau hadn't read what was really there, as if it said something entirely different. But von Hausburg said nothing, only took back his paper and crumpled it up.

What did Schmettau's fortune say?

I don't remember. I think it was something good. Something quite clear and auspicious, unlike mine and von Hausburg's, which were neither good nor bad but merely unclear. At least they were still unclear at the time.

No, I wasn't surprised that Count Schmettau knew Chinese. He liked the Chinese, anything from China. Everyone knew. He would often say, 'How close we are here to the East', then stare off into one of the Chinese paintings that hung at the palace. Bamboo ink on silk, enigmatic paintings of Chinese landscapes. I think looking at such pictures calmed him. It wasn't often that I met him, but when I did he was almost always lost in thought in front of one of those paintings.

5

The steps . . . Yes, the steps.

'Have I ever told you about the time on the steps, when I was following Fishmouth on the way to Golgotha, and I caught up with Mary Magdalene? Now there was a soul, the kind of soul you rarely meet. I've seen my share of multitudes, and even I couldn't resist such a suffering soul. Love . . .'

'Master, why are you telling me this? Do you really think you can tell a story? And a love story at that? Why, you're the last one to be telling love stories. And why? First of all, because you have no idea how to love. You may know how to put a story together, but if you don't know how to love, all that skill and cleverness don't mean a thing.'

'You're talking nonsense,' I answered sharply. 'If that were true then only murderers could speak about killing, only traitors about betrayal, only yours truly about evil and only an angel about good.'

'It's half true, master.'

'How so?'

'Because only the Devil doesn't improve with the telling.'

'I don't understand.'

'It's very simple, master. A storyteller must learn from the tale he's telling: the character who loves must learn to love better, the murderer to repent, the traitor to fall on his face before the king. That kind of story is the only real kind.'

'Everything else is merely the truth,' I laughed.

Novak lit his pipe. It was filled with the good Virginia tobacco from my own supplies that I'd let him have. He looked back at me as if he were smoking hashish.

'Why shouldn't I be able to tell a love story? I've been in love, too, you know.'

'There you have it, master. How do you mean, in love? Have you ever been ready to give yourself up to the woman you love, without a second thought, without a single qualm? Have you ever been able to believe in love without hiding behind sneering words that don't mean what they say?'

'No, of course not. Women are all mortal creatures.'

'I understand, master. Everyone thinks that way: I'll never die, and all the rest of you are just passing through and falling to ruin, and it's always someone else's fault that we hold back. Don't laugh, master. It's a woeful thing.'

'So?' I asked.

'So it's a poor storyteller that doesn't know how to end his tale. Even if he's able to put it all together, he doesn't know how to take it apart again. A bad story never ends, and that's the mark of a bad storyteller.'

'We've got ourselves a little Aristotle here!'

'Even better maybe. I do know a bit more about some things than he does. I know the twists and turns of the story are like a question, and the way it plays out is like an answer. Anyone can ask the question, but not everyone can give the answer. That takes a bit more work and skill. As far as I can see, it's all the same to you. You'll never learn a thing, ever. That's what makes you the Devil.'

'Well, now I know,' I said.

But he said no more, only puffed away at the Virginia tobacco and regarded the ground at his feet. I lit my own pipe, and we sat and smoked together.

6

Count Schmettau brought the meal to a close. He did so rather oddly, almost imperceptibly, in a way that for Schmettau was quite out of character. It was then that I understood for the first time the greatness of not calling attention to oneself. Schmettau suffered from greatness, as you yourself may have perceived. He was afflicted with an indescribable sense of his own importance. It was not enough for him that Count Marulli, who was obviously one of his protectors, would be coming to replace my husband. Rather, in some way I could not fathom, it had to do with his own position, which at the moment was different from ours, above ours. But Schmettau couldn't have known this yet.

In any case, the meal was finished, and Radetzky stood up, bowed slightly and announced the decision that he was to stay the night at the mill.

That bow, I saw later, marked the beginning of Act Two. It was then that an unknown artist, ill-disposed towards us for reasons we could not fathom, took our fates in hand and set to work. That afternoon everything still seemed the same, no worse than any unrehearsed scene from a minor drama. Tired from the day, we made ready for a short rest; but the day was short, and it was, in fact, time for bed. I was sure that the day to come would be no different from all the days before. I expected nothing from the morning but that which daybreak always brings: tasks to attend to rather than thoughts, certainty rather than doubt. At least that's what I was thinking. Perhaps the others had something else in mind. I mean to say, perhaps some among us were ready to encounter the vampires.

Throughout our lives we learn how to uncover false words, to turn them over and find the truth beneath them. When at last we come face to face with truth itself, we are helpless. Because falsehoods make sense, and truth does not. I was not expecting vampires.

7

'I don't know why you're being so harsh about this. First of all, you can trust my stories. I always tell you just what everyone said, even Fishmouth. I tell you everything that happened and how it happened. True, I sometimes get ahead of my own tale, and sometimes I fall behind, but I do that to make things more interesting for you to hear so you'll enjoy the story more.'

'Hmph, you don't say. Your stories are all meant to show how clever you are, and that's that. I can't remember a single story of yours where Christ gets the last word.'

'Naturally. That would be pointless. How could anyone believe in all those dire omens and threats, the sudden turnabouts, the heartfelt lessons and inspirations? And that's just what Fishmouth is always going on and on about. I tell you, the most the hero can hope for is a minor victory, a foolish bit of insight, a pathetic little treasure. Believe you me, even that's asking a lot.'

'But –'

'A good storyteller takes his time as he comes to the most important events then springs them on the reader whose eyelids are starting to droop from all the philosophical toing and froing. After the boredom, surprise. Then one surprise after another. What an ironic twist that makes! I'm telling you, irony is not of this world. There, you see? That's the kind of storyteller *I* am.'

8

We followed after Radetzky. He went striding ahead of us courageously. His chest out. Soon we reached the mill. It would be a dark place at any time of day, at any time of year. The water-wheel was black, enormous, rotting.

The mill itself was a hovel of wattle and daub.

Now Klaus Radetzky removed his wig and his short coat and was left wearing only his white shirt. He rolled up his sleeves as if settling to work. Until tomorrow, he said.

He went inside, and the door closed behind him. We stood there, watching. Nothing happened, but I felt uneasy. Some time went by before any of us spoke. It was then that I noticed the peasants who had also been watching as Radetzky went inside. After all, the whole thing was for their benefit. That's what I believed.

Still, even as we spoke, none of us took our eyes off the mill. For a long time we stood there, and the conversation slowly died down. At one moment it ceased entirely. Silence reigned, but not for long. Soon we heard snoring. From inside the mill. It was Radetzky, no doubt tired from the ball, now fast asleep.

9

When we arrived at Dedejsko Selo night was already falling. Baron Schmeddlesome gave the order for our meal to be laid out of doors. Nasty Chinese food with nasty fortunes baked inside nasty little biscuits. Nothing will convince me that Count Schmettau didn't make up the fortunes himself (he knew Chinese, that one), then arrange for everyone to get the prediction he thought most fitting, or closest to what he hoped our fate would be. I could hardly wait for the signal to be given that the meal was over. There was a signal all right, but hardly the usual one: Count Schmettau spilled some wine on his trousers and had to leave the table. Quick as could be, Radetzky stood up and said he had to make ready for his night at the mill. Everyone seemed to feel a bit odd, no doubt from the Chinese confections. One by one they left the table. Only the princess and Baron Schmidlin stayed put, prattling and giggling away – her like a minx and him like an old hen.

Radetzky came back shortly afterwards, all bristling with youthful courage. Schmidlin jumped to his feet, bowed low to the princess and with a courteous gesture invited the young man to take the lead. Radetzky stood there in confusion, not knowing where to go. That is, he knew he was supposed to go the mill, but he didn't know the way. Since Radetzky had also been brought up in the Vienna school of manners he made his own courteous gesture for Schmidlin to go first. Baron Schmidlin, being a Viennese article himself, made another little show of letting Radetzky take the lead. That's when Radetzky abandoned his good breeding, a sure sign he wasn't as cool-headed as he was trying to seem, and raised his voice, 'I don't know the way!'

'I beg your pardon,' murmured Schmidlin, bowing slightly to Radetzky, before setting off rather uncertainly in one direction.

The mill wasn't far. Maybe two hundred paces from the table at which we'd just eaten. Radetzky took off his riding-coat, stripping down to his white shirt. He rolled up his sleeves and, without another look at us, went right inside. I noticed that the peasants around us were watching closely. We stood and talked for quite some time. I didn't talk. I was casting my eye about for a suitable place to hide so I could come back later and keep watch on the mill. I just didn't trust the Serbs or the young man from Požarevac – not to mention being far from convinced that there were no vampires.

Some fifty paces from the mill stood a great oak tree, mostly dead wood. Its short main trunk forked into two thick branches that had long since stopped growing, but each was still topped by a leafy crown. I'd already made up my mind that I'd come back and climb up high enough to keep an eye on whatever might happen that night at the mill. But first I'd have to go back with everyone else to the hut in which we were to spend the night and then steal away later. And I'd have to do it before the witching-hour, of course. As Novak had explained, midnight and the wee hours were believed by the peasantry to be the best time for vampires.

As I stood there thinking the conversation around me stopped. It had suddenly fallen quiet, the sort of quiet one sometimes finds in Hell.

And then we heard the snoring. It was Radetzky, inside the mill, his fear conquered by exhaustion. Or else it was a display of snoring, I thought, a show for the peasants, or perhaps for the rest of us, to prove there was no danger.

Someone spoke. 'Radetzky's asleep!'

FOUR
The Vienna Agreements

1

And he never woke up again.

But, of course, you know that, otherwise we wouldn't be having this belated investigation now.

I don't know why he fell asleep so quickly. It might not have been him snoring after all; it could have been someone else behind the mill, someone who wanted us to hear the sound. Don't forget that Vuk Isakovič was nowhere to be seen.

I'm not accusing anyone. I'm merely saying what happened.

Perhaps the secret ingredient in the Chinese recipe was poison for Radetzky. One strong enough to send him to sleep right after eating but not strong enough to kill him at once. Whatever the case may be, we took the snoring as a sign to leave. We set off for the hut. It made me ill to think of the dirt and smell that awaited. And I wasn't in much of a hurry. Several times I turned to look back. I noticed that the peasants were beginning to go their separate ways.

I thought how brave Radetzky was. I thought how much my husband would appreciate the snoring we'd heard. Alexander despised anything in moderation. He was always trying to make his life the way he wanted it, or talking himself into believing that it was the most thrilling, the most beautiful, the mightiest and bravest, or nothing. For him there was no such thing as the journey between two points, no middle ground. He was always at one extreme or the other: the peak of excitement or the depths of despair. He was fond of saying that moderation was for cowards. I still admired him then, and so it simply never occurred to me to consider Radetzky a fool.

I had nearly reached the hut when Count Schmettau approached me. I was glad to have someone to talk to, if only to stay outside a bit longer.

'Picture, if you will,' said Count Schmettau, 'an army that has yet to be defeated with Doxat riding at its head, climbing towards Serbia, while its great tail sweeps across Austria. And the closer its snout comes to Belgrade, the more Turkish land is swept free behind it. Behind it flows a Danube of men and women in flight, a Sava of Turkish spies. They are now one day closer to Belgrade. And meanwhile the treasonous head waits within the city walls for the hand to reach it.'

'What are you trying to say?' I asked.

'I mean what I say, nothing more. You don't know, but I do. But you should know. If you only knew it all, how the groundwork was laid for treason, how the cursed cistern was dug, on the direct orders of Doxat, to his own plan and with your husband's approval, and how everything stands ready for the final act: the surrender of Niš and then of Belgrade. But, mark my words, while I yet live I shall fight against it. Belgrade shall not fall, even if I have to block up the cistern myself.'

I made no answer. To this day I wouldn't know what to say.

Although, of course, we were all aware of the same thing. We all knew the army and the refugees were on their way to the city. We had even calculated how many days they would take to arrive. Seven days, that's what Baron Schmidlin and von Hausburg were saying. Count Schmettau was saying five. Everyone else considered this out of the question. From Niš to Belgrade is thirty miles, meaning all those people would have to cover six miles a day to arrive in such a short time. People with little children, old people, the sick and injured. People carrying their belongings and bundles. People with no desire to go anywhere, who had been ordered out as part of Doxat's agreement with the Turks.

2

The night was bright under the full moon.

There were no windows in the room where the men slept, and only the smouldering fire in the hearth cast its red glow around us and the objects in the room. If the fires of Hell were to die down the effect would be the same. It felt like hours waiting for everyone to fall asleep so I could sneak out. But the costume ball and the late meal took their toll, and even I drifted off.

When I awoke the fire had gone out, and it was pitch black. I tried to sit up without making any noise. I sat for some time, allowing my eyes to adjust to the dark. In the moonlight that still made its way through the chinks in the roof and walls I was able to make out the sleeping bodies. I counted them, just to make sure. There were three of them besides myself, meaning that someone was not in the room. Novak, of course, was with the other servants.

Slowly and quietly I got up and looked at the nearest sleeper. It was the blond-wigged one from the commission. Beside him lay the red-wigged one. Two long steps brought me to the side of the third man. He was lying face down. No sooner had I crouched down beside him to have a closer look than he changed position. I drew back, worried I might wake him. When he had settled down, I crept closer. I nearly brushed against his ear. I held my breath. He shifted again. I drew back once more. Now he was covering his face with one arm. He may have been awake. Could be Schmettau. Or maybe Schmidlin. I gave up on him, whoever he was, and made my way to the door, or what these people used as a door. Once I stepped outside, I was blinded for a moment by the moonlight. As soon as I was a safe distance from the hut I lit my pipe. That calmed me down.

In no time at all I had found my way to the oak tree. Climbing wasn't as easy as it used to be, and I nearly fell when a desiccated branch gave way under me. It made a loud crack, and for a few moments I hung in the air, clinging to two other branches, not daring to move to find a new foothold in case I made any more noise. Only when my hands and arms started to hurt did I swing over to a living branch where I could place my feet. The failure to fall must have given me new confidence, for with surprising dexterity I climbed several branches higher, coming to rest in a fork at a good distance from the ground.

I was pleased with my hiding-place, counting above all on people's disinclination to ever look up. From there I had a clear view of the mill and, more importantly, anyone coming in or out.

I had no idea of the time, except to reckon that I hadn't slept long and that it couldn't be much later than nine or ten o'clock. Although I was on a thick branch it was still quite uncomfortable. This may be why the hours seemed to crawl by so slowly.

Sometimes sheer exhaustion is stronger than fear. Or an excess of fear merely dulls its own edge. Whatever the case, I soon fell asleep again. It was a miracle I didn't fall. Who knows how much longer the miracle would have held out had a sudden noise not awoken me.

I looked down and saw a group of five men sitting next to the oak. They were dressed in white. And speaking Serbian. I recognized one of them immediately – Vuk Isakovič. In white, he seemed like a bear disguised as a miller. They spoke in hushed voices. Isakovič would raise his voice at times, but I could make out no more than a word here and there, without being able to understand what they were talking about. I dared not move. I was barely breathing.

I couldn't say why I suddenly looked away from them. But I did. That's when I saw the man in crimson coming out of the mill. I thought I would scream. I bit my knuckles. The man in crimson never even turned around. He came down the few rungs of the mill-ladder as if he were descending the palace steps, as if a throng of loyal subjects were waiting below to catch a glimpse of him.

In a few dignified strides he made his way across the small clearing and vanished into the woods. He must have entered the mill while I was sleeping. But no matter how his appearance had startled and upset me, I tried to be reasonable and see that he must be a figment of my imagination. For Novak had not seen him, and he must therefore not be real. No one else had seen him either – not the first time, and not the second time, when the apparition had ridden alongside me.

Vuk Isakovič had seen him, though, when we were returning to the city, no doubt about that, and he had been afraid. This time, talking away, he had noticed nothing. I hoped that no one but Isakovič and I would be subjected to the sight of him.

And then I had a brilliant idea. What if the man in crimson *was* a vampire? It certainly made sense. From everything I'd heard vampires wouldn't enter the city, and the man had conveniently disappeared just before the gates had opened. So there *had* been a point to all that talk of cities and walls I'd been hearing since my arrival. Hadn't Schmettau mentioned, in one of his never-ending explanations, that the real purpose of cities was not to protect the inhabitants from marauding bandits but from the dead? Ramparts and water, the water in the moats, served as a barrier against visitors from beyond the grave. Belgrade could certainly count its blessings there. So, a vampire was preying on people in the mill, and here was the man in crimson. The peasants would describe vampires as being red with the blood of their victims, always wrapped in their burial shroud, and here was the man in crimson never without his cloak.

If it were true, then Radetzky was already dead. The man in crimson was, in fact, Sava Savanović. And the dead truly were beginning to rise. The Last Judgement. The end of days. The end.

But no. Not yet. Maybe there was a way to stop the vampires. They couldn't enter the city. The ramparts would keep them at bay. Water! But how? Why couldn't they? If I only knew I could destroy them. Pound the stake in. Stop the whole thing. Stop the twisted resurrection they heralded. Prevent the coming of the Antichrist and with it the coming of Christ himself.

And, as these courageous thoughts went through my mind, I happened to look down again. The five men were still beneath the tree, carrying on a heated discussion. They couldn't have seen the man in crimson. Again I could make out several words here and there.

'Great ballad . . . Kosovo . . . seek . . . swore . . . white . . . heroes . . . white . . . for ever . . . never . . . white . . . white . . .'

They were the very picture of conspirators. But who could they be plotting against, if not Austria? Perhaps they wanted to put the regent to death, which would explain the mention of Kosovo and heroes. I liked the idea of them doing the regent in. Lovely. Isakovič would look every bit the killer, all in white – a colour I've always hated – as he ran the Austrian Murad through with his magnificent Solingen sabre, a sword I watched him cradling like a child.

I strained to hear. At times their voices were louder, and then I could make out certain words; other times, no doubt when they were in agreement, their voices remained low and practically inaudible. There was nothing to be done about it other than to hope for an argument to break out.

And so, during one of their moments of general agreement about the need for the Serbian people to stick together, I looked back at the mill. And again there was something to see.

This time it was Maria Augusta, Princess of Thurn and Taxis.

3

She was behind a tree, no doubt imagining herself to be cleverly concealed. I'd been watching the Serbs for some time, so she could easily have gone into the mill and come back out without my noticing. Or she might have just been standing there, in full sight of any of the people near by. It was becoming quite the little crowd.

The foolish woman was waving at me. She'd spotted me. I tried to wave her away, but she just waved back. She obviously wasn't worried about the five men under the tree, which could only mean one thing: they were connected to her in some way. But then, why would she be waving at me? Maybe it wasn't me she was waving at. Maybe she was giving them sort of sign? She might have wanted to get rid of her lover. She must have suggested spending the night at the mill, and when Württemberg cleverly turned the offer down she'd made a deal with the Serbs to do him in.

Or maybe she was trying to signal them that I was in the branches overhead. Fortunately, they didn't notice. If they did notice, though, I was done for. Climbing this high would cost me my life. I held on tight.

Maria Augusta had stopped waving. But she might start up again any moment. I looked down again, and when I raised my eyes, I saw something halfway between myself and the princess. It was in the shadows cast by the moonlight among the dense trees, and I couldn't quite make it out. Again I looked towards the princess, but she was gone. I looked back at the unknown figure, just in time to see it vanish into the woods.

The place was getting as crowded as Hell.

The princess must have been waving at the mysterious figure. I could let go of my conspiracy theories about assassinating Württemberg and concentrate on the theory that he was being cuckolded. Although it was an odd choice of place for a rendezvous, even by my standards.

As for the Serbs, if they weren't talking murder, what *were* they talking about? Whatever it was, it was obviously gripping enough to make them blind and deaf to all the members of the nobility and the undead running around the place.

I felt I'd seen enough. All I had to do now was wait for the Serbs either to come to an agreement or have an argument and leave their spot under the oak tree. I was awfully tired. The men were still going on about 'Kosovo' and something 'white', which made me want to shout out 'black'. After all, isn't Kosovo dark ground for the Serbs?

And then, of course, it occurred to me that the princess's lover must be either Schmeticulous or Schmeddlesome. One of them had been missing from the room. If the Serbs would only get it over with and let me get back, then I could see who was left in the room. The two lovebirds would hardly be done before the Serbs.

As it happened, it wasn't long before the conspirators began to stand up. They exchanged a few more words as they stood there, then went their separate ways. Each one in a different direction. Vuk Isakovič headed off towards our hut.

I had just started to climb down when a voice stopped me. The voice did not come from the ground. It came from on high. It came from above:

> 'Where hast thou wandered, O morning star?
> Where oh where hast thou dallied?
> And dallied these three days bright?'

It was a man's voice, deep and powerful, yet tender as the softest damask. For a moment I thought it might be . . . But no. I thought it might be the voice of . . . But no. Impossible. There was nothing above but the moon and the stars. But from above came the response:

> 'Oh wander and tarry did I
> In Bijograd-town of white,
> And filled my eyes with wonder . . .'

It was a woman's voice, high, perhaps a bit strong, but vulnerable and full of feeling. Again it sang out:

> 'The Devil went down to Belgrade-town,
> And tricked the false commission,
> They all believe, but only one knows,
> If that one leaves . . .'

And there the voice stopped. I peered up into the sky, trying to figure out what had just happened but saw only a dark cloud that had suddenly appeared. For a long time I looked up without hearing anything else from above. I hopped down and set off for the hut. From time to time I would stop and look up, but there was nothing, only more and more clouds gathering. Damned clouds! Cold and free, with no native land, no exile.

I thought about the two voices I had heard. They'd been speaking the Ijekavian dialect, the speech of Bosnia and epic poetry and the

Bible. Why? Everyone in 'the white city' of Belgrade and the surrounding areas spoke the Ekavian dialect. Was it to keep the right number of syllables in the metre? And what was the bit about leaving Belgrade supposed to mean? Of all the places for the verse to stop.

Oh, I was fed up. It was all too much for one night. Nothing had gone according to plan. Just wait till I get my hands on that boy from Požarevac, I told myself.

I could have gone back to see what had happened to Radetzky, but somehow I didn't want to. I was cold. It's always coldest just before the dawn. When I found out in the morning, at least I'd be able to look genuinely surprised.

As quietly as I could I crept back into the hut. I counted the sleeping bodies. They were all there. The princess and her lover had made devilishly quick work of it, if I do say so myself. I went straight to my bed but could not fall asleep. The more I knew, the less I knew. And to think how innocently it had all begun: at a ball in Vienna a month before Belgrade.

Some ten paces away from me stood a group of three Jesuits. They were keeping a close eye on everything that happened at the ball. Naturally, they wore enormous crucifixes on chains around their necks. One day, when faith has nearly faded away, thanks to me, the crosses will be even bigger. They'll have to make them life-sized, which is nothing to sneeze at, if I remember correctly.

The sun hit me straight in the eyes whenever I looked up at the three crosses. I could get no closer to the summit of Golgotha: an entire centurion's detachment was guarding the site of the crucifixion. I could only look up, into the burning sun of Nisan, shining as if it were an entirely different month in the Jewish calendar – I forget all their names. It seemed as if the crosses and the crucified figures were ablaze. Several times I looked away. A great crowd of people pressed ahead of me, some of them quite tall – most likely from another province. The Jews could scarcely see a thing. I had to stand on my tip-toes. The whole thing was dull, but I still had to be there. To do what I could, to rescue him, to prolong his agony. For there was still a chance that Pontius Pilate might change his mind and pardon him, have him brought down from the cross. A chance that he might not die and come back from the dead. True, the procurator had twice refused to see me. I hadn't even made it past the first sentry. I elbowed my way through the crowd. I knew that the Magdalene would be there, probably close by. And so she was.

'What are you after now?' she cried.

'Listen, it's not too late. Here's some vinegar mixed with gall, give it to the soldiers for him to drink. He won't take it from me, but he might take it from you. You're a woman. He understands your frailty. He has a weakness for you himself.'

'Why would *you* help him?' Her black eyes flashed. That's how she was before Fishmouth took her heart: full of fire.

'Come now,' I said. 'Put me out of your mind. It's him you should be thinking of. I'm going back to Pilate, there may still be hope.'

'But why *you*?'

'There's no one else.'

'I won't do it,' she said shrilly. There was no point in trying to persuade her. I could see that. She wasn't one for debates. Hadn't we had our times together in the taverns of Jerusalem, the olive groves and healing springs? The days would draw to a close; the nights lay open. Sometimes her soul would slip my grasp; her body never did.

I had been waiting for Fishmouth. Weeks, new moons, I couldn't complain. Rome had no need of me; Jerusalem was preparing for my foe. She had a terrible temper. Everything had to be her way or else. Never have I been so indulgent. That's why I hated her and loved her all the more. It brought back memories, that flash of fire in her, like three years earlier.

I gave the vinegar to an old woman. The soldier merely nodded without saying a word. He wetted a rag. Stuck it on the end of a lance. And held it up to Fishmouth's lips. The legionary had to raise the lance high above his head, that's how tall the cross stood.

I drew closer to the Jesuits without attracting attention to myself. I was approaching them from behind and couldn't tell for sure who was speaking, but it didn't really matter. As I might have guessed, they were gossiping.

'Everyone in Belgrade knows . . .'

'Won't be long before it gets out in Vienna.'

'More's the pity. If His Imperial Majesty should learn of what's been happening there he might replace the ecclesiastical authorities – meaning us.'

'And put the Franciscans in charge of the Belgrade parish.'

'Which we cannot allow.'

'So then, we must find a way to restore the peace.'

'How do you propose to go about it, my dear count?'

'I am related to the princess. I shall use all of my influence, both as count and as bishop.'

Aha, so one of them was Bishop-Count of Thurn and Valsassina. The German nobility sometimes had two surnames: one for the family and the other for their lands. Where was Valsassina? I didn't know, but I'd been wanting to meet the fellow for some time now.

I joined the three churchmen.

'Your Grace and Excellency, I am honoured to meet the Bishop-Count of Thurn and Valsassina. I am Count Otto von Hausburg.'

The long face, with its Spanish pedigree and Moorish blood, twisted itself into something known at the English court as a 'smile'. In the German princedoms and southern lands, this would be considered a disagreeable spasm. I twisted my own features in much the same way. The bishop-count's face twitched again, which I took as a sign of satisfaction with our similarity. I bowed and kissed his ring-bedecked hand. His diamonds outnumbered his years, and since he was quite young, there couldn't have been more than thirty of them.

'I leave soon for Belgrade.' I don't know why I said this. I must have had a presentiment.

'My son,' asked the bishop. 'what has the Good Lord appointed for you in Belgrade?'

Mad as a hatter.

'Nothing, Your Grace. I fear it's the other one at work.'

'Surely not, my son?'

'The court at Vienna is all astir with the latest news.'

'Oh!' was the only answer the bishop-count made. He wasn't sure how much I knew, and he didn't want to say anything else. I bowed once more and glided away.

4

I woke up feeling tired from the uncomfortable bed. It was a dark morning with black clouds hanging low. The sky seemed to have been blotted out. I stepped outside, where I was greeted by breakfast and Baron Schmidlin. He bowed. 'How did you sleep, Your Highness?'

'Very poorly, Baron.'

'Ah, let us hope that this business will soon be over and that we shall be on the way to Belgrade within the hour.'

'Let us hope so,' I answered without believing what I was saying. I had no hope at all.

We were joined by Count Schmettau. 'Have you noticed that here in the country it feels colder than in the city, and yet also warmer than in the city – that one feels everything more strongly than in the city. The city does away with the sense of difference.'

'I should think it's *nature* that the city does away with.'

'Perhaps you are right, Princess,' he laughed, 'but you must know that people move from the country to the city and not the other way round.'

'And where do they go from the cities?' asked the poor simple baron.

Schmettau suddenly stiffened, as if he had seen a ghost. He made an awful face and pinched his nose as if there were a nasty smell.

'From the cities, Baron? There is only one place left to go after the cities: to the madhouse.'

'How very reassuring,' said the baron rather foolishly, for lack of anything else to say.

'You find that reassuring, do you, Baron?' asked Schmettau accusingly.

'Well, I don't know . . .' Schmidlin stammered.

'You're a country-born man, meant for nature, aren't you? You've got everything you could ask for right here, all your favourites: beer, women, food to stuff your face with . . . And then there's always your *diskrecija* –'

I had to interrupt Schmettau. 'Discretion? What do you mean? What could be discreet about the countryside?'

'Oh, Princess! "Discretion" has a new meaning for our beloved administration – nothing to do with polite society or with being unobtrusive and inconspicuous. Rather, it's the *cost* of being unobtrusive and inconspicuous. And of polite society, if you like. *Diskrecija* is bribery. Bribes, my dear Princess. Bribes that Schmidlin takes from the Serbs to keep them politely and unobtrusively informed of everything that goes on at your husband's court. Goings-on that aren't inconspicuous at all, much less fit for polite society, as we all know quite well,' said Schmettau.

'I cannot believe it,' I exclaimed, although I believed every word.

'Rubbish!' shouted Schmidlin, the first time I had ever heard him raise his voice. 'Rubbish! Rubbish! I'm the one paying the Serbs to report back to me everything that happens at the metropolitan's court. And all of my discretions, sir, are on the books, all accounted for – who, when, how much and for what. You know that perfectly well. But that doesn't suit your purposes. You'd rather have everyone be just as low and crooked as that little man you –'

Schmettau had seized Schmidlin by the windpipe and was throttling him. The baron was gasping for air, and for a moment I had to step out of character as a princess: I struck Schmettau a blow across the head. That brought him to his senses. He released the baron. He turned towards me, bowed and went off to the hut.

'Thank you, Your Highness, you saved my life,' said the baron.

I don't know why we didn't go directly to the mill, but we seemed to be waiting for someone or something. I paced back and forth. Schmettau sat on a three-legged stool in front of the hut. Beside him sat Vuk Isakovič and Novak with another man I didn't know. In the middle I saw tiles for playing the Chinese game of mah-jong. When I was a little girl the Thurn and Taxis couriers once brought me a beautiful box of tiles covered in Chinese characters.

What were you saying?

The rules of the game don't matter now. True, Schmettau did seem to be explaining, as far as I could hear, the rules and strategies, what they were allowed to do, what they ought to do and what they must do. I don't think the other three were particularly keen on playing. Novak the servant had to play, what with being a servant. Vuk Isakovič was an *Oberkapitän* and therefore subordinate to Count Schmettau, who I believe held some sort of rank in the artillery. The third man was a Serb. His nationality and low birth had landed him in the middle of a game he didn't know how to win, one that couldn't possibly interest him.

Schmettau liked the other players to make good moves, even if it put him at a disadvantage, and he would rap their knuckles for making mistakes. Isakovič was becoming angrier and angrier. Even from a distance I could see him struggling to restrain himself. From afar it seemed that Novak was coming out ahead. He was disciplined less often than the others, and the smile never left his face. It may have been that unseemly grin, or an especially clever move on his part accompanied by a delighted cry from Schmettau, that finally provoked Isakovič into punching Novak in the face.

'You devil!' shouted Isakovič. 'No one but a devil could play this! Christians can only lose.' He finished speaking, stood up, bowed deeply to Schmettau and strode off towards the forest.

Schmettau gave a great laugh and began to gather up the tiles. Once he'd put them back in the box he got up and walked away as if nothing had happened. The third man also got up as Novak sat there bleeding from the nose, struck him in the chest and ran off after Isakovič.

I don't think anyone but me saw this happen.

Soon afterwards the baron told me we were going to the mill. Von Hausburg and I went first with the other two members of the commission and the baron. When we reached the mill Schmettau was already there, leaning against a dying oak tree that had split into two great trunks. There were also some peasants scattered about, waiting. No one spoke. A strange stillness had fallen over everything. I think even the birds had stopped singing. Schmidlin nodded towards me. I didn't know what his gesture meant, and in my unease I was the first to break the silence.

'Why doesn't he come out? Can he still be sleeping?' I asked the two from the commission. They only shrugged and remained where they were.

'Let's go in, then,' I said to Schmidlin.

He gave no answer and looked away.

'Shall we go in?' I asked von Hausburg.

'I'll follow,' he said, and crossed his arms. His gesture was at odds with his words.

'Shall we go in?' I asked, turning to Schmettau.

'I have no intention of it,' he answered honestly.

'Right then,' I said at last, 'I'll do it myself.'

'Don't!' said the baron.

I headed towards the mill. I turned around to look. Not one of them had moved. I stood at the threshold. I turned to look. None of them moved. I opened the door. I turned to look. No one moved. I stepped inside.

5

Radetzky was lying on the floor, his arms spread wide and his legs together. His white shirt lay beside him. His body was white, not a drop of blood. Eyes open.

I screamed.

Poor man, I thought. He was obviously dead. And then the others came running. People crowded into the mill. Everyone was speaking at once. The man in the red wig fainted. Schmidlin and the other man from the commission carried him outside. Then came the servants.

They wrapped Radetzky in a sheet and carried him out. I followed them.

Outside, von Hausburg asked me in a frightened voice, 'What now?' I didn't know what to say.

We all went back to the hut. It felt as though we were coming home. But I didn't want to go in, I just took a chair at the table, which was set for breakfast. My eyes wandered over the plates, over the forks and knives and spoons, and I realized in an absent-minded way that it was to be a normal breakfast not a Chinese meal. Why had Schmettau ordered it, I wondered.

Sorry?

Yes, sometimes, in difficult moments, something entirely different comes to mind, something unrelated to the suffering. Or perhaps it wasn't a coincidence that I should think of Schmettau just then.

No, I wasn't thinking of my husband. I couldn't say why not. I simply wasn't. Do I think about my husband? Well, he went to his Maker long ago, you know. But, yes, I did think of him recently. When the revolution broke out in Paris.

Am I thinking of Alexander right now? No, but when the noble heads began to roll on the Place de la Concorde I remembered something, something that may have some bearing on the story. You know, my husband believed that all the European nobility were descendants of the ancient Roman nobility, who were descended from Aeneas, who came from the Greek and Roman gods. Yes, quite: not a very Christian thing to believe. But that's what he believed. And that's why von Hausburg made him so furious. Yes, just a minor incident from the costume ball. Alexander had brought up Aeneas, and von Hausburg began to speak.

'Picture this, if you will: Troy is burning, its towers thrown down, soldiers everywhere, killing, raping, looting. Where there's no fire, there's smoke. What I mean to say is, everything is either burning or has already gone up in flames. Cassandra is wailing like a circus performer and everyone is watching and listening to her, paying more attention to her than to the destruction around them. The nobles of

Troy have been slain, and Aeneas lies dead in a cellar among great jars of olive oil.

'But there's one servant, the very same man who carried all of those clay jars into the cellar – no mean feat, I might add – who knows where Aeneas is and what has become of him. I'm not saying the servant murdered the prince. No, he simply knows what's happened, that's all. And wrongdoing sometimes begins with knowing.

'With the nimble fingers of all servants he strips the dead Greek of his battle dress and slinks off through the narrow streets towards the harbour. Along the way he runs into several others of his ilk. He eyes a ship that fits all of Homer's specifications for ocean journeys. When he spots his chance, he climbs aboard, ambushes and kills the sentries and then weighs anchor. It simply must be by night: the flames make such a marvellous picture, lapping at the stars and the moon's pale crescent. And off he sails, westward.

'Many mishaps and setbacks later he comes ashore. The news of Troy's destruction has preceded him and taken hold in people's minds. "Everyone is dead, yes, but I, Aeneas, have escaped." And from such noble beginnings, the nobility of Rome and Europe.'

'You talk as though you'd seen it with your own eyes,' said my husband, scoffing but furious.

'Of course not. I heard it from others who did,' responded von Hausburg, and Alexander punched him in the face. Von Hausburg fell down and that was the end of it.

I wasn't surprised. I thought von Hausburg had drunk some courage with his wine and was having a laugh at my husband's expense, foolishly provoking him.

That's what made me think of Alexander. How fortunate it was that he didn't live to see what happened in France. It's a great irony, isn't it? The rabble in Paris clamouring for the heads of those same descendants – just more servants after all, with only a bit more cunning and skill than the rest of them. That is, if you believe von Hausburg. And why not? I don't see *him* under interrogation, unlike me. Next they'll be saying it's me you can't believe.

Get back to the story? But I never left it.

So there I was sitting at the table and thinking about Chinese cuisine, when the blond one from the commission sat down beside me. I can't remember his name. Or the red-haired one's either.

He looked like a whiter shade of the pale Radetzky.

I wanted to help him somehow.

'Be not anxious,' I said. 'Try to remain calm. Surely you anticipated that this might occur and can now take the appropriate steps. I know that His Imperial Majesty's commissions are always well-prepared for any contingency.'

He looked at me as if I were raving mad.

'This contingency was not anticipated,' he answered after a short pause.

'It wasn't?' I asked. 'But if you came here to find out whether vampires exist or not you'd have to account for the possibility – no matter how slight – that they did and that they might even attack the members of the commission.'

'Perhaps,' he said, after thinking this over. 'But our task was not to establish the existence of vampires. Although we have ended up doing just that, rather unexpectedly.'

'What are you here for then?' I asked in surprise.

'Our assignment was . . . you can be told now . . . there's hardly any point in . . . We were members of a commission with full imperial authorization, charged with finding the murderer of Count Ludwig Wittgenau.'

FIVE
Schmidlin's Debt

1

Now we're heading into the heart of darkness? Is that what you said? I wouldn't put it like that. It's all darkness to you. You can't see the light.

Where we're heading is someplace you've never been, and never will be. What good does it do you to wear those vestments and that heavy cross?

Did I have faith? Yes, make no doubt about it. Why shouldn't I? Faith can only be lost in happiness and plenty, never in hard times and sorrow. Von Hausburg had something to say in that regard. I don't remember the occasion.

'Can you imagine what it must be like for him up there? Nothing reaching his ears but complaints and anguished cries. You think anyone turns to him when there's plenty of food and drink on the table, when love is in the air? He's the first thing they forget when everything's going well. It's the poor and the forsaken who always have his name on their lips. If I were him, it would drive me mad. I'd destroy everything I'd created – the ones crying out *and* the ones saying nothing.'

That's what he said.

But getting back to the story.

Baron Schmidlin listened attentively and didn't seem surprised when I told him about the commission. It did occur to me that everyone seemed to be in the know yet still knew nothing.

'What are we to do?' I asked him.

He shrugged and said, 'Shall we return to the city?' And just as he was saying this, everyone gathered around.

Schmettau had returned from who knows where, von Hausburg had been close by the whole time and the two remaining members of the commission had been listening carefully.

'I am for fighting,' said Schmettau.

'Fighting whom?' said the baron scornfully.

'The vampires,' Schmettau shouted.

'Count me in,' piped up von Hausburg.

'And me,' I said. 'Only how?'

'The Serbs know how to handle these things. They've got experience with vampires. Let me get my servant. He's a Serb. He can tell us.' Von Hausburg went to fetch his servant. He must not have been able to find Novak right away, and the rest of us had to wait uneasily for them to return. No one spoke. I suppose no one had anything to say.

When they finally came Novak went right to the centre of the circle we'd happened to form. He didn't know which way to face, and so he eyed each of us in turn, even twisting around to get a better look. This struck me as a piece of impudence on his part. Von Hausburg spoke to him in Serbian, although his servant knew German. Novak would stop and wait for von Hausburg to catch up with the translation. The frown never left the baron's face as he listened, whether because he could understand Serbian or for some other reason.

What did he say? Well, you know what he said. What he said is what ended up happening. We'd have to find the vampire's grave by daylight. And for that we'd need a black horse with no markings. Then we'd have to dig up the vampire, sprinkle it with holy water and drive a stake of hawthorn through its heart – all the while making sure a moth-like creature, something called a *leptirak*, didn't escape from its jaws. If we followed all of these rules, the vampire would be destroyed.

Even so, somehow I still didn't believe it was vampires we were up against. I was hoping Radetzky's death would turn out to be the work of other powers, mortal powers closer to hand. That's why I was glad we were going to dig up the alleged vampire. When we found nothing but bones in the grave instead of a preserved corpse, it would prove that vampires didn't exist and that Radetzky had been murdered by cunning foes working against Vienna and my husband.

There was no discussion. We all agreed to do what must be done.

I don't know why he chose that particular moment, but von Hausburg came to me and whispered something. 'Count Schmettau is quite the talker, isn't he? Have you noticed that he never actually *does* anything, just wags his tongue?'

'I had noticed, yes,' I answered frankly.

'That worries me.'

'How so?'

'My greatest fear is people who do nothing, who only talk. The ones with nothing to say usually have nothing on their minds either. But the ones with ideas, who only talk and never do anything, they're the ones who'll surprise you when they finally spring into action. Can you just imagine all the hare-brained schemes knocking around in the heads of people who spend hours and days doing nothing but thinking? Beware of Count Schmettau, my dear Princess. I am your friend, and I wish to help you. In every way.'

I didn't like the way he said 'in every way', but I said nothing.

2

After everything that had happened I couldn't sleep. I felt like smoking. I stepped outside, not bothering to conceal myself. What difference did it make? Presumably it was all over by now. For some reason I didn't want to be near the hut, so I stepped a bit further off – but away from the mill, just to be on the safe side.

I'd gone a few dozen paces, if I remember correctly, in the direction of the city, and stopped in the middle of a small clearing. The clouds were thick overhead. I couldn't see the moon, only a hint of its gleam in the western sky. The morning star was nowhere to be seen.

I filled my pipe and struck a match. No sooner had I taken the first few puffs than I heard a rustling in the undergrowth behind me. I was out in the open, and whoever it was must have seen me already. There would be no point in hiding, and so I decided to pretend I hadn't heard anything. I stood there puffing away, seemingly cool as a cucumber but actually all hot under the collar.

The noises were coming closer then suddenly stopped. Whoever it was, they were holding still. Waiting.

I was waiting, too. Of all the times to come outside for a smoke.

The noises started up again. Then stopped. 'Psst!' I heard.

'Psst,' I responded obligingly.

'It's me, master – Novak.'

Oh, the fool. What a fright he'd given me!

'What do you want?'

'Nothing. I came outside to have a smoke and stretch my legs. I can't sleep.' He came closer, still keeping his voice down. 'I hardly recognized you. I thought it might be the vampire.'

'You and your vampires!' I said, raising my hand to strike him.

'Master, no. Here, I've brought you something.'

'What?'

'A bit of hashish. I swapped the Virginia tobacco for it with the hajduks.'

'You did, eh? And how do they come by it?'

'From hajduks in Turkey.'

'Right, let's have it.'

We stepped out of the clearing and sat by a good-sized oak tree at the edge. We lit the hashish. For a long time we smoked in silence.

Clouds like lumps of dough. Bake me no loaves, baker's man. So much talking, so many heroic verses.

> . . . Great laughter was in Heav'n
> And looking down, to see the hubbub strange
> And hear the din; thus was the building left
> Ridiculous, and the work Confusion named . . .

'Doves. *Pigeons*,' said Novak, all in a haze.

Not me. Anybody hear cooing? The Holy Spirit? In present company?

'What do you mean, doves and pigeons?'

'Skandaroons. That's what I mean. Skan-da-roons.'

'Skan-da-roons,' I repeated, syllable by syllable. Not in metre, though. No metres yet, still yards.

'In Iskanderun, skandaroons. Skandaroons in Iskanderun.'

'Bet you can't say that three times fast.'

'Don't pay to play.'

I gave him a swift backhand.

'Say it.'

'Not gonna. We're small as hell, but still we fell . . .'

'Chirp, chirp. Stop singing and start paying. Paying attention, I mean. Go ahead, make my day. Even though it's still night-time. I think. What's a skandaroon?'

'A pigeon.'

'Aha. So that's it, then: a *stool* pigeon . . . In disguise, were you? At the costume ball? Hm?'

'Everyone at a costume ball is in disguise. So there.'

'Servants are for serving. No disguises.'

'All right. Let me just get some sleep.'

Nothing from the sky. All clouds. Where's the moon? I'll catch the morning star. The two of them know. They know, and I don't. They're not here to sing to me. Soft voices in my ear, in the oak tree.

'Wake up! Wake up, you!'

Great dumb brute, smoked himself into a stupor. Needs a proper kicking. That's good for you, that is: better than a shiatsu massage in Japan, cherry blossoms under Fukoyama and all the rest of it.

'Get up, skandaroon. Start singing.'

'The skandaroon's a pigeon that flies, flies away, fly away home, ladybird.'

The ladybird was asleep. The Devil was asleep.

3

When I came to it was still night-time. My head hurt. I nudged Novak.

'Get up. You've slept long enough. On your feet.'

'All right, all right. I'm getting up.'

'Skandaroons! Start talking, I should be getting back to the hut.'

'Skandaroons? Where did you hear about *them*?'

'From you. Before you fell asleep.'

'I fell *asleep*?'

'Of course you did. If you're just waking up now, try to imagine what had to happen first.'

'I fell asleep.'

'Right you are.'

'But hashish doesn't make you fall asleep. It must have been laced with something. And the hajduks told me to make sure you had some, too.'

'Would that be the two with the Rs?'

'Yes, how did you know?'

'I know everything. Now start talking. Skandaroons.'

'I used to keep pigeons back in Belgrade. Carrier pigeons. I remember there was a Turk once who came with some birds. They were skandaroons. That's what they call them because they're from Iskenderun . . .'

'You mean İskenderiye?'

'Well, I don't know every last detail. They're only found in northern Africa, and they're only kept by the Ottoman army. And you know how they train them? They take the mother-bird out to sea and release her, and she has to find her own way back to her nestlings. Each time they take her further and further out, right to the middle of the deep-blue Mediterranean . . .'

'I see. Now pay attention. You've had quite a pipeful. What *about* the skandaroons?'

'Nothing, except I've seen them here in Belgrade, at the fortress. Up at the top near the cistern, there's a coop.'

'You say they're only kept by the Turkish army.'

'I've never seen them before in Christian lands.'

'Right. Good. Excellent. Off with you now.'

I also headed back to the hut. No one else was stirring, and I was able to slip back into my place unnoticed. Staying up all night hadn't been such a bad idea, after all. I pulled the covers over my eyes, pleased with myself. I managed to sleep until the first cock-crow. Infernal creatures! Whose idea was it to create *them*?

4

The baron had suddenly regained the upper hand and began hurrying the servants along, as though we had to leave right away. The servants were flustered, as servants always are when anything needs doing, and began running into each other and dropping things. By itself this wouldn't have been so vexing – after all, one is rather used to servants being all fingers and thumbs – if they hadn't managed by an extraordinary stroke of ill luck to knock over a small chest containing jars of Chinese spices.

Now, the entire cuisine of China is based on spices. Spices and finely sliced meat. The Chinese don't let just anyone have a knife either. The meat must be cut up beforehand. Count Schmettau knew all about it, how for centuries the Chinese emperors would wait on their subjects by cutting up their meat for them, thereby preventing shameful incidents like those in England and Holland and now in France as well. Such a form of government is unsurpassable, unless you eliminate meat entirely or cut it into even smaller portions. Of course, the Chinese prepare each person's meal individually, Schmettau would add; there are no large pots or pans, and each person is aware that his dish is meant for him alone, which helps him overlook the fact that his meat has been cut in advance.

A people such as the Serbs, on the other hand, know only one utensil – the knife – and each cuts his own. Besides that, since everything is served from a common pot – just the opposite of the Chinese – everyone grabs whatever he can, and no one knows what's really meant for him. Clearly, Schmettau would conclude, a better government for the Serbs would provide either bigger knives or a deeper pot.

However, Schmettau would say, the Serbs and the Chinese do have one thing in common, which is that their lives aren't worth a cent to their lords and masters. And so they set no store by their own lives either. Actually, his explanation for this had nothing to do with cookery or tableware.

And my reason for telling you this has nothing to do with the Serbs or, indeed, the Chinese. I mention it because Schmettau was terribly upset about the spices. He cried out and struck the servants, then hurled the vilest curses at them; he wept, tore his hair, dropped to his knees, then sprang up and ran in a circle around us, wailing, cursing and staggering about. What made it distasteful was not the overreaction to a trifling matter but the gaping discrepancy – made only more egregious by the short time that had passed – between his impassive acceptance of Radetzky's death and his inexpressible grief over some wasted Chinese seasonings.

In the end Schmettau smeared himself with the spices, wailing that all was lost. When he'd covered himself with as much as he could he suddenly turned towards me and began speaking as if delivering a lecture.

'It is good that it should be so. At last I have understood.' He leaped to his feet (he'd been kneeling until now) and came towards me saying, 'The Lord giveth, and the Lord taketh away. And we also get things and discard them. We have to keep throwing things out or we'd be up to our eyes in rubbish, wouldn't we?'

In my bewilderment I said yes.

'Cities have sewers, and men to sweep and cart away our rubbish. Isn't that so? But in the countryside there's none of that. Nothing gets thrown away out here. Whatever's no longer wanted goes on the fields as manure. That's what happens. You see, Princess, you cannot love all the ones you've ever loved. Or feel all the things you've ever felt. You have to keep sweeping it away. Destroying it. That's why the city is in equilibrium: a heavenly place, with high walls to keep the rest of the world at bay. The rest is Hell. Which is where we are right now.'

'You mean to say,' I stammered, 'that God has . . . abandoned us?'

He turned away, as if longer needing another person to talk to but continued speaking as he headed off towards the woods.

'There's more than one. Ha, ha, ha.'

He stepped among the trees and was lost to sight. When I think about Schmettau now I realize he must have been one of those people who cannot tolerate imperfection of any sort, especially in its chief aspect: life. He simply wasn't lazy enough. Because laziness is more than a certain dullness of heart and mind, it is also necessary for survival. Necessary, in fact, for happiness. For most people achieving happiness in life is a natural ability. It's almost something they're born with, and they don't need to think about it or learn how to do it. Whenever we are obliged to learn something there's always the question of whether – perhaps because of bad teachers, or faulty books, or that we are lazy, dull-witted students – we can ever learn it well enough. Worst of all, if the lessons being taught are utterly wrong. Learning to be happy after you've already ceased to be so, for whatever reason, is hard work. The chances of succeeding are so slim.

I was already tired, although it was only morning. But I wasn't to have even a moment's peace. Baron Schmidlin came to me and asked whether I wanted to go with the others to see the old woman.

'What old woman?' I asked.

'The only one who knows where the vampire lies buried.'

We set off. Without any escort, I noticed. Baron Schmidlin led the way, followed by the two men from the commission, Count von Hausburg, his servant and myself. I couldn't tell you what path we took; my mind was elsewhere, and I wasn't keeping track. Still, it didn't take us more than half an hour. Since we'd started at the top of one hill, I think we must have gone all the way down and then back up another. We were heading eastwards.

We came to a small village at the top of the hill, and it didn't take long to find the old woman. As a matter of fact, we found two old women. Both were exceedingly old. They were perched on stools: one woman never stopped talking, while the other said not a word. Each of them was more than a hundred years old and no doubt nearly deaf and blind.

The servant shouted, 'Which one of you is Mirjana?'

Nothing happened. The one who was speaking kept up her stream of words, while the one who was silent said nothing.

'Which one of you is Mirjana?' the servant repeated.

'What's all this racket?' squawked the woman who had been sitting quietly. 'Can't hear a word you're saying anyway. You should be whispering, not shouting.'

I understood at once how cantankerous she must be. My husband would have much to say on the topic of nasty old crones. Later, of course.

Novak went to her and whispered something in her ear. She grinned, revealing a mouthful of unexpectedly strong teeth.

'Well now, I'm not going to tell you. So there.' Then von Hausburg spoke to her.

'You're Mirjana?'

She nodded. 'But I'm not telling.'

'Why not, grandmother?'

'Because. That's why. So you'll have to stay right here and deal with me. Have to ask me nicely, sit and talk with me. That's why. It's no fun for me here on my own. Go on, bribe it out of me. Come on.'

'You'll be famous if you tell us,' said von Hausburg. Again she laughed, showing her strong yellow teeth. 'I'll be famous if I *don't* tell you, too.'

The baron was silent. As were the two men from the commission. Novak stood off to one side as though the conversation had nothing to do with him. Von Hausburg chuckled and winked at me. He was enjoying the give and take.

'You'll be even *more* famous if you do.'

The old woman laughed again, a hearty, brazen laugh. The other old woman joined her. Then the laughter spread to the two men from the commission, the baron, then Novak and von Hausburg. In the end even I joined in, not knowing why.

The old woman said, 'That's enough.' And as if at her command, we all fell silent. 'Sava Savanović lies in the crooked valley under the spreading elm.'

5

They were keeping me from sleeping, and I needed my rest because I knew important things were about to happen. I couldn't very well go around yawning, tired and not at my best. I tried counting sheep. It didn't work. I counted all sorts of things. In the end I gave up counting. I tried to empty my mind of all thoughts. They say that's the best thing to do, the only way to fall asleep. Your dreams try to get even with you afterwards, but by then it's too late.

The harder I tried not to think, the more I kept seeing Thurn and Valsassina, the bishop-count with his ugly face and mincing speech, going on about his travels and art and the inquisitions he'd presided over, such a young man and already so *good*. I had no use for him this morning, and yet he kept pushing his way into my thoughts, over and over, as if he were the answer to all my problems. Around and around he flew, trying to find a way in, just like all feelings. Only he wasn't a feeling; he was a man – of a sort. And feelings were always doing that: always in the air, in other people, in things, breaking free of their owners and homes and running loose through the world. Attacking me, trying to get inside, attempting to cross the line of my individual self, to scale the ramparts and enter my heart. But I wouldn't give in. I did whatever I could to fight off feelings. Not even if they broke through a wall would I surrender, for where could my armies go, where could they carry their weapons? Where is *my* Niš?

Love can dig all the trenches it wants to undermine my defences. Still I am protected behind wall after towering wall, behind blind ditches and deep moats, stagnant water hiding spikes at the bottom, waiting to impale that daring invader known as humility, to fend off the battering-ram of modesty and shame.

And so this morning I was under attack by Bishop-Count of Thurn and Valsassina. I must admit I found him hard to resist: he was, after all, a two-faced clergyman. That's why I let him in for a bit.

We had already met several times. In Vienna, of course. On one occasion, in my crafty way, I'd managed to manoeuvre him into talking about vampires. He wasn't happy about it, that much was clear, and I was starting to congratulate myself on a job well done. His face suddenly twisted into its famous smile, and I knew then and there (well, obviously) that he was going to try to trick me.

'Did you know, I've already encountered vampires?'

'No, Your Grace. Really?'

'Oh yes indeed. And do you know where? In Mexico, of all places. None other than Mexico. And you mustn't think of me as losing my purity out there among the Indians, those outlandish Aztecs and Maya. Why, they haven't the faintest idea about vampires. They're much more interested in plumed serpents and such things.' He was silent for a moment, and then continued. 'We had ordered a heretic to be burnt at the stake, don't you know. Nothing out of the ordinary, except that her paintings were to be burnt with her. She was a lover of heresy in all its guises. As the Holy Father so wisely puts it, "All heresies are but one." Her name was Remedios Varo. Her works of impiety had begun in Spain, if memory serves, before she imagined she could elude us by fleeing across the ocean. Once in Mexico, of course, she persisted in her old ways. She painted as if possessed. Come to think of it, she probably was.'

'What year was this?'

'Recently.'

'Ah.'

'Why am I telling you all this, you may ask? Because one of her paintings was titled *Vegetarian Vampires*. The painting depicted three vampires, three creatures, sitting around a small table and each using a straw – a straw, mind you! – to sip the juice from a watermelon, a rose and a tomato. The hats they wore seemed to be sprouting wings, and all three figures were gaunt and emaciated. Only to be expected, I suppose, if they didn't eat meat. Now, as I watched the painting burn, the thought did cross my mind that maybe these vampires aren't so bad after all, by God, if they feed on nothing but fruits and flowers. Nevertheless, the entire composition reminded me of an icon I'd seen in Russia, the work of a man named Rublev, entitled *The Holy Trinity*. As soon as I set eyes on that icon I felt an overpowering desire to burn it. I couldn't, of course. For political reasons, don't you know. But still I felt a double satisfaction in watching those vegetarian vampires go up in flames.'

'I understand completely.'

'I'm so glad.'

'How is it, though, that Remedios Varo isn't more widely known? I mean, heretics usually make such a noise. And they're in such demand nowadays among the clever set, aren't they?' I asked.

'Come now, Herr Graf. Remedios Varo was a woman and a beautiful one at that. And who thinks highly of beautiful women, especially in Mexico? No one took her seriously, what with her being so lovely and graceful, but *we* do not succumb to the wiles of nature. We took her very seriously indeed, and we nearly caught her in Madrid. She managed to slip away again in Barcelona, but we finally got her in the New World.'

Suddenly he gave a start, as if something had occurred to him. 'Are you working for the Inquisition now?'

'Always and for ever,' I replied.

That was quite enough of Thurn and Valsassina, I told myself, then turned over and fell fast asleep. I slept on for another two or three hours, until the others began to stir and roused me from the sweetest of slumbers.

6

That's what the old woman said, and her words seemed as straight-forward as the task that lay before us. At the time I believed that nothing could be simpler than a ritual (and laying a vampire to rest is, after all, a ritual), because the rubrics are all set out beforehand, with every last detail provided for, and not even a fool can get it wrong. Back then I never doubted the efficacy of any ritual.

Now I know that no ritual, no matter how time-honoured or up-to-date, can withstand intentional errors, the distortion of its essence, the deliberate perversion of the ritual itself. But those who twist a ritual out of shape are overlooking one fact: they're not really making a mockery of the ritual, as they think. Instead, they're taking the other side, the side the ritual was meant to protect us from. You know who I mean, the ones who sneer at the prayers of the simple, at smooth-talking priests, at the moneychangers in the temple, or at faith itself, saying that God does not hear us. The Devil hears our mocking voices as clear as a bell. And rejoices.

We went with the peasants to gather what we'd need to slay the vampire. We all went together, and Schmettau reappeared as if from nowhere. He must have wanted to see the sharpened stake. The final end of the vampire. He was obsessed with endings, you see. He'd even complain when a book came to an end. He was searching for completion, for an explanation to end all explanations, and a stake through the heart of the vampire must have seemed as final a solution as any.

For some reason I couldn't fathom, he liked to be near me, to talk to me. No, it's not what you might be thinking, I assure you. Count Schmettau was so preoccupied with the meaning of life that he could easily forget about life itself. He wasn't in love with me, and he didn't love anyone else. He may have loved Count Wittgenau – not as a friend, of course, but as someone similar to himself. He cared only for those who shared his way of thinking, and such people were rather thin on the ground. Understandably so.

So then, in spite of the task at hand, which should have been strange and unusual enough for anyone's attention, Schmettau was going on and on about his own experiences.

'Have you ever played mah-jong? You have? So have I. With Chinamen, of course. It's a Chinese game. Do you know, the Chinese very wisely refrained from telling me the rules and the object of the game. They wanted me to learn by myself. They would merely give me a sign if I made a wrong move. And I worked hard to learn it. First and foremost, the moves a player may or may not make, only afterwards moving on to the point of the game. And do you know what I got out of it?'

'You learned how to play.'

'No! Or rather, yes, I learned how to play. What I meant was . . .'

Just then the peasants cried out. I looked, but could not see what was happening. Until they brought the horse. A pure black horse with no markings. *Unclean*, they were saying; that's how Baron Schmidlin translated it. Only a horse of purest black could identify the vampire's grave. That is, the horse would stop and refuse to cross it. Behind the horse came a Serbian priest, a great wooden cross around his neck. He was bald with a jet-black beard. He was carrying an aspergillum of holy water.

Leading the way, head held high, came the young man who'd been playing mah-jong that morning with Schmettau, Isakovič and Novak. He was carrying a sharpened stake and a heavy mallet.

Everyone was in place at last.

Schmettau fell quiet, as if affected for once by something taking place outside his own thoughts. We went in silence for a long time, following the peasants. They had no idea which way to go, I could see that much. They were looking for elm trees and not finding them; they were finding valleys and gullies, even crooked ones, but still no elms.

'You know,' Schmettau said, picking up where he'd left off, 'in learning how to play the game I learned the most awful truth of all. I came to know the rules and to understand the object of the game. And what a pleasure it was, discovering the various kinds of tiles, the ways of taking them out of play, the strategies for offence and defence – the whole point of it was becoming clear! And what a terrible thing it was to have finally mastered it all. I began to recognize weaknesses and limitations, to see defeat coming before it became inevitable, to know how to win all too easily and all too soon. The thrill was gone.'

'I see,' I said.

He made no reply. We walked along without speaking, thank God. I was too anxious and uneasy to lend an ear to any more of Schmettau and his talk.

From time to time we'd halt, and the peasants would start digging, as if there were graves all around us and a body would be sure to turn up no matter where you stuck a spade. We'd pace back and forth and wait apprehensively. Silently the peasants would dig then stop, shovel the earth back in and move on. There hadn't been a single whinny from the horse. The young man with the stake would sit and lean on it like a walking-stick, keeping a close eye on the mallet beside him as if worried that someone might steal it.

We didn't do much talking. I suppose none of us really felt like it. Baron Schmidlin seemed to watch all that digging more closely than anyone.

'Do you know what the Serbs believe?' he said, on one of the few occasions the silence was broken that day. 'When the dead are disturbed and their bones unearthed great evil shall follow. It's not good to lay hands on the dead.'

'Do you think it's better not to search for the vampire?'

'Often,' interjected von Hausburg, 'when they can't do anything to the living they go after the dead.'

'The Serbs?' I asked.

'As if the other hell weren't enough for the dead and they should suffer this one besides,' he answered, avoiding the question.

The peasants began to shout, and Schmidlin ran to join them. Von Hausburg and I watched him go, but we didn't move. I was sure it would be nothing but another false alarm, and I continued my conversation with von Hausburg.

'This hell and the other?'

'Well, yes,' he said, taken aback. 'We stand at the furthermost point of Hell, although Hell knows no boundaries and therefore *has* no furthermost point.'

'I'm afraid I don't understand.'

'Don't be afraid of not understanding. Be afraid when you *do* understand.'

7

Of course, I didn't think von Hausburg was the Devil – I didn't believe the Devil would be able simply to go about his business as if he were a normal human. Besides, he seemed to talk like any other philosopher – particularly concerning things he couldn't have known anything about. Unfortunately, regarding what he *could* have known, he was mistaken. Like him, many believe that knowledge and intelligence are the swiftest road to misfortune, that the more people know and the more intelligent they are, the harder their lives. But blessed are the ignorant and foolish, they'd say.

Dull-witted, simple-minded people are doomed to base and foolish pleasures. They have no idea of all the wonderful, fascinating, *thrilling* things the world holds. And sooner or later, everyone must grow bored of even the choicest pheasant, the best French vintage, the most arousing entertainments in the boudoir and the most inventive gossip. What stupid people find pleasurable can fit on a very short list. And once they've worked their way to the bottom of it there's no end to their misery and woe. Even if they're rich, their money is useless, for it can only buy them more things that have lost all meaning.

They hate change. They especially hate anything that's different, and that's why they're all the same. They think their lives are a vale of tears, that each day is no different from the one that came before, that everyone else is just like them and that they themselves can never change. They're unhappy because they're all the same.

All unhappy people are the same. Anyone who is happy must be happy in his own way. Because happy people, the ones who use their minds, who have learned something and even understand a thing or two, know how to enjoy little things, uncommon things, quick ideas, books and more books and how to be glad when something changes or when they uncover a new side of something, some rare beauty. Clever people simply have more ways of satisfying themselves and in more unusual ways. They're not slaves to habit, their own or anyone else's.

And that's why they're a hundred times more likely to be happy.

Von Hausburg was wrong when he said I should fear understanding. Could the Devil make such a mistake?

A deliberate lie?

Why should the Devil lie? The Devil is the only one who always and everywhere tells the truth. He's the only one who stands to benefit from it.

I asked him about Hell.

And this is what he told me, 'Hell is vast and never ends. Greater than infinity is Hell. Beyond its seven seas, beyond its seven mountains, lie seven more and seven more, and on and on for ever. The reaches of Hell are not measured in yards or any other measurement of latitude and longitude (for do not forget that the mountains and seas of Hell are endless); rather, they are *counted*, in hours and days and years and centuries and millennia and all the other ways we have of marking time, and yet, he who roams in Hell must know, never shall he meet another soul, not even with all eternity before him. Can there be a greater punishment, a longer sentence? The truth is also that Hell is small, smaller than nothing. In that one speck, that most infinitesimal shadow of the inconceivable inexistent, all the souls of all the sinners of all ages and places must press together tightly. There is no movement, for there is nowhere to go, and the souls are together for ever and are nearly as one. Not a single soul can be itself, an individual. Can there be a greater punishment, a longer sentence?'

'Then how can we be standing at the furthermost point of Hell?'

'I never said Hell has no gates,' he answered, laughing.

8

It was growing dark. They told me the deed must be done before the first stars appeared in the sky, for vampires emerge by starlight and cannot be overpowered then. The night belongs to them. We hurried along, at times even breaking into a run. I was sweating, gasping for breath. The baron reassured me that it would all be over soon and we could go back to the city and put the whole thing behind us as if it had never happened.

Our hopes were fading with the sun's last rays when the horse let out a whinny. Whinnied and dug its hooves in. And then began to rear up. The sweaty black hide was tinged with red by the setting sun.

The peasants seized their mattocks and spades. Shovelling quickly, they soon struck something solid. We were in turmoil and began shouting over one another. One of the peasants fainted from excitement, from exhaustion or from too much *rakija*. The others dragged him swiftly out of the way. Again the mattock made a hollow thud. The coffin, we hoped. Someone shouted to be careful, not to wake the vampire, for the light was almost gone and we would be at his mercy. Gingerly the peasants cleared the remaining dirt away.

It was nothing but an old tree stump.

Disappointed, the young man sat with his tools on a nearby stone, propping himself up with the stake. The priest, meanwhile, leaned in for a better look.

'An elm in youth, in her old age a stump.'

'The stump of the old elm tree!' the peasants cried. Baron Schmidlin's voice joined them. We all joined in.

'Keep digging,' the baron commanded. The sun had nearly slipped below the horizon.

Don't go, I thought to myself. Oh stay, damn you. And then you can set for two whole days.

The peasants dug on, frenzied and lathered with sweat. Again and again they wiped their brows.

Soon the spades were scraping against wood. We all drew near. They had reached the coffin. The man with the stake was jumping for joy. The coffin had already begun to fall apart. It was unpainted, of common planks. The peasants dug it out quickly and hoisted it to the surface. Their courage had not yet left them, for some daylight still remained. Baron Schmidlin ordered them to remove the lid. At their touch the rotten wood crumbled away. Slowly they pulled back the lid.

The man inside was firm and ruddy in the face, as if he were sleeping and on the verge of waking up. And yet he had been lying dead for ninety years. What surprised me most was that face. I'd been expecting something formless, loathsome, belonging to nobody. And Sava had the face of a man, but not just any face. Sharply defined features. A nose to remember. Open eyes. Mouth. Hair. Cheeks. Even a smile. Slanting eyebrows. If only I could have looked a little longer. It was the face of someone who was somebody.

'The vampire!' cried the peasants.

I said nothing. I wanted to say Sava Savanović.

There was no time to waste. Soon it would be night. The priest began to chant in his nasal voice. He hadn't even finished chanting when he flung the water in Sava's face. The young man with the stake waited eagerly. The sun was going down. He pushed the priest aside to everyone's approval.

He held the stake to Sava's heart. With his other hand he raised the mallet high. He struck the stake, pounding it in. Through the heart it went, and up came the blood. Gushing and gushing and gushing. Spreading towards my feet. Spotting my boots. I stepped back. The others remained where they were.

When it was over, nothing remained of Sava but a shrivelled white corpse. And then – I couldn't see it, because I had stepped back – they began to shout.

'*Leptirak!*'

'*Leptirak!*'

9

The peasants surrounded Schmidlin. They raised their spades and mattocks. The young man pulled the stake out of Sava and advanced on Schmidlin. I didn't know what was happening. They dared not strike him, not yet. He was reasoning with them in a frightened voice. They didn't seem to heed him. Closer and closer they came, angrily brandishing their tools. The one with the stake and mallet struck the baron on the head. The baron collapsed. And then they were upon him. I picked up a rock and gave the nearest peasant a blow to the back of the head, knocking him down. Blood began to flow. Novak struck down another peasant, I saw. Count Schmettau never moved.

A shot rang out. Von Hausburg's little pistol was smoking. Another peasant lay on the ground. The others froze. Von Hausburg took aim at the nearest one.

He said something in Serbian and reluctantly they dropped their weapons. They glared at us with hatred, but still they turned and went away. I ran to the baron's side.

'Changed my trousers. Something . . . on them. Spilled. Handkerchief . . . in my other trousers. The peasants said . . . cover the vampire's mouth . . . so the . . . *leptirak* . . . can't get out . . . Forgot my . . . hand-kerchief . . . Afraid . . .' – the blood was pouring now – 'to put my hand . . . my bare hand . . .' I could barely make out what he was saying. He gripped my hand. 'You! I . . . I . . . love . . .'

And then he was gone.

'So, the peasants turned on him for letting the *leptirak* get away,' said von Hausburg.

'Not good, not good,' Novak was saying. 'Now someone else will be turning into a vampire.'

I looked at the unfortunate baron. He seemed quite different now, and not just because he was dead but because he was different. I had trouble standing up, and the two men from the commission had to help me to my feet.

'Just how many vampires *are* there?' I asked.

No one answered. Which was an answer of sorts.

'How many vampires are there?' echoed Schmidlin.

He got the same response.

'And can anyone guarantee that they'll stay in Serbia and not cross the Prince-Eugene line?' Schmettau persisted. The answer this time was no different.

'I didn't believe in vampires,' Schmettau said in agitation. 'I really didn't. I thought it was something your husband had made up. I thought evil was of this world only. This is another matter entirely. And where's the *leptirak*? It could have bitten anybody. Any one of us! Not me, though. I'm no vampire. I'm not! I'm not!'

And shouting that he wasn't a vampire, off he ran. None of us moved, and none of us wanted to go after him. Soon he was lost to sight.

10

Was it the face of evil?

11

'I think it would be best to return to the house where we spent the night to avoid the journey to Belgrade by dark,' said the red-wigged member of the commission.

I disliked having to sleep in that dank hovel again, but after all that had happened I certainly didn't want to travel by night. With fear at our heels, we returned to the hut.

It didn't take us long. In fact, it was all quite close. I must have been mistaken in thinking we'd ranged far and wide in search of the vampire's grave. We'd probably been going around in circles the whole time. I can think of no other explanation.

SIX
In the Subsequent
Course of Events

1

Now that I've told you so much of the story, may I have a peek at that book? Don't you think I've earned it? I know I still haven't told you the most important part, but since I've come this far do you really think I'll start misleading you or lying about the rest?

Thank you.

Let's see, I'll just open it at random. Like when you're feeling sad or hopeless, don't you know, and you open the Bible *au hasard* and read something that comforts you in your distress. I'm partial to the New Testament, the bits towards the end.

Now then, let's see what it says:

> Thus ends our tale of the events at Belgrade. All that remains is to apprise the gentle reader of the fate of our heroes and heroine.
>
> Count Josef Schmettau remained in Belgrade. Earlier we neglected to tell you the count's Christian name, it having entirely slipped our minds, but now, along with his name, there has occurred to us the possibility that you may mistake him for another count, one by the name of Schmettau – Waldemar Schmettau. Count Waldemar Schmettau is an entirely different person, although it is true he had some connection with Serbia, having been the first to propose the reinstatement of that country as a partially autonomous state under Turkish vassalage. This proposal was submitted through official channels of the French

government, by which we mean His Majesty's now-defunct rule and not the current revolutionary administration. This was in 1774 and, as you are undoubtedly aware, led to naught. But let us leave Waldemar and return to Josef Schmettau.

It so happens that our worthy count, among his other marks of distinction, also held the rank of general in the artillery, master of defence for fortified cities. Within a year of the events of our tale he had already undertaken the defence of Belgrade. With consummate knowledge and skill he made provision for the defenders of the principle rampart and bastion. In the projecting fortifications ringing the city he stationed small but strong detachments. Indeed, his first victory came with the failed Turkish attack on the Danubeside redoubt. The count was convinced that the city could be held, and he prepared with equal assiduity for a prolonged siege as for a surprise counterattack. There was but one eventuality for which he remained unready, the one that no one has been able to foresee since time began.

Betrayal.

Although betrayal, as you know, is never simply an internal affair. For Austrian treachery, as witnessed throughout these pages, thrived on Serbian indifference (which has surely not escaped the reader's attention) and Turkish desire to penetrate close to the heart of Europe. A desire which, unfortunately, we have neither the time nor the space to relate.

Thus, although our count was told that the Austrian negotiators were not informed of the successful defence and had therefore hastily sued for peace with the Turks, the truth of the matter is that the negotiators were only too aware of what was happening.

Belgrade was surrendered without a true fight, following a mere month-long siege during which the Turks never attempted a direct attack on the city. At most there was the occasional bombardment – and from inferior Turkish cannon at that, with their tendency to explode into pieces, thereby posing a greater danger to the men who were firing them than to those on the receiving end.

The first stipulation of the peace treaty was that the Austrians must demolish everything they had built from 1717 onwards. This meant dismantling a line of bastions of such modern and superior design that Marshal Vauban himself would have been proud of them. They were required to level earthworks, to tear down curtain walls, to block up secret tunnels, even to raze the barracks within the fortress as well as the residence of the princess and all other such buildings in both the upper and lower town. The Prince-Eugene line was wiped from the face of the earth.

Only the cistern did not figure among the Turkish demands. Or perhaps the Austrians deliberately refrained from destroying it, and the Turks failed to notice. Or perhaps this was a last act of defiance by Count Josef Schmettau.

And then . . . as if Austria had never been: the mighty ramparts, the great bastions, the deep trenches, all as if they had never existed; the dances and costume balls, gone; the lofty nobles and their Shakespeare, gone; the cathedrals and seminaries, the schools, the great victory at Mali Mokri Lug, the Baroque looking-glasses – all, all of them gone. Even the great cistern itself would thereafter be known as the Roman Well as if unbuilt by Austrian hands.

As for the other heroes of our tale . . .

2

When I finally got up I was in a terrible mood. And why not? Running around all night with phantoms, vampires and adulterers, smoking bad hashish and remembering Bishop-Count of Thurn and Valsassina . . . none of it likely to put anyone in good humour.

Immediately after breakfast our little party came face to face with the result of the crimson man's visit to the watermill and to Radetzky. Everyone was dismayed, or at least pretended to be. The fellow with the blond wig went so far as to faint upon seeing the body on the floor. The princess displayed such presence of mind and spirit (what spirit?) that her innocence struck me as questionable. It was quite clear that she was involved with the Turks in some way or that her family had branched out from merely carrying letters to writing them as well. But treachery among the men and women of this world is a fine and useful thing, while conspiring with otherworldly creatures against one's fellow mortals is a transgression comparable only to certain incidents that I am understandably loath to discuss.

I didn't want to enter the mill. I could well imagine how Radetzky must look. Even the reliably pea-brained Schmeticulous hung back, while from Baron Schmeddlesome I expected nothing less than the laughable cowardice he, in fact, displayed.

As so often happens in life, you learn nothing from those who are content to keep their heads down and stay put; you have to wait for someone to come along and push their way to the front. And so it was that my princess of industry, in her burning desire to wreak good wherever she went, attempted to soothe the red baron with her sensible questions and her own sensible answers (because any conversation becomes senseless once you let other people respond). He must have realized that there was no longer any point in secrecy and blabbed the terrible secret of the commission's true assignment. Radetzky had even fooled *me* with his lies.

I didn't have much trouble convincing them all to enlist against the vampires. They seemed to jump at the idea. I went off to find Novak, although I knew where he was, of course. I needed to get away for a short while to think things over.

Wittgenstein had come to investigate the fortress and the cistern in particular. Then he'd disappeared. The commission had come to look into his disappearance, pretending to be investigating the reports of vampires. The hajduks who supposedly knew something about the vampires were in cahoots with the Austrians and – as I had overheard from the inevitable triangle, with the princess as hypotenuse, Schmettau on one side and Schmidlin on the other – the baron was bribing the Serbs, or the Serbs were bribing him, as you like, and the baron was the one I had seen on the night of the costume ball lit up by a flash of lightning as he stood with the hajduks. The hajduks, for their part, claimed that there were no vampires and that the whole thing had been an impractical joke.

But there *were* vampires. Meaning the hajduks were lying, that they hadn't done away with the tax-collector; he really had been bled dry by vampires. Why were the hajduks claiming responsibility for what the vampires had done? To seem bigger and stronger? The next question was what would vampires need with a tax-collector's purse? Vampires weren't exactly known for dealing in cold, hard cash.

Then, on the other hand, the triangle of commissioners had arranged to spend the night in the very same watermill where the vampires were said to be appearing. What for? To carry their deception as far as it would go? 'See, we really *are* looking for vampires.'

On yet another hand, the regent behaved as if there were no vampires, no commission, no Wittgenstein nosing around the fortress – as if, in a nutshell, nothing unusual was happening at all. Which made him a bad lot in my eyes.

And while I pondered, weak and weary, I came straight to the door of the alehouse. Novak had given me a description and directions. No sign hung over the entrance, whether because the owners wanted to avoid paying taxes or because they didn't know how to write, I couldn't say. As I stepped inside I was assailed by a stench so strong that my nose soon lost track of it.

Novak was propped up at a table, already pickled as a gherkin.

I sat down beside him.

'On your feet! We're off to find the vampire.'

He regarded me blearily.

'When I was little . . .' he slurred, 'when I was little my mother was a good woman. From a good family. A *good* woman. Believed in work. And I believed in everything, too. I did. In God and the Devil and good books and saying the Jesus Prayer. That's right, I believed in the great and holy prayer of transfiguration. Lord Jesus Christ, Lord God, have mercy on me, sinner that I am. Or however it goes. You don't know it? But I never believed in work. Ever. In *rakija*, sure. That came later. Also wine. And beer, too – just not as much. It's true. Even before that, I believed in all sorts of things I'd been taught. And books. What do you know? And there was my mother, believing in work. And you know what, we were rich. She didn't need to lift a finger. Ever. But she did. She'd take up her needle and thread and not mind a bit. Embroidered all my collars. Sat in the corner and trimmed all the linens with golden birds and flowers. And why? She'd say, so the servants know to fold back the sheets and tuck in the covers and pillow-cases, proper-like. And my collars, so I'd have something special to wear, a bit of cheer for myself and for others to see . . .' He began to weep. 'She thought there was only one way to bring all that whiteness to life, those damned plain white sheets, with her little flowers and little birds, so there'd be no mistaking the way the things ought to go, and they'd be a happier sight and everyone happier for it . . .' He was sobbing now, his tears mixing with the *rakija* he'd spilled on the table. 'She believed in all those little things she embroidered. And I believed in big things. Great big empty things. Master? Master, you're not crying, are you? Surely not you?'

'Be quiet, you fool. Pull yourself together. Silence.'

'And why should I be quiet? What's the use of keeping quiet? It's no better than talking.'

'Now get this through your thick skull,' I said furiously – servants understand nothing but direct commands and words of anger. 'We are going to track down Sava Savanović in his vampire hole. You are going to help us. You're one of the locals. It's no good sitting around snivelling. Your mind is rotten with drink and memories, and you haven't a thing in your life to show for it. Now, on your feet!'

He stood up reluctantly. I had to settle the bill. Once outside I forced him to vomit up what he'd been drinking. Then I splashed him with cold rainwater from a bucket that stood conveniently to hand. My efforts to sober him up were successful – somewhat. We took the long way back so I could tell Novak everything I'd seen and heard and hear what he thought.

He paid close attention, punctuated by an occasional sneeze.

3

Very well, if you won't let me go on, I'll stop reading.

I couldn't care less what it says, anyway. I'm the only one who knows what happened. The others can only make things up. If knowledge is a crime, you should have put me on trial long ago.

I'm old enough now that I simply don't care. Do what you like. Have me burned as a witch, pack me off to a nunnery, but I'll repent as I see fit, and there's not a thing you can do about it.

4

How can I be good when everyone else is so bad? Should I be the only one to suffer? To suffer all by myself in this hopelessly tangled web of lies and truth? There's only one thread to grab hold of, and whether it's the truth or not depends on which end you start at.

One thing's for sure, the knot can be solved by pounding a stake through the middle of it. Although, upon further reflection, that may not be the most felicitous metaphor. After cutting the Gordian knot, Alexander the Great did go on to conquer Asia only to die soon afterwards. No, I don't think I'll use that particular example.

'Don't you think, though, master, that there should be *more* signs of the coming end of the world besides just one vampire in Dedejsko Selo?'

'Such as?'

'I don't know, something like "In those days the sun shall be darkened . . ."'

Which is what Bishop-Count of Thurn and Valsassina had said. He looked along the length of the ballroom and, his eyes heavy from wine, sat down to rest with his head in his hands.

'I was in Rome a few months ago.' Angling for one of those silly-looking birettas, no doubt. 'I was shown some work by our astronomers. They had just finished calculating the date of the end of the world: 11 August 1999. Are you relieved to hear it? On that day there will be a total eclipse of the sun. You see, there's still time for you . . .' he laughed nastily.

'Time for what?'

'To fulfil Origen's prophecy.'

'Origen?'

'You know, Origen, the Christian from Alexandria who died in the Roman persecutions, but not before sharing with the world his idea of apocatastasis, universal repentance and salvation. Even the Devil. No Hell, everyone saved. Naturally we had him branded as a heretic.'

Everyone knew who I was.

But I didn't believe the bishop-count. I didn't believe that terrible things would be accompanied by signs and wonders or be heralded by calls and warnings. The terrible things were sufficient unto themselves. Why not a balmy spring day, birds warbling, crickets chirping, people lying, cherries blossoming, a light breeze ruffling the babbling brook, flowers dotting the meadow and, bang, end of the world. And Fishmouth standing there in his white robes, always those white robes, with all those little winged things flitting around him like fireflies, and he's bellowing *You're all going straight to Hell!*

'You know what crossed my mind as you were telling me about the man in crimson-purple?' asked Novak.

'What?'

'Do you know what the English mean by a purple passage?'

'Remind me.'

'A purple passage is a bit of masterful writing in an otherwise bad book. It stands out.'

'Well, he's certainly outstanding at what he does, no two ways about that. You should have seen the way he transformed into that Turk! But we'll soon fix him. With a stake. We're going to find him right now. You gather the peasants and make sure everything's ready, and we'll put an end to this vampire business once and for all.'

'There's one thing I forgot to mention.'

'Something I'll find useful?'

'I don't know.'

'What do you mean, you don't know? Foolish servant! Out with it, then.'

'The Russian we met, the one the peasants thought was the Archangel Michael . . .'

'Yes?'

'Well, they saw him making the sign of the cross. He was using two fingers. Two fingers – not an open hand like the Catholics, not three fingers like the Orthodox, just two fingers. Is that the Protestant way?'

'No, it's not! Heh, heh, heh. That's fiendishly good news, if I do say so myself.'

'How so?'

'Because the only ones who cross themselves with two fingers are the Russian Old Believers. Michael would never come in the guise of a heretic! Never. Which means he's not Michael. And if Michael isn't here then it's not the end of the world either. Very good news indeed. And now, to put an end to the master of purple.'

5

But the search dragged on. The peasants kept stopping to dig. It was exasperating. Especially since they'd brought along a priest, who was entirely surplus to requirements. Stupid Christians, they just don't get it. There's only one way to beat the forces of darkness, and that's with *more* darkness. At times I was terribly tempted to grab the stake and take matters into my own hands, but I refrained, thinking it best to remain in character as an Austrian count.

It was getting dark by the time we found the grave. At first it seemed to be yet another dead end, but the black horse wasn't fooled. It refused to take another step. I told Novak to buy the horse for me once it was all over. The priest started droning on and on, and I wanted to poke out my eardrums. Schmidlin had his assignment from the peasants, to stand by as the young man drove the stake through the heart and to cover the mouth of the finally departed so the *leptirak* couldn't get out and turn anyone else into a vampire. The baron seemed frightened, but he nodded his head and took his place alongside.

They brought up the coffin, and the young man with the stake got ready to strike the moment it was opened. Only one peasant stepped forward to remove the lid. It made a hideous scraping noise as he tried to draw it back.

The lid seemed to be unspeakably heavy, and (unable to stand by any longer) I leaped forward to help. We didn't have an easy time of it. I don't think we managed to budge it by more than an inch. I called for Novak. For some reason – perhaps his foolish Serbian superstitions – he had hung back, but one of the men from the commission came to our assistance. I was pleasantly surprised. The young man's strength made itself felt right away. Now the lid had moved by a foot. Then the other man from the commission joined in, and with one last push the coffin was open wide.

SEVEN
The Secret Chapter

Someone else lay inside.

He was ruddy and wearing a shroud, but it wasn't the man in crimson. The man in crimson had eluded me. The young man got straight to work with his stake. Blood everywhere, like a pig slaughter. And then the peasants were in an uproar. Instantly I realized that the *leptirak* had escaped after all. Schmidlin, of course, had failed.

Quite rightly, the peasants turned on him. It *was* his fault. Not only had we failed to find the crimson man but now someone else would be turning into a vampire. I didn't want to draw my pistol until I was sure they'd killed the baron. Only then did I fire. I got one of the peasants, but instantly regretted it. Why hadn't I shot the priest! And the baron was still alive, too.

As it turned out, things weren't as bad as they seemed. Schmidlin didn't survive. Although he did still have enough breath in him to say where he'd gone wrong, by leaving his handkerchief in the waistcoat he'd spilt something on at lunch. He was so used to that waistcoat, he explained, that he'd gone ahead as if he were still wearing it out of sheer habit. But he wasn't wearing it, and so he didn't have his handkerchief either. And when the moment came he hadn't dared to use his bare hand. Habit, they say, is second nature. A bad one. They also say *habit does not make the monk*, and I dare say this was true in Schmidlin's case. His habit had just made a monkey of him.

And he was in love with the princess, too. That's what he said, or confessed. Poor sap. The princess was in love with her husband. Loved him for no earthly reason. I remembered their conversation, the one

I'd overheard at the costume ball. Of course, it was only afterwards that I realized what disguise Maria Augusta had been wearing. At the time, during the ball, it was just a mask talking. The regent had brushed her off. Why wouldn't she leave him alone? Couldn't she see that he didn't want her? And she'd answered him by saying that he was the one. Which one? the regent had asked. And she'd said, did he remember the rug Count Schmettau had got from China? It was a masterpiece of weaving, a mysterious landscape the likes of which we'd never seen, and we all stood and stared at it in wonder. You were the only one who went ahead and – she stopped and then continued – stepped on it without thinking twice. You didn't even look at it. That's what makes you the one. The only prince. The regent shrugged. That's what rugs are for, for walking on. But he bowed and kissed her hand, saying, I do not understand. For the very first time I do not understand. Perhaps . . . he said, then turned abruptly and went away.

I think that 'perhaps' must have given her hope. Isn't it remarkable, how one little word can suffice for someone in love? Most likely there had been one such word from her lips, just one, addressed to Schmidlin. That had been enough for him. The fool. He'd really had it coming. I can't protect fools from themselves.

SIX
In the Subsequent Course
of Events (continued)

6

'What would Our Dear Lord do without you? What would *we* do without you?' asked Thurn and Valsassina, then continued without waiting for an answer. 'According to Dionysius the Areopagite, at the very heart of light there is always a point representing the divine darkness. Without it pure light would be utter blackness. And that point is you.'

'It is,' I confirmed. 'And if you ascend high enough into the endless boring light you will fall far enough into yourself to find me.'

'Do you think I haven't? Dionysius goes on to say that knowledge is union between the knower and the known. I knew you at once. Anyone who recognizes you has already journeyed to the depths of his soul. How many persons of this sort do you meet?'

'Lots!'

'Excellent!'

'Are you really that encouraged by the prospect of so many fallen souls?'

'Ah but, *caro maestro,* for those who have known you there is hope of repentance and the knowledge of God. Those who have never seen you have nothing to repent. And those who have nothing to repent are merely deceiving themselves.'

Not a sound could be heard. Not even a moan. Only silence. An otherworldly silence. The stillness of Hell in which there are no sounds, no nightingales, no cries of torment; no mortal words in the first language, or words in any language, or purring of cats, or death-rattles; no wind in the fields, nor thunder, nor lyres, nor sneezing; no sanding and rasping, no weeping. No breathing either. That kind of silence. Even Mary Magdalene was quiet. The sun beat down. Was this really the month of Nisan? The first new moon after the spring equinox. And Friday? I looked into his eyes. Flames. In his pupils, a roaring fire. I had to turn and look. Jerusalem was burning. Herod's white walls ringed the fires around. Who could ever put them out again? On Mount Moriah the flames encroached on the temple from all four sides. I couldn't see the priests anywhere. The fire had passed through the courts and was at the door. I looked towards the Mount of Olives, where vats of boiling oil coursed down the hillsides towards the scorched valley. The heat was unbearable. All the aqueducts in the empire couldn't bring enough water to quench it. Now again on Moriah the whole temple had gone up. Flames reaching to the sky. It was all lost to sight: the humble houses to the east, the palaces to the west; the hills had turned to funeral pyres. The temple burned most fiercely. Salvation lay outside the walls. All the water in the empire wouldn't be enough now. I turned my back on Jerusalem. Again I could see his eyes. And in them the flames. Even he can't put this fire out. And then his eyes grew dimmer. Dark. He laughed. Laughed at me.

'It is finished.'

'That's what he said?'

'That's what he said: *It is finished.* And then he died. I turned around again, and there was the city. Just as it had been. To the west, the untouched palaces and villas of the Romans, Pharisees and Sadducees;

to the east, the houses of the poor. The groves on the Mount of Olives unscathed. The temple unchanged in its power and glory. The air was filled with sounds. All the sounds that exist, the softest and the loudest: cocks crowing, tax-collectors threatening, judges passing sentence, all the unbearable, harsh and terrible sounds. Just like in Hell, I couldn't hear myself think. But I understood: nothing had happened. On that Friday, nothing had actually happened.

'I know that, master. What happened on Friday, that wasn't the most important part. The most important thing happened on the Sunday. Isn't that right?'

'Are you looking for another argument? Nothing happened on the Sunday either. So there.'

'If nothing happened on that Sunday then what are you afraid of?'

'The story! That's what, oh servant of mine. The *story* that something did.'

Part the Third
THE CISTERN

ONE
First, into the City

1

I don't know why it took us so long to realize that the servants were gone. None of them had waited for us: not my two maids, not the Chinese cook, not the various other attendants we'd brought with us. They were simply gone. Von Hausburg said only one word – 'Schmettau' – although he probably meant to say more. I had no doubts myself, although the thing made no sense. We only believe absolutely in what we can never understand.

Eternal salvation?

I wouldn't go so far as to say that Count Schmettau was on a par with the divine in our inability to comprehend him, any more than I would compare his running away with our servants to an act of God. Even so, Schmettau's actions certainly had an effect on my eternal salvation. Certainly more than the actions of my nearest and dearest.

Oh yes, of course, it's coming back to me now. Von Hausburg said afterwards how the banishment from the Garden of Eden must have looked just like our departure from Belgrade.

'But we haven't done anything wrong,' I answered, 'and we left of our own free will.'

'The matter of sin is beside the point. And as for our leaving voluntarily, it's not true. Each of us is here because he must be. Just as each of us came to Belgrade because he had to.'

I tried to argue again, but he wasn't listening.

But getting back to the plot. When we saw the situation we were in – no servants, no food, surrounded by hostile peasants – we decided to take turns keeping watch overnight. The first watch, from nightfall to the second hour after midnight, fell to von Hausburg and the red count. The second watch, until daybreak, would be the blond count and Vuk Isakovič.

I had trouble sleeping. I dozed off quickly enough but woke up soon after. Something had disturbed my light sleep, some noise I couldn't identify in my tired state. After that it took me a long time to get back to sleep. Normally I'd read for a while, but I hadn't brought a book with me. Besides, there wasn't enough light for reading. True, the moon was bright in the sky, but the peasants had covered up the tiny window with a cloth. The cloth made a poor curtain, and a thin ray of moonlight still found its way in, landing on the floor not far from where I lay.

I was alone in the room, with nothing to break the silence but my own movements and the occasional creaking of the old house around me. Such a lonely night. I don't know how long it was before I fell asleep again, but I think the stillness and the occasional noises gave me no rest. I might still have been awake just after midnight.

2

When I opened my eyes, it was already morning. Outside I could hear voices and the usual morning bustle. I confess I was reluctant to get up, having slept so poorly. I had not yet left the room when I heard the scream. Without stopping to think I ran outside. The first thing I saw was von Hausburg and the red commissioner. Beside them was Novak, kneeling. I moved towards them, and only then did I see the two bodies. On his back lay Vuk Isakovič, a sabre jutting from his chest. His white shirt was clotted with blood. Face down beside him, as if reaching out towards him, lay the blond commissioner. He had no wounds, at least not that I could see. Novak turned him over, looked at him, then returned him to his original position, on his stomach. Again his face was concealed.

Von Hausburg looked at me and said, 'Enough. We're going back at once!'

The red commissioner murmured that we must bring the bodies to the city. I knew right away that we would neglect this duty and that von Hausburg would recommend sending someone from the fortress to retrieve the bodies later. And so it was. Novak hurried to saddle the horses. We spurred them on and galloped away. None of us spoke. I didn't know what to think. The two deaths seemed unrelated to the vampires, and I couldn't see the connection. It was then that I felt the desire to discover what lay behind these sinister happenings – felt it even more strongly than the urge to be back behind the thick walls and never ask another question.

But still I drove my horse onwards, riding at breakneck speed not because I wanted to reach Belgrade, but because I didn't. I was afraid of my own self.

We seemed to ride for hours. My legs were sore, and my hand was stiff from gripping the reins.

We made our way to the top of a hill – unnecessarily, as we found out later, for it was not the shortest route to the city. Even though we were following a sort of road, we had gone out of our way. It may have been deliberate on the part of whoever was leading. I never found out who it was. The baron was dead, Isakovič was dead, and the only ones left were a guest, a foreigner and myself – and I'd never been outside the city walls. Novak rode behind us, I noticed, and I wanted to ask why he wasn't leading the way. But I didn't.

When we got to the top of the hill all my suspicions vanished. Before my eyes lay the city, extending to the north. There was the first low wall, and behind it the huts of the poor, the gallows, the graveyard. The second wall was the Prince-Eugene line with its massive Baroque gates, its thick high ramparts running east and west. Behind it stood the larger, better residences, my palace, the Serbian church and several of our own churches. The third wall was the rampart of the fortress itself. I could make out the bastions, each named for a saint, and the two ravelins and the two curtain walls. Further than that I could not see.

I realized then that Belgrade was protected within three concentric circles, each one stronger and more unyielding than the last. Any outlander, any wayfarer, any enemy at the gates would have to conquer all three to reach the city's heart.

And there, at the very heart of Belgrade, was my husband as ruler. Everything I desired was there. No vampires. The triple defences protected me and kept them at bay, whoever they were.

We sped forward on our horses. Down the hill they galloped. The trees on either side were thinning out. A branch or two lashed at me in passing. We were flying along and I no longer minded the chill in the air. Below us lay the city, and we were coming back.

I didn't hear the first shot.

3

The horses stopped short. The red commissioner on his black mount nearly flew head over heels from the saddle. The next shot I did hear. Someone shouted.

'Turn back!'

I saw where the shot had come from. The smoke was curling into the air above a guard on the wall. He was still aiming the musket at us. Some dozen yards from him, another guard also had us in his sights.

I turned my horse around. I dug in the spurs, but the beast could only struggle uphill, its sides heaving. We didn't stop or say a word until we'd reached the top of the hill again.

'Who are they firing at?' asked the red count.

'At the four of us,' answered Novak.

'But why?' he asked.

'Because!' spat out von Hausburg.

The red count looked at me, I looked at von Hausburg, von Hausburg looked at Novak and Novak looked at the red count.

'They won't let us in,' I said at last.

'But why?' repeated the red count.

'Because they've been given orders,' said von Hausburg.

'But why?' he persisted.

'Because they think we're vampires,' I said. To this day I don't why it occurred to me to say that. At the time I thought I was speaking too hastily without stopping to think. I knew it was true, though. It just might not have been strictly necessary to say so.

'Schmettau!' said Novak.

'Schmettau,' I said, picking up where he'd left off. 'Schmettau came back to the city, raving about Sava Savanović and Radetzky and Schmidlin and the *leptirak* and all the rest of it, and somehow convinced them that we've turned into vampires.'

But how could Alexander have believed it? I asked myself. How could my husband say nothing as I was left to fend for myself with Serbia and the vampires? How could he bar my way to safety? How could he leave me like that?

TWO

1

I wandered empty and alone. The moon was low in the sky, and my shadow trailed at my heels. But not for long. Soon the clouds gathered, blacker than the night, and it began to rain. A real spring rain, heavy and falling fast. Despite my hood I quickly became soaked to the skin. My wandering might have seemed aimless, but it turned out not to be. When I found myself in front of the tavern I knew so well I realized it had been my destination all along.

The rain was pouring down, and I made my way through sheets of water. I knocked three times with the heavy brass ring, waited, knocked again twice, waited, and then knocked twice more. The door swung back on its creaking hinges.

The faces were all familiar. I'd often seen them of a Friday evening. Just the right time for all those who have fallen away from faith and family. They might go drinking and whoring every night of the week, and probably did, but nothing was so sweet as breaking the Sabbath. They knew it's not enough simply to sin: you have to *plan* your sinning not just go about it randomly. Not only do you need to justify your sinning in advance, you need to be angry that others don't join you, and to believe that what you're doing is noble and proper. And to keep at it until the need for sin – a need which, no matter what others may say, is not of the body but of the spirit – grows into a new religion with its own priests and its own philosophers who are responsible for thinking up yet more ways to sin.

Such people never repent. It's easy to beat your breast over a night here and there, a woman here, a man there, a gold piece or two; it's not at all easy to feel sorry because of the very meaning of your life.

I took a quick look around: some drunkards and whores, two sailors, some of Barabbas's henchmen, one spy for the Romans and one spy for the Sanhedrin. I could tell they were spies by how well they were dressed and how poorly they were drinking: the service may have provided their tunics, but the drinks were coming out of their own pockets. The imperial spy was practically regimental in his crisp Caesar cut, while the spy for the Sanhedrin was trying hard not to break the Sabbath any more than necessary. He kept calling the tavern-keeper to fill his small clay goblet from the great jug of wine.

I sat at an empty table and ordered some sweet Samarian wine. The wench brought it right away. It was an inferior wine, watered down, and the night was only just beginning. I ordered more, for the longer the dark lasted, the less it would matter how much water and how much wine was served. That's how it always goes, whether new wineskins or old.

At the next table sat a sailor, regaling two drunkards and a whore with tales. What was he doing so far from the sea? Lying his way from one place to another in hopes of wine, something to do at night, passing the time – what else?

I knew she wouldn't be there yet. How well I remembered her time, the late evening, after the day's work was done, when she'd come to make merry. Only this day had brought no work. Nor would there be any merry-making. But I knew she would still come, for habit is a refuge like no other.

'Call me Ishmael,' said the sailor.

'I know that story,' I remarked. 'It's long and dull.'

He ignored me, continuing his tale. The others listened raptly.

I called for more wine. I didn't want to get drunk, so I merely sipped it. But I was starting to get a headache. From the stale air in the tavern. From the change in the weather. It was always changing. And the sailor was going on and on. I stood up and spoke to the sailor's audience.

'Just so you know, the whale gets it in the end.'

He moved to strike me, but I dodged him. Everyone stood up. The tavern-keeper stepped between us. A jug fell. Curses flew. The other sailor came at me. A whore was laughing. Barabbas's men had their hands on the daggers at their breasts. The spies were taking it all in. The whore laughed again. The sailors looked at each other and nodded. The tale-teller pulled out a crooked knife.

And then *she* was at the door. Hair unbound, wet. Dripping with rain. Her eyes with the same old fire in them. The hour was mine.

The sailor spoke her name in a low voice. 'Mary.'

2

Mary. Maria. Maria Augusta. She lay there in all her helplessness. How does that Serb put it in that poem they're always quoting? *She sleeps, perhaps. / Her eyes outside all evil.* But the vampire wouldn't let her. And, outside, evil was standing watch. The red count sat beside me, quite unconcerned. He was twirling one of the many curls of his red wig.

'Herr Graf,' I said, 'it will be easier to bear our guard duty with some conversation rather than in silence.'

'But if we're talking we won't be able to hear the enemy sneaking up on us,' he answered cannily.

'The dangerous enemies are the ones who can't be heard, and I dare say vampires move without making a sound. So let's at least talk a bit, for fear is always sharper in silence. Why, all of these new stories coming out in German, the ones you call Gothic – the terrifying bits have no dialogue at all, just dark and stormy descriptions. As soon as the sun comes up or the characters pluck up their courage, that's when you get direct speech.

'What shall we talk about?' he asked politely. 'About Wittgenstein.'

'Who's that?'

'The one who came to investigate the cistern.'

'Ah, you mean Count Wittgenau.'

It's all in the name, I thought; even a rose would reek if it were called stinkweed.

'The count had discovered . . . Well, I think I can go ahead and tell you. I mean, it hardly matters now . . . So, the count had found out, don't ask me how, that the regent had arranged with the Turks, in exchange for the right sum of gold, to deliver Serbia into their hands. He'd been told – Count Wittgenau, I mean – that the regent's mistresses and hunting companions and drinking bouts were costing him more than he could wring out of Serbia in taxes. Serbia is a poor country . . .'

'Mistresses and companions are rich indulgences,' I said helpfully.

'What? I suppose. I wouldn't know. In any case –'

'And the world is all that is the case,' I added.

'What? I don't know that one. In any event, Count Wittgenau found out that the regent had hidden the gold in that cistern at Kalemegdan. Several times he tried to get to the bottom of it, in both senses of the word, but the cistern is well guarded. He quickly saw that it would be impossible to enter the cistern from the fortress. But he also quickly heard of the old Roman aqueduct that runs from some village near Belgrade all the way to the cistern at Kalemegdan. The aqueduct is partly underground and partly above. It's encased in brick along its entire length, and is mostly a canal with water no deeper than the average man's height. Some Serbs told the count where to go outside the city in order to enter the aqueduct, and what turnings to take along the various conduits in order to reach the fortress. One early morning the count rode out of Belgrade. He was disguised as a tax-collector . . .'

'Not a very wise choice.'

'He was escorted by several soldiers. They went slowly, for it had to appear that they were travelling far from the capital, and yet they didn't want to go out of their way. They spent the night at an inn not far from the watermill. The next morning the count was nowhere to be found, and the soldiers were drunk and seemed to remember nothing. The investigation, carried out at the regent's orders, also discovered nothing. This came as no surprise to us in Vienna. What *did* surprise us was the sudden reappearance of Wittgenau's body six months later at the same inn where he'd gone missing. The corpse was perfectly preserved, as though not long dead. In fact, it almost seemed alive. Vampire-like. Now do you understand? Myself, I'm just beginning to understand. The regent directed that the body be prepared for Christian burial, but, in fact, he ordered that a stake be driven through its heart, as we ourselves recently witnessed, and that it be burned. And so we lost our most important piece of evidence.'

'Evidence that the regent was a traitor or that the count was a vampire?'

'The two are not mutually exclusive.'

The moon had come back out.

'You wouldn't really seize a vampire as evidence and take it back to Vienna?'

'Certainly. How else to prove the existence of vampires other than by showing the emperor a genuine specimen?'

'But then the vampires would spread!'

'Ah, but we're men of science and would keep matters under strict control. But we could never allow science and emperor to be deprived of such an important discovery.'

'Keeping that control would give you the very devil of a time.'

'The Devil is beyond our purview. You mistake me.'

'You...' I sputtered. 'If you were to find another vampire, you mean you would pack it up and ship it off to Vienna?'

'Without a second thought!'

'Why didn't you then, when we found Sava Savanović?'

'We couldn't, not in front of all those peasants. But that's why we ordered Schmidlin not to cover the vampire's mouth with his hand so that the *leptirak* could fly free and . . .'

I jumped on him and seized him by the neck, shouting. 'You . . . madmen . . . turning the whole world into vampires . . . the final judgement . . . final judgement . . .'

He was thrashing about, trying to kick me away, to bite me, but I squeezed and I squeezed and I squeezed. My hands and fingers hurt. I gritted my teeth. My nostrils flared. I hated him. He struck at my head with his fists, his wig fell off, and I was strangling him. Let the vampires out of Serbia. Conquer everything in their path. And I should come to an end for science! My whole world come to an end!

Wasn't it Socrates who said *Ego scire me non scirem*, meaning 'The science did not teach me anything'?

He didn't struggle long. The moment came when he just slumped. I let go of him, and he fell to the ground and lay there.

The vampires are not getting out of Serbia, not while I'm still alive.

THREE
The Convocation

1

How could Alexander believe Schmettau and leave me to the mercy of the vampires and the Serbs? I felt sick. I wanted to retch. I covered my mouth with my hand. The tears wouldn't come. Neither would the words. All I could feel was the sweat that had broken out on my face and body. Enormous beads of sweat. I was soaking wet. I was trembling, shaking.

The red count was saying something.

'There must be a gap in the defences somewhere. A place where we can slip in or break through, by force of arms if need be.'

'You're mad!' shouted von Hausburg. 'Mad! From the moment I set foot in Belgrade everyone's been going on and on about how impregnable the fortress is. All the Turks in the world couldn't take it. A *pigeon* couldn't land inside the walls without permission. We'll never get in. And we don't even need to. I think we should just keep going right around the city, find a place to cross the Sava and then we'll be in Europe. Once we're on the other side, we'll figure out what to do next. We're all counts and princesses here. I'm sure we'll manage.'

'That's out of the question,' I said. 'My regent is in the city. I won't leave him. I want to show him that I'm not a vampire. I want to prove that Schmettau is a liar and a madman . . .'

'If we do make it inside your husband will be waiting for us, stake in hand, to give us the same welcome he gave Wittgenstein.'

'What Wittgenstein?' I asked.

'I think the princess is right,' said the red count, speaking up again. 'We must get back to Belgrade. We're not vampires. If we flee to Austria they're liable to issue a warrant for us, or whatever they do for vampires. We have to show them that we're *not* vampires. And we have to do it in Belgrade. Because it's from Belgrade that the news of vampires will spread. And it's only in Belgrade that we can stop it.'

'I know a way into the city,' said Novak.

Von Hausburg glared at him but said nothing.

'There's an old Roman aqueduct, partly above ground and partly under, that runs from Mali Mokri Lug, a village to the east of here, all the way to the heart of the fortress. It's still in use and passable all the way. When I was a boy I used to play in the tunnel. The water runs through a channel cut into the bottom, and the walls are only a bit lower than the average man's height. We'll just have to stoop a bit. From the outside, no one will be able to see us, and on the inside there's nobody at all.'

'Schmettau knows all that, too, because he told me himself that when a city is preparing for a siege, you block off all access, any secret tunnels and mine them so no one can get through,' said von Hausburg, all in one breath.

'They can't cut off their own water supply,' I objected.

'Yes they can,' von Hausburg answered. 'They've got a whole cistern full of water, as you know perfectly well. They certainly won't be needing fresh spring water piped in from Mali Mokri Lug.'

'I'm going through the aqueduct,' I said.

'So am I,' said the red count, joining me.

'Me, too,' said Novak.

Von Hausburg shook his head furiously. He said nothing.

'Lead the way!' I said to Novak.

He nodded. He rode forward on his horse then stopped to think. He headed east and we followed. I turned around once more while we were still on high ground, at the top of the hill, to look back at Belgrade. It seemed to be burning in the morning light. An unnatural gleam lay over all. The city seemed to be ringed with a protective fire that was keeping out the rest of the world.

We rode for more than an hour. Novak could not find the aqueduct. We were going in circles, as we had done when searching for the vampire. Novak spoke with some peasants. Then we wandered some more. Wherever we were going, it wasn't towards the city, for I never caught sight of the walls again. Perhaps we were going further and further away instead of coming closer. Meaning that when we finally found the tunnel we'd have a longer trek ahead of us. Again Novak stopped to talk with the Serbs. Again we urged the horses forward. Then we slowed our pace, realizing we still hadn't arrived. I thought we must be in the area where the aqueduct runs underground, and that's why we couldn't find it.

However, I said nothing. No one spoke, except for Novak. Von Hausburg was silent because he was offended and sulking, the red count was silent because he was afraid and I was silent because I didn't know what else to do. I no longer remember all the thoughts that were passing through my mind just then. I felt both spent and invigorated at the same time.

Novak spoke to a peasant woman then turned to us. 'It appears the place is guarded,' he said.

'Guarded!' we all exclaimed.

'True, the aqueduct has no guards as we know them. No matter how closely we look, we shall see no armed young men, whether in uniform or not. The guards are none other than peasant women at their washing near by, lanky children playing leap-frog, a lad and lass trading looks as they mowed, two or three scowling old men, then traders from Ottoman lands with their bundles of flying carpets, genies in bottles, books printed from right to left, hashish and halva, then yet more traders from Austrian lands, and others still from Novi Pazar, whose wares compare not unfavourably with those of the West, and a handful of gypsies, and even a lady from the city, with a great number of those who can read and write, and a priest besides, and several deacons, some cantankerous old crones and, finally, above them all, by night, the moon and the evening star. These stand watch, and guard the entrance to the aqueduct and to the city.'

'Quite the crowd,' observed the red count.

Von Hausburg hissed. 'Quite the speech! What was that supposed to be? A purple passage? Who cares who they are? They can't do a thing to stop us, except possibly the priests and deacons.'

'I don't understand any of this,' I said. 'All of those people are there to prevent anyone from getting into the city?'

'No, Princess,' answered Novak. 'They're not there to stop people getting *in;* they're there to stop anyone getting *out.*'

2

Mary Magdalene. I knew she'd come. On that terrible night. My hour was nigh. I pretended not to see her. Let her come to me, I figured.

There she stood, shining in my eyes. Mary Magdalene, a soul that once was mine. Everyone gathered around her. Asked her questions. She was answering. I couldn't hear what, and I wasn't listening. There was wailing and whispering and great commotion, as if they had lost their nearest and dearest one. He *is* everyone's nearest and dearest, Novak would say – but you still won't be saved by your connections, I would add. They couldn't seem to make up their minds. Should they be angry? Start a riot? Seek revenge, mourn, despair? Resign themselves? As though it really affected them.

They were play-acting.

When they'd had their fill of sanctimony they invited her to sit with them. It was her tavern, her circle of friends, and soon they were drinking and talking just like any other night.

I didn't want to approach her. I knew it would be overplaying my hand; it would seem as though I were following her, hounding her. Carefully I measured out my sips of wine and kept quiet. More and more time went by. I called for a plate of falafel so the wine wouldn't go to my head.

The conversation was dying down. They'd been through it all, retelling the past, bemoaning the passing, predicting what was yet to come. In a matter of hours they'd used up all the tenses in their pride, their self-importance, and come to the end – or to eternity, which is their name for the end.

They were all so sure of their predictions for this world. The Roman spy was prophesying the end of the empire. 'It won't be hordes of barbarians that bring the walls down – it'll be the soul of Rome itself: once the rot has set in the gates will swing wide open . . .' He hadn't even finished speaking and already the others were agreeing with him. She looked over at me.

It wasn't an angry look, but it wasn't a greeting either. She didn't make any other sign that she'd seen me. She continued to listen to the others.

'There will be no Jews,' the spy from the Sanhedrin was saying. 'The heavenly Jerusalem . . .'

Hear, hear! the others chimed in.

What did they need a city for? A city is a place that gives protection from attackers. Up there, in the heavenly Jerusalem, there will be no need for ramparts, for bastions, high towers, Greek fire, regiments or cannon. For who will ever launch an attack against it with catapults, battering-rams, siege ladders – what mercenaries, what crusaders?

No attack and no defence either. No barriers, no walls, no boundaries, no form. When you do away with the walls that separate the city from the world, the city *is* the world. One city, the whole world. Everyone in it. And no one in it, with no way to tell the city apart from everything else. Or from nothing at all. And everyone crowding together in the same place, inasmuch as the world is one. And everyone far apart from everyone else, inasmuch as the world has no end.

Isn't that Hell itself?

Somehow, I don't know how, that madman Schmettau had seen the truth of it.

From somewhere in Asia came the dawn, darker than the night. A ray of light cut into the earthen floor of the tavern. All was still, and most of the Christians were slumbering. Ishmael was muttering in his sleep. That story of his just wouldn't stop until he got it all out.

Poor fellow.

The Tiberian spy had long since gone to submit his report. A report that would be glanced at by some sour-faced imperial functionary, who would then file it neatly away – never suspecting that there's no better way to forget things than with a well-organized filing system. But every empire, every kingdom and princedom, every republic especially, will preserve an unshakeable faith in such systems, all those ingenious ways of classifying and shelving things to make them easy to find. And even easier to forget.

All the rest of them were still there. His wine under lock and key, the tavern-keeper slept with one eye open, for you never knew with that crowd. I waited.

And she did rise from her seat. With unwavering step she came straight towards me, her gaze sharp and clear. And impossible to read – because of the sleepless night, the events of the previous day, the fact that I had once known Mary, and she was different and yet still not different.

She came and sat beside me. So close that I could feel her warm breath on my neck, so close that the air between us shimmered and became her skin, became her hand caressing me.

She hadn't even touched me.

'There's still hope for you,' she said softly.

'Hope? I'm celebrating my victory.'

'All alone? And here of all places?'

'I wanted you to see me. To see who was the last one standing. Who's here, and who's dead.'

'Liar!' she hissed, her old self again. 'You've come here because you're pitiful and lonely. You've come to be sorry. That's why you're here.'

'Sorry? For *you* to see?' I laughed, but carefully, to avoid waking the others.

'That's right. You've come to see me. It was me you were running from, and it's me you've come back to.'

'I wasn't running away . . .'

'Because I loved you.'

'Why should I be afraid of love?'

'It's not love you're afraid of. It's losing love. That's the beginning and end of all your fears. But you still came. So there's still hope for you. Listen, it's getting light. Go and get some sleep. Nothing will happen today. Tomorrow, Sunday, in the morning, at sunrise, come to the fountain at Gethsemane. I'll be waiting for you.'

3

'What I figured, Princess, was that if we see anyone who matches that description, we'll know we're near the aqueduct,' said Novak.

'We'll see hundreds of them,' snapped von Hausburg, but Novak made no answer, only spurred his horse forward. I set off after him. The red count hung back for a bit, then followed along. Von Hausburg was the last to make up his mind and brought up the rear.

We saw washerwomen and lads and lasses and children and old men and crones, even priests, peddlers of every description and gypsies, but the aqueduct was nowhere to be found.

We rode for a long time, around and around and straight ahead, up hill and down dale, through fields and orchards. We were greeted by peasants, glared at by peasants; some gave us directions as best they could, others merely shook their heads. The day was fading, and we feared the coming night.

Then, suddenly, it was as if the sun had risen anew. An otherworldly light broke over us from the west, blinding us. For several moments I dared not look. I felt as though I'd already been there once, although I could no longer see it. As if I knew that light, that squinting, as if I knew what was happening.

When I opened my eyes the light was softer, gentler, and the air was shimmering and enfolding us like the soft touch of a loved one's hands. Alexander's. But Alexander wasn't there.

On a great cube of stone sat an angel. Attired in white. Neither male nor female. Nor something in between. One wing was bent downwards, the feathers at the tip almost sticking into the earth, while the other pointed upwards to the heavens. The halo shone like gold, if gold were made of air and had no weight and could never be used to buy and sell things. Rosy and greenish lights played over the angel's face. It was sitting rather insouciantly, I thought: of good cheer, free of care. That's when I recognized it. It was the White Angel, the one who met the women at Christ's tomb.

Pardon?

How do I know it was *that* angel?

I'd seen a fresco in Belgrade at a Serbian church. I was told it was merely a copy of the original fresco, which was somewhere deep inside Turkish territory. I remembered the face. A face serenely announcing the greatest of all victories.

Sorry? I can't hear you. You want to know how the Orthodox painters knew what the angel looked like? I don't know. You think I was just imagining it. That I'd think any angel looked like the White Angel. Ah, but that would only be true if the Serbs had managed to paint the White Angel as more beautiful than actual angels.

But let's continue.

It was waiting for us. In its right hand it held a long staff. Its left hand rested in its lap. When we had drawn near, it raised its left hand and pointed to something on the right. On every finger it wore a ring of precious stones in all the colours of the rainbow.

It was pointing the way.

Into the aqueduct.

A dark and empty place.

None of us spoke. We didn't so much as look at one another. We weren't even looking at the angel any more. We dismounted and without a second thought stepped straight inside. I went first, then Novak, then the red count. Von Hausburg took up the rear.

FOUR
The Aqueduct

1

He lay there, strangled, looking up at me with wide-open scientific eyes. The red wig lay beside him.

What should I do? I could raise the alarm by shouting *Vampires!* But it would be too straightforward, somehow not quite right, rather beneath me. And I'd nearly forgotten. There was the other count to deal with, too, the blond one. He was also a man of science, ready to destroy my world in his quest for renown and scientific truth. What was the best way to get rid of him? He was sleeping in the hut with Novak and Vuk Isakovič. Of course, Novak wouldn't be any trouble. But Isakovič could wake up any moment, might not even be asleep. And the Serb was fierce and strong.

I decided to lure the blond one outside, throttle him and go back to bed. Vuk Isakovič would either sleep through his turn at guard duty or wake up in time – and to find what? The two counts with their necks wrung in the night, a night teeming with vampires. And me, sleeping like a baby.

It was a good plan.

I crept into the hut. That's when my plan hit the first snag. The dark was so thick I couldn't even see the others, let alone tell them apart. Although the moon was bright, I couldn't see a thing inside. I thought the blond one might be lying by the door. I raised my hand to hit him, but not before putting my other hand over his mouth. He woke up struggling, but I kept him quiet by hissing into his ear, 'The vampires are just outside.'

I felt a shiver pass through him, and then he jumped to his feet. Together we went outside.

Only then did I understand the mistake I'd made. It was Vuk Isakovič.

For a moment I was at a loss, but then I thought of something. Isakovič had unsheathed his sabre as soon as he'd spotted the red count on the ground. And I went back inside to wake the blond count. As I was leading him outside, I whispered, 'Isakovič has turned into a vampire and killed your companion. There he is, crouching over him and drinking his blood.'

The blond one didn't stop to think. He drew his sword and lunged at the Serb. Fortunately, Isakovič didn't make a sound. Quite the valiant death.

I said to the blond one, 'Don't worry, you got him straight through the heart. That's just as good as staking.'

And then I started thinking. If I killed the blond one, too, wouldn't it seem a bit fishy, what with me surviving while vampires picked off the other three? Much better for one team of guards to perish together. But how to pull it off now that we were mismatched, with me from the first watch and the blond count from the second?

Much better to have killed the blond one and left the red one alive. I looked at the red wig on the ground. I looked at the blond wig on the head. Then back at the red wig. Then back at the blond wig.

'Listen,' I said. 'No one will believe that Isakovič turned into a vampire and killed our friend in the red wig. They'll want proof. You know what the princess is like.'

He only nodded. He seemed truly frightened.

'But they might believe that *both* of them were killed by vampires,' I continued, moving my head up and down, too. I figured, if he can't be talked into it, he can at least be nodded into it.

He nodded again.

'And you and Isakovič were to be on second watch, weren't you?

It would be much better if the two of them' – I pointed at the bodies – 'had been serving guard duty together.'

'But they weren't,' he argued. That was a good sign. Arguing always means thinking. And it's always the wrong kind of thinking, which is just what I needed then.

'But if we switch the wigs around – you take the red one, and our deceased compatriot gets the blond one – then it will be the *blond* count and Vuk Isakovič who died at the hands of vampires on the second watch.'

'We can't just change wigs and be different people.'

'Oh, but you can, believe me. No one knows your name, and the only thing people remember about you is the colour of your wig.'

'What about my sword?'

'We just give *your* sword a little tug,' I said, yanking it out of Isakovič, 'and pop in *this* one – Vuk's sabre – in its place. There, now it's clear that when facing the vampires he chose to take his own life and risk eternal damnation rather than become one of the creatures himself.'

Then I picked up the red wig and handed it to the blond count, who then and there ceased to be blond. I took the blond wig and stuck it on the head of the red count, who now had a new posthumous personality. Then I sent the red count back inside the hut while I kept an eye out. I promised myself that the very next day, at the very first opportunity, I would get rid of him, too.

2

Not the real entrance. It was a crumbling side branch that led to the main channel of the aqueduct. Because it was falling to pieces, the passageway's structure was laid bare. Later, when there was nothing overhead but a barrel-vault of solid masonry, we would be unable to see a thing. The darkness would be absolute, and we would have to feel our way.

But there at the start we could see a tunnel of Roman bricks, red with patches of whitewash. Water gurgled along a square-cut channel in the floor. To me it seemed as though the jaws of some enormous creature gaped open before us. We were in a red cavern, white teeth on either side of us, walking down the middle – the tongue. Harsh noises scraped from the palate as we stumbled along, the rushing air made moaning vowels, the whitewash chittered with toothy sounds, the holes in the walls hummed and droned. And we were heading into the very centre of it all, to the place where the sounds originated, where the flow was carrying us. Led by the tongue to the city.

It was damp and slippery. We had to stoop as we went, and after some time we took to crawling rather than walking. But even crawling is hard to keep up for long.

How long? A long time. In the dark, making your way on hands and knees, you lose track of time. You only remember that the entrance is far behind you. Everything after that first moment is an hour, a day, a week, a year, a – whatever you want to call it. And the time has already gone by, it's been night and day and night again, and Saturday has been and gone, and the costume ball, and all the other things that have happened, one right after the other.

There I was, crawling along, leading the way from start to finish, because I had been the first to enter, and now it was too narrow to change places. Behind me was Novak, followed by the red count, and finally von Hausburg.

Nothing was really happening. We made our way along the tunnel, bent over, straightening up as far as the ceiling would allow, falling to our knees . . . You could hear the creaking of our backbones.

I've heard from Muslim pilgrims about the Church of the Nativity in Bethlehem. The Empress Helena had it built with massive doors. The invading Persians galloped right through those doors and into the church. But they didn't destroy it, unlike other Christian holy places, because of the image painted above the doors: three wise men dressed in traditional Persian garb. They recognized themselves and were unwilling to destroy their own image. When the Christians returned, during the Crusades, they lowered and narrowed the doors so no one could enter the church on horseback again. But that didn't stop the Turks, wielding their yataghans, from entering the church on foot. Everyone has a mother, though, and everyone is glad when a child is born. And so the Turks also bowed to the Mother of God. And made the doors even lower and narrower. Now to enter the church you must stoop, the doors have been set so low. That's what the tunnel made me think of: a long entrance into church. And whether we wanted to or not, we had to go on bended knee. To be humble all the way.

What do you say to that, my dear cousin? Are we called upon to be humble?

Oh, you're the one asking the questions, and I'm here to answer them?

If I do ask the occasional question, I'll be sure to throw in the answer as well.

Allow me to continue. We made our way without too much difficulty. True, it was a strain on our bodies, but at least our minds were free, and we weren't thinking about anything. At least I wasn't. What *can* one think about, after all, when the very next step might mean dashing one's head against the wall or slipping and breaking an arm or leg. I don't know how far we'd gone before we were faced with the first decision.

The tunnel branched off into three. Novak explained it: only one of the branches led to the city, while the other two supplied the outlying villages. He said that even if we made the wrong choice, it was nothing to worry about: we'd just come out somewhere and get our bearings, and then, if it was a wrong turning, we'd make our way back and try our luck down another branch.

'Easy for you to say,' von Hausburg shouted, his voice echoing all around us. 'You fool! It hasn't even occurred to you that this might be only the first of many junctures. The decisions will get harder and harder, the options will multiply a hundredfold and a single wrong turn will lead us out into a wasteland, into empty fields, into enemy countryside teeming with vampires. The sun may have set already for all we know, crawling around down here in the dark.'

'But there are only three lines,' said Novak stubbornly.

'And a thousand possible decisions, of which nine hundred and ninety-nine will take us down the two wrong paths. And only one . . .'

'That's life for you,' said the red count, and everyone fell silent.

There was an incessant dripping on the back of my neck, especially bothersome when I wasn't moving. I wanted to keep going, any direction at all, as long as it meant not standing still.

'Let's take the left branch,' Novak said.

'Right, let's go, even if it's the wrong one,' I said.

I was seized with a desire to run, so badly did I want to know what lay at the end. But I was hampered by tiredness and the need to stoop and could only quicken my pace to a swift walk. Novak hurried to keep up, huffing and puffing, but made no complaint. The red count was a nobleman, as was von Hausburg, and the nobility do not grumble or make a fuss. Complaining is a trait of commoners, who even make a habit of it.

We were relieved to find that the tunnel ran straight on with no more side-branches. It was somewhat narrower than the first tunnel we'd come down, and that troubled me. From experience, one knows that the minor byways are smaller in every sense. The lack of side-branches was another clear indication of the tunnel's unimportance. Just as in life, the wrong path can be recognized by an absence of difficult decisions after the first wrong turning. It all seems to go so smoothly after that. But I said nothing and simply kept going, not speaking up, just like everyone else.

And when I saw light ahead, for the first time since we'd gone underground, I knew it would turn out to be some village, not the fortress. And I was right – but the day was already fading, and night was coming on. Still, we were glad of the chance to get out and straighten up. Everyone stretched, and I even lay down in the grass to ease my aching bones. I was cold and hungry. Hungry for the very first time.

Novak reconnoitred a bit and told us that we had probably reached Mali Mokri Lug, and that we must get back into the tunnel soon, for it was nearly dark.

'As if we'll be any safer from the vampires down *there*,' von Hausburg said. Then he exclaimed, 'Water!'

'What do you mean, water?' we asked.

'Water! The vampires are attracted to water. They gather around it. In the watermill. Don't you see? We're safer out in the open.'

'The aqueduct leads to the city. Vampires can't enter the city. We know that much. If there were any vampires in the tunnels, they'd have shown up in the city by now,' Novak replied.

Von Hausburg had been out-argued, and only retorted sarcastically, 'Maybe they're as lost as we are.'

The discussion was getting us nowhere, and I turned and went back into the tunnel. After the first few steps I heard something splashing at my heels. I assumed it was Novak. Just then, a scream rang out. And, after the scream, the words *Oh God*. I turned around. Novak was already dashing outside. When I came out, I saw von Hausburg peering down at something. I raced to his side. Only then did I see that we were standing on the edge of a sheer drop. Down at the bottom of the gorge lay the shattered body of the red count. The wig lay beside the body, and blood was seeping out in every direction.

'We didn't even know we were standing on the edge,' von Hausburg gasped. 'He slipped and fell. I couldn't keep hold of him.'

'Oh God!' I said.

'Just what I said,' von Hausburg responded.

'We have to keep moving,' I decided. 'There's nothing we can do for him now.'

I stepped back into the tunnel. Behind me came Novak and von Hausburg.

3

I stepped back into the hut, somehow knowing that it would be a long night. Novak was sleeping peacefully, snoring; the new red count was tossing and turning. If any vampires came around he'd be sure to hear them. I don't know why, but being indoors made me less afraid of the vampires, as if the walls could really offer any protection. I hadn't forgotten that Radetzky met his death indoors, but that was a watermill, and this was a hut. And maybe they'd had enough by now; the corpses were piling up, and they could have their pick of the next one to become a vampire. No sense bothering with the living. I closed my eyes, but sleep wouldn't come. At one point I was in that curious state that is like a foretaste of true sleep, when you no longer know where the lights and sounds are coming from – whether from within, which is sleep, or from without, which is the real world. But soon my eyes flew open, and I was staring into the dark, more awake than ever, angry and exhausted. When I jolt awake like that I know that sleep will be a long time coming. I was lying on an ordinary bedroll on the hard ground, and I was sore from head to toe. I sat up. I didn't want to get up all the way, just to prop myself up a bit.

That's when I saw him. My first thought was that he was a vampire. But he sat calmly in the Turkish manner looking at me in surprise. As if *I* were a vampire.

I thought about jumping up and running outside, but his henchmen Isakovič and the blond count might be waiting for me, now that they'd had plenty of time to cross over to the other side. I didn't move. And he continued to stare at me with his eyes wide open.

After a while he spoke but without opening his mouth. I could hear him, although there was nothing to hear.

'So you *do* exist then?'

'Not only do I exist, I am also very, very powerful.' I spoke softly, trying to make up for being at a disadvantage.

'I was sure you were purely imaginary, but now I know you're not.' Perhaps the words were only in my mind, for the old man had not spoken aloud, had not even moved his lips as in a ventriloquist's trick.

'I don't know whether you are to be congratulated or pitied,' I said, noncommittally enough to maintain the upper hand.

'Neither do I,' he said with what struck me as modesty. 'But now that I know for sure, Isaac – now that I know, it must be for the best that you do exist.'

Why was he calling me Isaac? Ishak, he pronounced it, the Bosnian way. What nonsense the old man was coming out with, and all without opening his mouth? I made no answer, only waited for him to (not) say something else that would tell me which Isaac he thought I was. And sure enough, he didn't stop there.

'But if you are so powerful, why did you rebel?'

Why did I rebel? How should I know why Isaac rebelled? I could only explain my own reasons for rebelling. I took a closer look at the old man. Only then did I realize that he was some sort of dervish.

'Listen here, dervish,' I said. 'All acts of rebellion are the same in the end. Why did Shaitan rise up against Allah?'

He nodded. This was meant to show that he understood. 'Yes. And rebelling always makes another devil of us. We started out believing in justice and goodness and ended in evil. I know that better than anyone.'

'Pride,' I said. 'It was pride that we began in, and when we ended it was in despair . . .'

Then came the thought, as the words were leaving my mouth, that this was the man in crimson. In the guise of a dervish. The arch-vampire. Or archangel. Michael.

FIVE
The End of the Story

1

I could hear my heart beating. *He* could hear it. Was this truly the last
night? Would dawn bring with it the Day of Wrath? Michael, archangel,
servant. The humblest servant of all. I hadn't seen him for aeons.
Aeons. The last time, before all that fog outside Belgrade, I had seen
him at the beginning of the world. And now I was seeing him again,
here at the end. I was hopeless. Hopeless. I'd been so remiss, so wrong,
so foolish. I buried my face in my hands. The palms grew wet. I lowered
my hands. Looked around. He was gone. No dervish, no Michael . . .
Whoever he was, he was gone. I crawled to the door. Peeked outside.
It was dark but empty, with no one in sight. I looked back at the room
and saw only Novak and the red count. I didn't understand. Who was
he? Did he even exist? Perhaps I was . . . breaking down? Losing my
mind? I had another look around. Everything seemed real and matter-
of-fact. I had to think. Think hard. The only way out of this was by
thinking long and hard and getting it right. But nothing was coming
to mind. My head had never been emptier. I sat on the ground and
trembled. I don't know what would have become of my mind if Novak
hadn't woken up just then.

'Master, why aren't you sleeping?'

'Novak, my one and only Novak, talk to me. Tell me something,
anything.'

'What would you like to hear, master?'

'Tell me about . . . Do you remember how I was telling you about Mary Magdalene, how we arranged to meet that Sunday morning at the fountain in the garden of Gethsemane?'

'But you never finished telling me that story. You got as far as the part in the tavern when you were making plans to meet on the Sunday.'

'I didn't tell you about that Sunday?'

'No.'

'All right, let's go outside. I don't want anyone else to hear.'

We stepped outside. Novak's eyes fell immediately on Isakovič and the blond count. I suddenly remembered that I should also be surprised.

'This doesn't seem like the work of vampires,' he was saying. 'Looks more like they did each other in. Or someone else did it for them. Definitely a man, not a vampire. Not you by any chance, master?'

'Why would I do such a thing? What had they ever done to me? You know I don't like it when you accuse me of things.'

'Maybe the peasants then. It's no mystery why they'd kill Isakovič. He was bleeding them dry. He was a hundred times worse than the Austrians. The blond one would have had to go, too, because he was with Isakovič.'

'What shall we do with them?' I asked. People like it when you ask them questions. Makes them feel powerful.

Novak looked at me in surprise. 'Not a thing. We'll leave 'em right where they are. It's no more than Isakovič deserved. Tomorrow when the princess wakes up, let *her* figure something out.'

We lit the Virginia tobacco and decided it was safest not to go in a straight line, because we might easily lose our way. We agreed to go around in circles, with the hut at the centre, but far enough away to prevent anyone inside from overhearing.

During the first circle we did not speak. The second circle seemed a bit narrower, a bit closer to the hut. Still we said nothing, only puffed at our pipes. The third circle was even more narrow, I could have sworn it. The path we were following was a spiral, winding closer and closer to the hut at its centre. I couldn't say whether Novak was doing it on purpose.

'Are you going to tell me the story?' he asked at the beginning of the fourth circle.

2

All that Saturday I slept. I was so tired. I did keep waking up, but then I'd fall asleep again. I woke up for good sometime after midnight. It was Sunday already. I knew that dawn was hours away, and I tried to go back to sleep but couldn't. Naturally I was thinking about Fishmouth's promise to rise again from the dead on the third day. I had no doubt that Mary Magdalene was convinced of his resurrection and wanted me there to witness it. No, I never tried to back out of going. Didn't even cross my mind. I didn't believe in any resurrection, and I wasn't about to start believing either. I knew we'd find the tomb with the body still in it. I just wanted Mary to see it, too. Because once she'd understood that all of Fishmouth's stories were nothing but hot air, that he was gone and wasn't coming back, and that I was there and always would be, then she'd come back to me . . .

'But weren't you the one who left her?'

'Me? Leave her? She was the one who left. That's the truth. But it doesn't matter now who left, don't you see?'

I got through those early hours as best as I could, thinking heavy thoughts, tossing and turning, taking sips of water. In the end I got out of bed. Earlier than I needed to. I paced the room. I couldn't very well go out and wander the streets of Jerusalem yet. I clearly wasn't drunk, and only drunks and whores aroused no suspicions at that hour among the Roman patrols. Those hours seemed to last longer than Christianity itself would afterwards. All the priests and churches in the world pale in comparison to that kind of *if*.

'But didn't you just say you were sure there'd be no resurrection?'

'Quiet, foolish servant. I don't know what I'm saying at this ungodly hour. Of course I was sure. I'm always sure. Now you've gone and interrupted me. Where was I?'

The first ray of sunlight fell into my room. I waited a bit longer so I wouldn't be out on the streets before anyone else. And then I finally stepped outside. I'd never been up and about the city at such an early hour. I'd never met the people I met that morning. Poor souls whose troubles drove them out of bed while others slept on. Frail, thin women making their way to the well, messengers galloping in from far-off places, the slaves of especially wicked masters already casting out the rubbish – as if the day's first task was to separate good from bad – and the poor who pounced on that same rubbish, hoping to find something good among all that badness, and the soldiers of the day's first watch ... I could see the whole world of mankind. I wonder, did anyone else see it besides me?

At the fountain, people were already waiting. Mostly women. They were shivering; mornings are chilly in Jerusalem except at the very height of summer. Jerusalem is built on the hilltops, on high. They filled their jars and waterskins, the fountain gushed, the line of people grew longer and longer. I couldn't see Mary Magdalene. She was often late.

I bounced up and down to keep warm, even though I was wearing better and thicker clothes than anyone else. The women didn't even look at me; they waited patiently, stepped up to the fountain when it was their turn, filled their containers and left. It occurred to me that she might not come at all. That would be the easy way out, instead of having me as a witness to her disappointment. It's human nature not to face up to things. I understood her completely. The Sanhedrin had sealed the tomb with such a stone that half a cohort wouldn't be able to budge it, let alone that little band of starveling disciples scraping by on goodwill and handouts. And even if they could, Mary Magdalene wasn't the woman to go along with any kind of deception. If the apostles somehow did manage to move the stone and steal the body she'd be the first to repudiate them.

'Let's go!' It was her voice. So she had come after all. There were two other women with her. They were carrying jars and strips of linen.

I sniffed the air. Myrrh and spices. So they'd come to wash and embalm the body. Even *they* didn't believe in the resurrection. We set off. Mary led the way, the two women came after and I brought up the rear. Every once in a while I turned around, suspecting that Peter and the others might be following us. But there was no one.

We didn't head straight towards Golgotha. We took the long way round. It seemed as though Mary Magdalene wanted to circle back on her tracks to throw someone off. Slowly but surely the circles were getting narrower and narrower. It was starting to annoy me. I was sure there was no one after us. If anyone were lying in wait it could only be at the top. And if the ambush was going to be at the grave it made no sense for us to be going around in circles. The spiral was narrowing, and up and up we went. The morning was wearing on, and it was getting warmer. At one point I caught sight of the tomb and the stone blocking its entrance. It was enormous. Verily. We went past it, Mary now walking so quickly that I had to break into a run to keep up.

The next time around, as soon as the tomb was in sight, Mary interrupted her roundabout route and charged directly uphill. I saw no one else. It was just the four of us, all alone. At the very top of the hill gleamed three bare crosses. The tomb wasn't far from them, perhaps a hundred paces or so.

The women with the myrrh stopped in their tracks. So did I but without knowing why. I wanted to ask Mary, but my voice failed. That's when I saw him.

He was in white, one wing touching the ground, the other pointing up almost as if in flight. In his right hand he held a staff. With his left hand he was pointing to the right. At the tomb.

Only then did I notice: the stone had been rolled back. Not much, but enough to fit a body through. Mary went right in. Without stopping to think. After her, with some hesitation, went the other two women. I stayed put. I looked at the angel. He looked at me. Then he smiled, hopped down from the rock he'd been sitting on and simply strode off. I kept him in sight as long as I could, and when his wing finally disappeared behind an outcropping I turned my attention back to the stone at the mouth of the tomb.

Mary was peering out. She beckoned me to come closer. I shook my head. She stepped out and came to me.

'He has risen,' she said.

'He's been snatched,' I replied.

'What about the angel?'

'What about him? That was no angel. That was one of the apostles in disguise. Just some goose feathers stuck on. I watched him walk away. Why wouldn't he fly off if he's got the wings for it?'

'Now do you get it, Novak? The Resurrection was nothing but a hoax, plain and simple. Everyone was in on it. A costume ball for superstitious halfwits. Fishmouth came dressed as the Son of God. An apostle came as an angel. Mary came as the woman who had loved me . . . Now do you get it?'

We were in the seventh circle now, and the hut was only thirty paces away.

'Shall we go back inside?' Novak said.

'Yes, let's. I've finished my story anyway. I've nothing left to tell you. That's the end.'

3

We went back into the hut. I lay down and fell right asleep. The bracing air must have gone to my head. And the walk. I didn't open my eyes again until morning, when they came to tell me that Isakovič and the blond count were dead. We hurried to get ready. There was no explanation. Everyone must have had enough.

It was time to return to Belgrade, the white city, the dark place where it might all come to an end. I didn't want it to be over. I didn't long for anything that hadn't actually happened. There was me, and there was them; rather, there was me, and there was the other. Too many faces, so many masks, and all of them merging into one. And all of the decisions were really but one decision: them or me, the other or me. Charles Kinbote says somewhere that mutability is of the Devil, while unchanging sameness is of God.

Novak saddled the horses, and we started back. No one asked any questions or had anything to say. Everyone thought the red count was the red count; perhaps he thought so himself.

We rode for more than an hour. I wasn't sure we were going the right way. We seemed to be taking the long way round, bypassing unseen obstacles, wandering down paths that didn't lead to the city. More than once I began to doubt we'd ever make it back to safety behind the gates. It wasn't the gates themselves I cared about so much. I wanted to cross the Danube and the Sava and keep on going.

After we'd climbed the umpteenth hill and come to a clearing I looked out and saw the city. It was Belgrade, no doubt about it. There's no other big town like it in all of Serbia. Under the thick chimney-smoke and the dust from its winding streets, it made a dark spot in the broad daylight. It wasn't hard to recognize from afar. Once inside it looked like any other overgrown backwater in the East, with the thinnest veneer of Europe. Impossible to tell it apart from all the others. From outside, of course, it could never be mistaken for Paris, for London, let alone for one of those newfangled cities in America with their grid-like streets. But by a trick of the eye I might think I was looking at Jerusalem. Built on hills, all its highways and byways tangled together and set on land that in other cities would have fallen to the newest and poorest arrivals. Belgrade was east and south, those two less-desirable corners of the world (for it stayed on its own side of the rivers, and anyone inside was the poorer for it).

We dug in our spurs, although the horses were picking their way carefully down the last hill. As soon as they felt level ground under their hooves they began galloping towards the city. I looked back over my shoulder. Not a living soul in sight. Only the hill.

The guard tower was coming into view. The sentries observed us expressionlessly. As soon as they recognized Maria Augusta, they ran to open the gates.

The way lay open before us, and I galloped in at full speed. Behind me came the princess, Novak and the red count. Now we were approaching the Prince-Eugene Line. I looked back over my shoulder. The guards were closing the gates with quick, sure movements.

There was no one behind us. The guards were hurrying because of their training not because of any urgency.

I cracked the whip. Filthy men and women leaped out of our way. Again and again I looked back over my shoulder. Woe to him who knows four things – up, down, backwards, forward. Too far forward, yes. But just a little forward, and there was the outermost city gate. The moat was deepening. The fortifications seemed stronger now than when we'd first left the city. Only a few dozen yards to the Prince-Eugene Line. The line the vampires wouldn't cross. The princess was waving ahead, clever thing. And sure enough, the sentries had seen her.

The wooden drawbridge was coming down as we galloped towards it. It was creaking and groaning. I didn't wait for it to touch the ground, but goaded my horse to jump. We pounded across and swept through the armoured gates. They were barely open, but still wide enough for horse and rider to pass through. We flew inside. I looked back. The drawbridge was being raised on its thick chains – faster than it had been lowered, I thought. Two guards on each side were pushing the massive inner gates shut. I dug the spurs in deep. I heard the drawbridge thud into place against the wall.

I knew I was saved.

So you think it makes me happy to finish a story? Ha! I feel just like Old What's-His-Name on the first Sunday. For I created this world. Even John Damascene says so, and he's a saint. This whole world is mine. My lie. Apart from me it doesn't exist. I am the good storyteller who made it up and said what it looked like – this horse, the reins, the hand that holds them. And the ramparts behind and the city ahead. And the princess and her prince and even a frog if needs be . . .

I turned around once more.

The gates swung shut behind me.

SIX
The Creation of the World

1

I couldn't spare a thought for the red count. Simply couldn't. I had to keep going, to get back to the city. And the city was only a few right decisions away. At least now we had identified one of the wrong turns. I assumed it was already night outside, but this made no difference to us, to me, since we couldn't see a thing in the tunnels anyway. The ceiling was lower again. I crawled along, my hands and arms in pain. My fingers were sticky with blood. My eyes ached from staring into the total darkness. I should have kept them shut, but I couldn't – not while I was still making my way forward on hands and knees. I feared I would fall asleep if I closed my eyes. And it's no good going about with one's eyes shut, no matter how thick the darkness.

No one spoke. We were all too exhausted. Oh, how I hated water just then! We would come to another juncture, grope at it in the dark, and without consulting the others I would say which way to go: left or right, and sometimes straight ahead if we were faced with three choices. But we rarely were. I was thinking how easily we might lose our way. One wrong turn, I knew, and we'd find ourselves down another dead end. We might spend our entire lives down in those tunnels, worming our silent way, each time making just one wrong choice. But somewhere deep inside I felt – I *just knew* – that it would not be so. Hadn't the angel shown us the way? Would an angel really point us to a labyrinth with no way out? Why, that would be as if the

Good Lord had created us only for endless wandering, for nothing but suffering and falsehood.

Pardon?

You know I'm hard of hearing, cousin. You'll have to speak up.

I don't how long we were at it. Hours, no doubt. There was no way to keep track of time, for nothing was actually happening. And then Novak said he couldn't go on, that we must stop and rest. I was grateful to him for that. My conscience could remain clear while my body rested. I sat with my back against the tunnel wall and extended my legs across the channel in the floor. In this position I was still cramped and bent, my legs aching, but I couldn't lie flat without rubbing against the sharp edges of the channel. And yet, despite the discomfort, I fell asleep almost at once. As did Novak and von Hausburg, I believe.

I slept heavily, a dead sleep. Not once did I open my eyes, either of my own accord or at any disturbance. No dreams came to me. I couldn't say how long I slept. A long time, I think.

I was awakened by the pain of a headache. From the damp, the stale air, the exertion, from everything that had been happening over the previous days. Every last bone and muscle was aching and throbbing. My limbs were so stiff that for a moment I feared I'd never take another step.

Of course, I had no way of knowing whether it was still night or whether Sunday morning had arrived. Actually, I *do* remember – quite well as a matter of fact. It was Sunday. I think you remember, too, because that was the day, early in the morning, when you came from Vienna to Belgrade. My, how many people arrived that day in the city. How many things happened.

I had trouble waking Novak and von Hausburg. They were dead to the world. No, no, you're mistaken. Novak was still alive then. Although I could barely get him to open his eyes. Von Hausburg slept more lightly than his servant. We took the time to warm up properly before setting off again.

We were crawling and crawling down one long tunnel now. There were no junctions. No decisions to make. Everything was simple again.

Novak kept saying that we must finally be in the main conduit and heading directly for the fortress. I was convinced. And I began to relax. To let my thoughts unwind. And just as I was successfully forming the first happy thought I'd had since going underground, I felt the tunnel branch in two. I wanted to scream, but merely said 'Fork'.

Novak crawled up beside me, saying he wanted to check.

'The left-hand tunnel slopes down. The right-hand tunnel rises,' he said.

'What does that mean?' I asked.

'Oh, what does *he* know,' von Hausburg said.

Novak continued. 'I think this is the last fork in the tunnel. If we go down, we'll end up in . . .'

'Hell,' von Hausburg interrupted.

'The lower tunnel,' Novak went on, 'carries water to the cistern. If we go this way, we'll come to a chamber below water level at the base of the spiral stairs, the bottom of the cistern. Then we'll have to take the stairs to come back up. We'd better . . .' he stopped for a moment. 'Do you hear that?'

'What?' von Hausburg and I asked at the same time. 'Shh, shh. Now, can you hear it?'

I listened. Nothing but the running water and our own breathing.

'I don't hear anything,' von Hausburg whispered.

And then I heard it. Distant voices. More of a rumbling. But many voices. And getting louder.

'Vampires!' cried Novak.

'Maybe . . .' Von Hausburg's voice trembled. 'Maybe not. It could be . . . the refugees from Niš. Why, sure. Just listen. There's so many of them. There couldn't be *that* many vampires. It must be the refugees. Schmettau said they'd be arriving today.'

'I don't know,' I said. 'We've got to keep moving. Head right.'

There were more and more voices. And they were coming closer and closer. Novak was ahead of me, and judging by the scrabbling sounds he was moving fast. I stuck up my hand and felt air, and with relief I realized that the tunnel was now high enough to allow us to walk. I'd still have to keep my head down, but at least I was on my feet and not my knees. Not only could I walk I could run. And run I did – bent over, my back straining with every step, but still running. Whether from the noise we made as we ran, or from the distance we were putting between us, the voices were harder to hear.

Suddenly I saw light ahead. It was weak and far off, but it was still light. The light of day, I hoped. We were nearly out. We stopped. Listened. Not a sound. Again we broke into a run. Von Hausburg slipped and fell, and Novak and I came back to help him up. He'd cut the palm of his hand, shielding his face from the sharp edges of the channel.

'A fine time to trip and fall, master, now that we're in the light.'

'You imbecile!' cried von Hausburg irritably. 'Everyone gets careless in the light. Most accidents happen close to home. Statistics show.'

Isn't that so, dear cousin?

After von Hausburg's fall there was no more running. Still stooping, we moved along at a normal pace. It wasn't exactly a leisurely stroll, more like the steps of those who know where they're going and where they'll end up. And the light *was* getting stronger all the time. It was strong and clear. Daylight. There was a gate of bars in our way. Novak tore it right off its rusty hinges.

I went first as we stepped outside. It was so glaringly bright that I had to squint.

2

As soon as I opened my eyes again I saw Alexander. He was standing only a few hundred feet away. Astonished.

'Maria Augusta!' he cried.

I flew into his arms. He held me tight.

'*Bist du ein Vampir?*' he whispered into my ear. Was I a vampire?

The first thing I noticed was that he had addressed me with the intimate *Du*. I made no answer. I knew what I must look like, bleeding in several places, covered in cuts and bruises. It was a wonder he'd recognized me in that filthy, tattered state. But he *had* recognized me. It was at that point that he noticed Novak and von Hausburg. Still holding me, he shouted, 'Seize them!'

Only then did I notice all the soldiers. Surrounding us. But none of them moved to obey Alexander's order. They merely stood there, glowering and full of menace, aiming their muskets. Von Hausburg spoke.

'Wait! We're not vampires. We're just like you. Look at us. Do we *look* like vampires?'

The soldiers looked and looked – not that it would do them much good, for they had never seen vampires before. I said as much.

Alexander smiled, then suddenly grew serious. 'They're down there!'

'Where?' I asked.

'In the cistern.'

'They've entered the *city*?' von Hausburg said, enunciating each syllable. 'Across the Prince-Eugene line?'

'Across every line in their path,' my husband said, jabbing his finger at Novak and von Hausburg. 'You two! If you've managed to survive the vampires this long, then you'll manage yet. It's you they're looking for. And it's you we're going to give them.'

'But,' I said. 'How can you be sure it's not me they're looking for?' I had also begun to address him in the familiar form. *Du*, Alexander.

'Because I know. They're after von Hausburg. Who else? And that's who they're going to get, with his servant besides.'

The soldiers prodded von Hausburg and Novak into motion. We'd all been standing at the mouth of the tunnel. To the right was the Vizier's Fountain, which is built into the north wall of the Upper Town. From there it was only a few dozen steps to the cistern, or rather the structure covering it. Von Hausburg and Novak moved slowly, the soldiers at their heels. Alexander and I followed. At one point von Hausburg stopped and turned around. He looked into my eyes. In this position he remained until the soldiers forced him on towards the cistern. I saw that he was carrying the small pistol at his waist, but he and I both knew that the powder was wet. And that he wouldn't have time to reload it. The only question was whether he preferred to die right then, in the light of the sun, looking out over the place where the Sava meets the Danube, or to face the vampires down below.

They had reached the entrance to the cistern. The soldiers made quick work of opening the doors, but von Hausburg and Novak held back. The soldiers pushed them forward with the butts of their muskets. I slipped out of Alexander's embrace.

'I'm going with them!'

'No!' cried my husband. 'No!'

'I am,' I said again. 'That's how we came, and that's how we'll go. An angel . . . An angel showed us the way. No evil can come of it.'

'An angel? You don't know what you're doing. What angel? Angels have never saved anyone from death. This is no time to start believing.'

'You don't understand. If I don't go down there I'll never be able to live with myself. This is my chance, I know it. My chance. It's not every day an angel comes along. And I've already seen a vampire. He was . . . His face was just like anyone else's. A face . . .'

Alexander looked at me, perplexed. The soldiers began to shout that the cistern doors must be secured. I pushed him away at last and followed von Hausburg and Novak inside. Behind me the doors slammed shut.

Torchlight. And the sound of voices. Thousands of voices. Louder and louder. We looked at each other. Von Hausburg drew his pistol.

'Your powder is damp,' I said, but he only glanced at me and gripped the pistol more tightly.

Novak took my arm. 'Princess, I'll go. You stay here. I'll go down. Maybe that will be enough for them.'

'Can't you hear them? There are thousands of them. Thousands. They haven't come by the thousands for just one. This is why I'm here. To go down there. Not to wait but to face it directly.'

'The master stays,' said Novak.

'Naturally. I never leave the high ground. You two go right ahead. I don't mind a bit.'

'Can you smell the brimstone?' I asked, imagining the stench of Hell wafting up towards us.

'Never mind the sulphur,' said Novak. 'Cisterns always smell a bit off.'

'That's right,' said von Hausburg, pressing his back against the doors. The pistol was at his heart. 'Novak, you're free to go. I've finished the story I had to tell. There's nothing left to hear. As for you, Princess, you've made your choice. Off you go.'

There was no more discussion. We crossed to a low wooden door that led to a stairwell. On the opposite side was a matching door and another set of stairs. One was meant for going down and the other for coming back up. They were only used when the water-screw was not working. The system was in good repair at the time, although no water was being drawn. I told Novak it would be best to split up, one to each stairwell, because if we both went the same way, we might go right past the vampires. I also said that I would take the up-staircase. I expected the vampires to be coming that way. That's why I wanted to go by myself to head them off. Novak didn't object; my reasons probably hadn't even occurred to him. Or else he didn't know what the different stairs were for. He turned to go, and I heard his steps echoing as he skirted the top edge of the cistern. I heard his door creaking open.

The voices were getting louder and louder. Merging into one great voice. One language. I couldn't understand the words – not just because it would have been Serbian but because every voice was saying something different, yet all in unison. Like the finest church choirs, the ones I'd heard at Orthodox churches during the high holy days: I'd been able to pick out each individual voice, and yet the chant as a whole made a perfect harmony.

I opened my door. I had to bend low to pass through it. The steps were slippery from the damp. The smell of sulphur was gone. Slowly I began to climb down. Painfully. It took as much effort as going up. After every few steps I would stop to rest, breathe deeply and gather my strength. Fortunately, there was quite enough light.

Out there was the angel who had pointed his jewel-bedecked finger at the entrance to the aqueduct. Out there was my husband who had taken me in his arms. Embraced me and asked me whether I had turned into a vampire. He hadn't run away. Hadn't pretended not to know me. Not to see me.

The voices were ringing in my head. I wanted to sing something, anything, as loud as I could, till I could hear only myself. So I'd know I was there, and that I could out-sing them all.

The steps spiralled around and around. One turn after another. The way down was becoming harder and harder. I felt the pain in every step, my calves, my thighs. I was short of breath. Now as I rested I gulped great mouthfuls of air, as if it were running out.

I thought I'd never reach the bottom. It felt like hours. I was soaked with sweat, my ears rang with the sound of the choir down below. It was as loud as someone shouting in your ear.

And then there were no more turns. No more steps. I looked through a slit in the wall and saw the surface of the water. I had arrived. Slowly I went a few steps forward. I saw an open space ahead. The voices were coming from there. I entered.

The space was immense. Beyond any I had ever seen. Its walls stretched so far on every side that they were lost to sight. It was full. Full of people. Or vampires. And all speaking at the same time. There was Vuk Isakovič. I spotted him at once. And there beside him was himself again, only much older. Even so, I knew him. Several feet away from him stood Sava Savanović. The voices grew so loud that I could no longer hear them. A perfect silence reigned.

From out of the many stepped one figure. I had never seen his face before. Nor would I ever see it again. From his shoulders hung a robe of royal crimson-purple.

SEVEN
The Secret Chapter

What are you saying? I can't hear you!

Oh, I owe you a story. The one about art. From the Chinese feast. And you want to hear it. It can't wait? Right now?

All right then.

Now, I can't take any credit for this story, even though I did tell it at the time. I heard from it someone else, you see.

Yes. At the costume ball. Told by someone dressed up as the Devil. My husband had been asking something, I don't remember what, or perhaps I didn't hear. And the Devil began to speak. What he said is what I repeated over lunch, trying to get the words just right.

He spoke as if he truly were the Devil and had taken part in the events he was describing. It was the best disguise at the ball. Because a disguise isn't a matter of what you're wearing, it's the story you tell.

And here's what he and I said, as follows:

'Do you know what art is? And the difference between art and the real world? I thought it up. Created it. No, I didn't say "Let there be art" – that's not the way I work. It was on the seventh day when he was resting. Resting from what? Really, I ask you, from what? For six days he spoke, let there be this, let there be that, tiring himself out. By the way, lest I forget: *I* was the first thing he spoke. Created. Because the first thing he said was "Let there be light", and there I was. For I am Lucifer, the light-bearer. And, do you know, the other angels could never forgive me for that. Especially Michael.

'So, it was the seventh day, and he was resting, and he called all the angels together and told us each to paint a picture, and once we'd finished he would choose the most beautiful one of all. And we set to work. I knew what I was going to make. True, at the very beginning it wasn't *quite* clear in my mind, but as the work progressed I understood it more and more.

'From time to time I'd look up from my work and steal a glance in his direction, at the ill-tempered old man with the glowering brow. He sat on his throne of granite, resting his chin in his hand, lost in thought, weary. Left eye blue, right eye brown. I wondered whether he regretted creating it all, whether he was having second thoughts and would he rather have everything the way it was before, as nothing? After being by himself for so long – only he knew how long – was he like any other old man who lives alone, losing his temper with noisy children, looking back wistfully on the peace and quiet he once knew? What was it he wanted to say to the rest of us? Let there *not* be any of you? Or, with a mocking smile, Oh, just let it be. I'm sure that afterwards, once the seventh day had ended, he was often sorry – although a bruised reed he would not break, as they say. Yes, that bearded old man we could never live up to – I'm sure he was sorry ever after.

'He had said, "Paint the world for me", and that's what we were doing. And it wouldn't be like me not to have a peek at what the other angels were doing. You should have seen the hamfisted nonsense Uriel was turning out. What a mess! Pure pandering to the audience. He'd depicted him as ostensibly happy upon his throne, a hundred times bigger than the rest of us. You men and women were the size of ants, while we angels with our wings could have passed for houseflies. There was no night in the picture, no seas.

'I also saw what some of the others were painting. They were doing *such* a meticulous job. Everything was exactly as it really is, and you could hardly tell the image apart from the real thing. I considered this another form of pandering.

'Unfortunately, Michael was too far away for me to see what he was up to. I thought and thought, trying to come up with an excuse to leave my work and casually saunter past. I couldn't think of anything. I was probably too wrapped up in the task at hand.

'The sweat ran as I worked. I put my head to one side. Liked what I saw. Or bit my lip. Retouched. Admired. Reconsidered. Rubbed out. I was creating from fog and darkness, feeling my way along. It was becoming clearer and clearer to me.

'At the very bottom I put the seas . . .'

'Were you using bamboo ink on silk?' whispered Joan of Arc.

'Was I *what*? On *silk*? And with bamboo ink no less.' He chortled. 'You haven't understood. My materials . . . Well, you'll see.

'So, down at the bottom are the never-ending waves of the sea and the coasts above them. On the water there's a ship, broken in two by the force of the waves. The sailors leap from the deck as it sinks. There are only a few rafts to cling to, but some reach the shore, and the shores are all different: from stretches of sand that slope gently down to the water's edge to jagged cliffs that end like certain mortal lives, plunging into the raging foam at the bottom of the picture. I've thought of everything. I've put in palm trees and cypresses and bushes growing from the rocks, the sweet smell of vineyards and stunted olive trees. Goats and donkeys and human limbs browned by the sun, and women biding their time. The picture rises to hills with plum groves and herds of swine. Villages are dotted here and there, people whistle, night falls. The moon and the morning star keep watch and see eye to eye. In a fair valley, extending part-way up the hills, the first city can be seen. Its walls are high and thick, messengers knock at its gates. Inside the walls, all is movement: the barking of dogs can be heard and the hammering of blacksmiths. In the air, the fragrance of sweetmeats, the stench of slops and swill. The streets are paved with cobblestones, carriages creak past. Children are at their games behind the houses. And no one sees the army approaching from the south, marching swiftly to the sound of fife and drum. But the army is still far off, somewhere in the valley between the high mountains. In another city sits a woman, fanning herself in the heat of the day. On her fan I've drawn everything I've already drawn. Another world just like the first, but immeasurably smaller and utterly false. *That's* the one I painted with bamboo ink on silk. A carriage passes a school where children are playing during breaktime. Stalks of wheat peer in as the carriage goes by. It's summertime and the living is easy, the cotton is high in the fields. The fish are jumping in the streams, and the serpent wends its way among the tall grass, ready to strike at any treading heel. Its eyes are green as emeralds, its scales smooth and lustrous. Not far off, a city is under siege. The army encamped outside its gates is in disarray, its fair-haired hero refusing to fight – although he'll change his mind when his comrade-at-arms and lover is killed. From there a man will make his way home, after a long journey, only to encounter his own wife's suitors. She weaves the world the way I made it, but every morning she undoes her work and with it goes the world. That world is also false, because it is made of wool. And because it can be destroyed. Far from where she sits at her loom I send great numbers on a journey. I trace the way ahead of them, the royal road that yearns for the horizon. Others struggle over mountains and through valleys, far from the cities of men, their destination uncharted on any map.

'Again I wanted to see what Michael was up to. I craned my neck, ambled about a bit, but I couldn't get close enough to see his handiwork.

'I turned my attention back to what I was doing. Solitude was standing beside the window; the woman came in to find it waiting for her. Not far from there a young man was making oil paintings – oil, you see, *not* bamboo ink – of Flemish masters, better than the ones in Europe. Never his own paintings, only the work of others. I sent a boy into Egypt to learn the tricks and illusions of sorcerers, to heal lepers in the marketplace with enchanted waters. He crossed the Sinai and came to Alexandria. There they taught him the secrets of the carpenter's trade. I sent for him again, but he never came back. I gave the king a lyre, and he broke out in song. I taught him major and minor, halleluia, halleluia, halleluia. I put in men and women who meet and know each other and who also go their separate ways like strangers at the crossroads. I put in the crossroads, too. Next came the peaks. I adorned them with pines and firs and put in monks with shaven heads and told them to believe in yin and yang. I never drew good and evil, not ever. That was added later by someone else. I only gave them red robes or yellow robes and sweeping vistas from the mountaintops. Silk scrolls. Brush tips dipped in bamboo ink. On the most forbidding cliff faces I set impregnable cities. The watchmen were on the lookout night and day. Waiting. The invading armies never came. No one ever came. High above their helmeted heads flew eagles, their wings barely moving, carried aloft on currents of air. Winds blowing from the four corners of the world – I painted them, too, in transparent colours. At the windswept heights I made bare mountaintops. Crystal streams bathing the rocks and a path winding to the summit. Wide enough for only one traveller and paved with yellow bricks. It led directly to the sky, for above the mountains I put the sky – blue here, black there, with sparkling points of white. And I hung the sun and allowed the moon to wax and wane and made the morning star to be first and last.

'Again I tried to see Michael's work. But again without success. And then the tired old man rose slowly to his feet. It was time, he muttered. His mood was dark, and I had to hurry to finish. I started making mistakes. My hand was trembling. Nostrils pinched. Eyes watering. Mouth dry. If only there'd been no end to the time I had, I could have made a perfect picture.

'I was adding details now. Strewing the scent of lavender across the open fields. Launching sailing ships across the grey oceans. The merchants aboard them travelled swiftly from land to land. In one village I put three brothers together, promising the fourth and youngest brother the very best of everything. In the end I put them in a courtroom, with judges dressed in black. I dug tunnels for water and put people in them. And princesses and dragons. Here and there I put stout-hearted heroes with finely tempered swords and poured them goblets of wine to quaff with their paramours. In other places I drew tracks on beds of crushed stone and sent locomotives chuffing down the undeviating parallel lines. As it arrives, its shrill whistle fills the winter air and the ears of the remaining passengers. And I made the grass gleam with frost and dew. I sowed tomatoes in tidy gardens.

'He said, "Enough. I would see."

'We all turned our pictures towards him. That's when I saw Michael's. It was blank. There was nothing on it. I tried to catch his eye, but he didn't deign to notice.

'The old man went slowly, not because he was paying close attention but because he could move no faster, and as he went he looked, listened, sniffed, chewed, drank. When he reached Michael's picture he stood for a long time. Saying nothing. Then he went around a bit more quickly, taking in the other angels and their creations along the way. From time to time he'd murmur something, nothing that made much sense, more like a word or two as he took a breath or cleared his throat. When he finally reached me, I stood poised between the most exalted satisfaction and the most profound despair. There was nothing more godlike than bringing something into existence, nothing more diabolical than casting it away. Aeons passed, the universe spinning and falling back in upon itself. When at last he raised his head, all the cosmos had contracted to the size of my fist.

'"I find favour with Michael's work."

'"What?" I hissed. "If it be thus, I go my way."

'And hurtling through the cloudless sky I went. When I landed, it was on the narrow road of yellow bricks. I made my way along the bare hilltops towards the first fortified cities. The monks in their yellow robes made no greeting as I passed. I looked around me, smelled the air. Listened. What's that line about the angel being new to the world and not seeing it with the world's eyes? And the poet tells the angel to sing the praises of the world, to speak of things the world knows not and to strike it dumb with amazement.

'Down and down I made my way. All around me mortal creatures were breathing their last, their death rattles rising heavenwards along the royal road.'

SIX
The Creation of the World
(continued)

3

Now back to the cistern, all right?

The man in crimson began to speak, but I heard no voice. At least not in the usual sense. I could hear him in my mind not outside it. And I wasn't out of my mind, no matter what you may be thinking. What language? Sorry? What language was he *speaking*? Well, I couldn't really say. I happened to hear it as German. But I think that Novak would have heard it as Serbian if he'd had the chance. *You* might very well have thought it was Latin.

'We bid you welcome,' he was saying.

'Are you a vampire?' I asked, surprised not to hear my own voice.

'What's in a name?' he countered.

'What do you want from us?'

'What do *we* want? But you're the one who's come to us, dear Princess. We don't go looking for people; they come to us. Not everyone, of course, only the best, the ones who have the courage and the skill.'

'You've killed so many people!'

'No, Princess, not a single one. Doctor Radetzky was murdered by the Serb who later took a stake, as you saw, and drove it through our friend Sava Savanović. The baron died as he did, as you yourself saw. The blond count died at the hands of von Hausburg, and Vuk Isakovič was run through by the red count, who in turn was pushed to his death by von Hausburg.'

'Dear God! But . . . what about Wittgenau?'

'Who?' The man in crimson seemed genuinely surprised.

He turned towards the others and spoke to them, but I couldn't make out their words in my mind. From their facial expressions the discussion seemed quite animated. I stood there and waited, limbs still stiff from my recent exertions, but self-assured. Watching them. There was a familiar face, an old woman dressed in beautiful raiments, her shoulders thrown back. She was strong, not stooped with age or weariness. Although she was standing far away among the vampires, I felt she was looking back at me. She regarded me sadly, and I thought I saw tears in her eyes. That's when I realized – it was myself. Much older. As you see me now. I wanted to cry out, but no sound would come. Soon she was lost to sight among the other vampires, and I felt a wave of relief. Seeing with one's own eyes is always more painful than just knowing.

Once he had consulted the others, the man in crimson turned towards me again.

'You must mean Wittgenstein.' The words stopped for a moment. 'He simply had to go, there was no other way.' He made a gesture. 'He was against us, hated us. He would say, *The world is not the totality of things but of facts.* You don't really think we could allow language to be greater than the actual world? To allow anyone at all to be God except God Himself?' The others were nodding in agreement as he spoke. 'And he came after us, but he came the wrong way. Here's what he did, unlike you: he left the city then made his way back along a tunnel from the outside.' He smiled, showing all his teeth. 'I know that you also went out, but you were wise enough to come back to Belgrade before coming down here, through the cistern, on the inside. That's the right way.'

'Do you mean to say you've been in the city all along?'

'In the city, most assuredly. I was even at the ball and had the pleasure of speaking to you.' He bowed.

'What's to become of me now?' I asked.

'Ah, dear Princess, for you this is only the beginning . . .' And with the word *beginning* still in me, I was struck blind by a great light. When

I was able to see again, the vampires were gone. Every last one of them, gone. Nothing remained but the endless reaches of that underground space, which seemed even greater now that it was empty.

Only then did I see that the walls were not bare but decked with the occasional halberd in that narrow-bladed Saxon style of Johann Georg I. There were also some tufted maces lying about, and some hussar sabres, and a pickaxe, nearly a dozen daggers, five or six rapiers, a two-handed broadsword that even Hercules would find cumbersome, a pair of yataghans, three katana, a set of Scottish flintlock pistols and one otherworldly Chinese landscape, on silk.

For a long time I stood taking it all in, still astonished at the vastness. I knew the vampires would never return. Slowly I turned and left. The damp air of the cistern hit me full in the face, and I had to stop for a moment. I can't tell you why, but some invisible power compelled me to raise my hand to my nostrils and make sure it didn't smell of brimstone. I detected nothing out of the ordinary.

I decided to take the down staircase, because that's where Novak was sure to be. I was worried he might have slipped on the damp steps and fallen. I moved quickly, as if flying. As if I weren't climbing at all, but running down the easiest flight of steps in the world. Just past the third turning I came upon Novak. He was struggling along, his right leg bleeding.

'Princess! Is everything all right now?'

'Don't worry, Novak. Everything's all right. You must come and see them, too. Don't be afraid, they're not evil. Here, just a few more steps to go. Easy does it.' I took his hand as we went.

Suddenly he pulled back.

'I don't think I want to, really.'

'There's nothing to be afraid of. Trust me.'

At the last turning he stopped again and looked me in the eye. I was not accustomed to such directness from servants.

'That's an order!' I said sternly.

Slowly we made our way to the very bottom. What I saw there took me by surprise. Only a short while ago the entrance had been completely unobstructed – yet now the way was blocked by a wooden door. I looked around to make sure, but there was nothing else there. Novak didn't know what I had seen, and he went to the door and tried to open it. It was locked.

He shook his head, as if he'd been expecting this to happen, yet no one would take his word for it.

'Princess, do you know what this is?'

'Yes, that's where the vampires were.'

'From what I hear this is the chamber where your husband keeps the gold he got from the Turks for his betrayal. Begging your pardon, but that's what I've heard. Count Wittgenau came to investigate. He found out, and your husband, or someone else from the court, paid some Serbian hajduks to kill him.'

'But what about the vampires?' I asked.

'The vampires are only make-believe. Nothing but a story. Listen now, it's time to go back up. And up there is my master, waiting. He's convinced that the vampires exist. When we come back alive he'll think we've turned into vampires, too. You know he's got a pistol . . .'

'The powder is damp.'

'So it is. But he's also got a dagger. First he'll try to shoot, and then he'll come at us with the knife. I'll make the first move. You stay behind me where it's safer. While he and I are going at it, you take this and . . .'

He picked up a stone that had fallen from the masonry and handed it to me.

'Don't go easy on him.'

We started up the down-staircase. Again I found myself able to run without effort, but I had to stop and wait for Novak to catch up. His leg was in pain, but still I hurried him along. I didn't want to remain in the cistern any longer than necessary. I felt it would not be good to spend too much time down below.

The ascent was quicker than the descent. A few steps from the top Novak stopped me and drew me to him. Again he looked into my eyes then nodded. I kissed his brow. Then he went ahead of me and pushed the door open with a mighty heave.

I was right behind him. Von Hausburg tried to fire, then threw his pistol aside and drew the dagger from his boot. He lunged at us with the knife. Novak wasn't fast enough. I heard the blade plunging into him. Carrying the stone, I stepped around Novak and struck von Hausburg in the head. He collapsed. I kneeled beside Novak where he lay bleeding. He was gripping the pommel of the dagger where it protruded from his abdomen.

I put my hand under his head. He was trying to say something. He couldn't get the words out. Blood was flowing from his mouth now. Once more he tried to say something, and then he breathed his last.

4

I still owe you something? But haven't I brought everything to its conclusion? Isn't the dragon vanquished and the princess happily settled? What more do you think you have coming to you, dear cousin? By the time all this was happening, you had already arrived in Belgrade. I called out from inside the cistern, and Alexander had the doors opened. I stepped outside. Covered in blood. I didn't say a word. He looked at Novak and von Hausburg lying on the ground.

What's that you say?

'Were they vampires?'

'No,' I answered. 'And von Hausburg is still alive.'

'What utter madness this whole thing turned out to be! Utter madness! And to think! Just to think!' he shouted, but gleefully.

'To think what?'

'Why, all those voices. The voices we were hearing. It was the army and the refugees, the first contingent from Niš. Not vampires at all, just our very own soldiers and refugees. They were outside the city gates. They all arrived today. Just like you. And your cousin, Bishop-Count Thurn and Valsassina.'

I looked at him in surprise, and suddenly he seemed shorter in my eyes, shorter than before. The light had gone out of his eyes. He was happy for the same reason as everyone else. He was ordinary, just like Schmettau in fact. And Schmidlin. And the blond count and the red count. And you, dear cousin.

That's when you appeared as if from nowhere but just in time. You came with your imperial orders. Although I never understood how you had managed the journey from Vienna to Belgrade in only five days. You looked at us all with such distaste. Alexander bowed deeply before you. You ordered them to take von Hausburg and to provide him with the best of care.

And then you announced that General Doxat had been sentenced to death for surrendering Niš and betraying Austria. You told us that you'd been sent to offer Doxat a chance to renounce his Protestant faith and become Catholic in return for his life.

That night Nicolas Doxat refused to become your eternal subject. The next morning, before the executioner had raised his axe, Doxat called out to the fortress, 'I made you, and now you take my life.'

The executioner made clumsy work of it. There was a great deal of chopping about. Is that what you wanted to hear? Is that what I still owed you?

Who?

Von Hausburg?

But you went with him yourself that Monday afternoon to Petrovaradin, and from there to Pest, to Vienna and on to Paris, I believe. Didn't you? He had his new servant with him, the Serb with the stake and mallet. He didn't even take his leave of me. He spent the whole time telling his servant about his first meeting with someone named Fishmouth. As if that story meant more to him than anything else.

As for me, I've nothing more to tell you. I've told you everything just as it was.

Now let's hear what *you* have to say.